<u>ALSO BY THE AUTHOR</u>

A BOOK OF LIGHT AND SHADOW
GOOD BOY
BELLA'S BOYS
THE DEATH LIST
THE GOD PROVIDES
A TRUNK OF FORGOTTEN LORE
SUMMERHOME
A PRAYER FROM THE DEAD
IMMORAL DILEMMAS

<u>COMING SOON:</u>

WHIRLWIND
THE CURSE OF KATIE ELDER
THE WITCH OF NOVEMBER
THE TELLING OF THE BEES

NIGHTSWAN PRESS
SYRACUSE, NY 2025

TABLE OF CONTENTS

FOREWORD

BY GARRETT COOK

I have been both teaching writing workshops for most of my adult life. Both of these tasks while executed differently have the same intent; to do your best so the student or client can do theirs. This task is only as difficult as the writer makes it, so it can be easy and pleasant or it can be Sisyphean because our best varies tremendously. Mike Tyson's best poem and Woody Allen's best uppercut share one thing in common: they ain't gonna do the job.

Teaching Thomas R Clark has made me sweat only because he has made me push myself to accommodate his best. I knew a success when I saw it and I knew that my teaching would have to improve to meet his talent. Tommy was gonna do the work and I had to as well. Every writer I've worked with since Tommy owes him a tremendous debt of gratitude. He is a cross section of passion, drive, curiosity and talent and you will see all these things in this volume.

Tommy wears his excitement and exuberance on his sleeve and dear reader, you will soon share in it. It is never a matter of debate or question whether Tommy loves someone or something, you will find the evidence readily available and you will find it incontrovertible and you will find it infectious.

I am lucky to know Thomas R Clark and his work and you, the holder of this volume, are lucky as well.

Garrett Cook
January 2025

THE BREEDERS

Driving through the foothills surrounding the Finger Lakes of upstate New York is typically an enviable task. Filled with wineries, farms, and beautiful, rustic homes, it's one of the more enjoyable things to do in the region. Doing so in the middle of the night while a rainstorm rages, however, isn't Gary McCarthy's idea of fun.

The clouds hang low to the ground and the elevation of the hills covers the roadway with a never-ending bank of fog. Gary's inability to use the Ford's high beams is the least of his worries. As it is, any traffic going either way nearly blinds him, reflecting off the road surface and through the windows of the truck's cab. But each swipe of the wipers smears the rain on the windshield, and lights in the oncoming left-hand lane turn this into an obfuscating rainbow.

With it being the middle of summer, and humid, regulating the defroster on the windshield is a chore. It's a pain in the ass, but Gary knows the drive here and back to his hotel in the shitty little city of Cortland will be worth it once he reaches this first destination. He smiles thinking about it. The euphoria lasts until his cell phone rings.

The caller ID on the truck's dashboard tells him his new employer is calling. Gary connects the call but doesn't speak.

"Mac?" the client asks after an uncomfortable silence.

"Yeah."

"How was the flight?"

"Like you'd expect from Dulles to Syracuse in this weather. Why are you calling me for small talk? You only paid for three burners," Gary says.

"Ya think I'd be usin' up a phone just to call and tell ya how pretty yer eyes are?"

"Okay, good point. What's up?"

"The information I gave ya earlier has changed. The, um, package, it's moved an' we can't locate it."

"Are you fucking kidding me? So what's the deal? You know the deposit is nonrefundable."

"I know. I know. The event isn't off. It's just, well, on hold."

"What happened?"

"She, I mean the package, we lost it yesterday."

"So you're telling me I flew all the way to this shithole, where I'm currently out in the middle of the night driving a rental around in a rainstorm, and—"

"Hey, Mac," the client says, interrupting Gary, who scowls at the act. "Don't forget I'm the banker here. The job wasn't until tomorrow. It's not my fault ya went out in this shit. It ain't supposed to rain tomorrow anyhoot."

"Whatever. If you need to know, I'm getting a new emotional support dog. My old one just died."

"Emotional support dog? Really?"

"Fuck you." Gary wishes this asshole was in front of him right now, with the barrel of a Desert Eagle in his mouth. "You try, um, checking tickets on people for a living. I'm busy. Call me tomorrow when you have an answer. Cycle the phones and don't fucking call me unless you have the location or you're calling it off, got that? And if it's the latter, there's no refunds." Gary doesn't wait for an answer. He ends the call, shaking his head in displeasure. He doesn't like the employer, not one bit. But he doesn't have to.

"There's more natural teeth in a maternity ward than there is in all of Cortland county," the mousey man who went by Dennis told him during their first meet. A stop at a gas station earlier in the day did nothing to disprove this theory. "Don't ferget yer in the asshole and armpit of the Appalachians. Bring plenty of teepee and deodorant with ya." The client pronounced it Apple-A-shuns, like the rest of New York's population did, which annoyed this West Virginia native living in Georgetown to no end.

The road swerves as he presses the button for the automated windows to go down. Wind whips rain into the cab, soaking him. Now the truck is on a straightaway with no bends or curves. With one hand on the wheel, Gary fishes a cell phone out of his pocket. He smashes it on the steering wheel and pulls out the SIM card before tossing them both out the window into the stormy darkness.

A few miles later, the GPS tells Gary to turn down an unmarked side road. There's no road on the map, only a waypoint indicated, seemingly in the middle of nowhere. It's quiet, and the rain lets up. The high beams light up the rural setting, revealing a serpentine, pothole-ridden gravel road, if you could call it thus, lined with gigantic oaks. A sign, hidden in the brush and listing to one side, declares this to be BONNEY FARMS. The top of the signpost is decorated with a trio of dog head sculptures.

Nothing bad has ever happened in these situations, he thinks to himself sarcastically as he recalls a night in Afghanistan over a decade ago when everything changed for Gary McCarthy. The night an insurgent's IED gave the Army Ranger a going home gift in the form of a titanium plate covering a majority of his forehead. The resulting PTSD had prompted Gary to adopt an emotional support dog after his recovery. That dog, Rambo, passed away a month ago after a decade at Gary's side.

Now, ahead of him, the brush of the wilderness bordering the gravel road subsides, unveiling the lights of the property. In the back of the F-150, a new dog crate rattles as the Ford hits the superfluous potholes filled with mud and captured water from the storm. The headlights reveal another country road bisecting the property next to a small creek flowing down from the surrounding hills. The stream runs under a wooden footbridge before disappearing into the darkness.

A homestead, or more correctly, a single-wide trailer on a concrete slab, sits on one side of the informal intersection. Following the creek, across the drive sit a half dozen steel and aluminum sheds and an ancient barn. Gary's lights illuminate most of the yard, and he can see half of the barn's roof is listing, with a gaping, black hole near the peak.

Gary finds a gravel drive adjacent to the trailer and parks the Ford next to a shiny, newish black Subaru Forester. The decals with the logos for Lyft and Uber peak his curiosity. Do these hicks drive rideshare? He wonders for a moment. Maybe it was how they supplemented their income? He considers the possibility, then disregards the thought. No, there's something more to this, he resolves and sits there for a few seconds, pondering the Subaru and mustering the strength to deal with a person and not kill them for the sake of it.

It'll only be long enough to get the dog, Gary mentally reminds himself. Tomorrow you can take it out on your mark and leave them dead and stinking in the water, his id adds as a consolation. Gary smiles at the thought. He pulls the card with the details out of his pocket. MELANIE BONNEY, BONNEY FARMS, BOX 2539, HOMER, NY. When he opens the door, the stench of a sulfurous musk immediately assaults him.

"A fuckin' polecat? Really?" He scans the area, making sure the skunk isn't nearby. The last thing he needs is to get sprayed. He walks down the path to the trailer's dilapidated porch. Charms and chimes hang from wires and twine, and the building smells worse than the skunk. It's a sickly sweet, nauseating combination of mildew, piss, and shit. The malodor waters his eyes and makes him wish the skunk would materialize and deodorize the place. Sweet Jesus. Gary keeps this thought to himself as he steps up onto the porch.

The shadow of a large dog standing in the corner of the porch catches Gary's eye. He steps back, not wanting to antagonize a mastiff. A curtain inside the trailer moves and light bleeds out, exposing the watchdog as something peculiar. Is that a stuffed dog? Gary wonders. Turning on his phone's flashlight, Gary confirms his suspicions. A taxidermized dog, with three poorly stitched together heads and marbles for eyes, silently stares back at him. That's all sorts of fucked up. What are these people? The welcoming committee for secondhand Hades, he thinks, shakes his head, and knocks on the door.

The rapping is greeted by a high-pitched barking, followed by a chorus of snarls and howls originating near the proximity of the metal sheds. At least I'm in the right place, Gary thinks, as the barking persists. The sounds of someone approaching the door from the interior follow. With each step, the trailer's frame buckles, the metal screaming in distress until he hears the tumblers of the lock fall.

The door opens and Gary is assaulted by a freshness of stench he can't believe possible. A monster of a woman stands before him, as wide as she is tall, dressed in a grease-stained purple housecoat. Her gray hair is thinned by alopecia, and the woman's face is riddled with oozing sores. At first he thinks she's crying, but then he realizes it's pus, not tears, dripping down from her left eyeball. She holds a ring of rusty keys in one swollen hand, and in the other, a coffee cup filled with some steaming liquid.

Behind her, a little ankle biter of a mutt that appears to have combined the worst traits of a pug and chihuahua growls and hisses. It's smaller and thinner than a typical pug, with the lean body of the chihuahua and the familiar anthropomorphic pug face. The dog reminds Gary of David Hedison's infamous last scene in the original version of The Fly, where the human-headed insect is trapped by a spider pleading for its life. This poor creature is no better off. A victim of cerebellar hypoplasia, the dog waddles sideways as it runs. Its tilted face is covered with swollen lesions.

Gary stifles a laugh, noting how much the dog and its master mirror each other. He smiles, recollecting how he and Rambo, too, shared similar traits. The correlation nearly kicks off an anxiety attack. He shuts it down with the only coping mechanism he knows to use, outside of killing the old woman outright. Humor.

I guess the commercials are right and shingles don't fucking care who or what you are, poor dog. Gary keeps the joke to his inner monologue. "Melanie Bonney?" he asks.

"Mmmmhmmm, but ya can call me Mamme Mel, it's what da kinfolk roun' here do," the woman replies, nodding.

More like Mamme Nasty Ass, he thinks, ignoring the lady's attempt to teach him her pet name. "Gary McCarthy. We spoke on the phone last week about the puppy."

"Mmmmhmmm. Ya da man who lost his support dog, righty? Y'all din' soun' like no darkie on da phone."

"Beg pardon?" Gary didn't appreciate the woman's verbiage, pointing out his mixed heritage. Gary's father was of Irish-American descent, his mother a dark-skinned Cuban dancer, and their son shared her mocha complexion. Say one more racist thing and give me an excuse to unload this Desert Eagle in your face, please.

"T'ain't 'portan'."

"And yes, my emotional support companion passed away. I'm just here for the puppy."

"Mmmmhmmm. Yes ya are, indeed, mmmmhmmm," she says, then shouts out, "emotional support. Hah! Eloy! Get out to da spring house an' get dat pup. Da man is here for it." Gary notes she has one tooth on her bottom jaw and no others. It juts up like a tusk when she closes her mouth. "Eloy's mah boy, he's a little daft, but he's good with da pups. Dis one yer getting, she's a prettyful one. Nice markings. That'ah be sick hunna, carsh."

"That's not a problem." Gary fetches a wad of bills from his pocket and hands it to the woman. Her fingernails are crusted filth and Gary is skeeved by her touch. It sends a shiver up his spine, and it requires all of his willpower to not pull the Desert Eagle out of its holster at the small of his back...

And empty it into her face.

She counts the money then adds, "It's airish tonight. Chillin' me to da bones. Lemme get ya da paperwork for da bloodline." She steps back into the trailer and shuffles through some papers on the kitchen island. The floor is covered in pages from newspapers and magazines, complete with piss stains. A Navy Jack (known to some as the Confederate flag or the flag of the Army of Northern Virginia), stained and torn, hangs on the wall above a sofa. The furniture and flag have seen better days.

Fucking wonderful, Gary thinks when he sees the tattered banner. The last thing I need to see tonight is that racist piece of shit flag. Gary knows there are two sorts of people who fly this flag, racists and idiots. He's mostly certain the Bonneys, being in Upstate New York, fall into the latter category. The longer Gary stands here, the more nauseous he gets and less patient. He's about to snap—and gut the old hag—when he hears the sniffling and whining of a puppy behind him. The pug-chihuahua's barking resumes.

"Peanut! Quitcher bawlin'!" the woman commands. The yapper doesn't listen. Gary turns around and the puppy comes into view, led by the man called Eloy, who is obviously Melanie Bonney's kin. But unlike Mamme Nasty Ass, the puppy does not resemble Eloy. Eloy's cleft lip was sewn up poorly when he was a child, and now his face appears askew.

The ugly didn't fall too far from the tree, Gary thinks. *Shit, it mighta hit the roots.*

The puppy is excited. Fawn colored, its tail wagging, the wee critter makes eye contact with

Gary. As he and the pup stare at one another, he feels the oxytocin course through his body with each second. This is the one, Gary thinks. He bends down at the knees, and the puppy charges to him, jumping into his arms and licking his face.

"Well hello there! Ain't you a sweetheart!" Gary tells the dog. All at once, months of apprehension and stress seem to leave his body. Not since Rambo's last days has Gary felt this good, this emotionally satisfied.

"Her name is Per-Per-Perseffff...Annie." Eloy manages to stutter out of his toothless mouth.

"Persephone?" Gary verifies the name. Eloy answers with an affirming nod.

"I think it's a beautiful name," Gary says, scratching the dog behind the ears. "We'll keep it."

The pup licks and nibbles at Gary's face. He lowers her down and stands up. "Come on Persephone!" He motions to the puppy to follow him to the truck. She obliges. He picks her up, opens the door, and scoops the little dog into the waiting crate where a new bed and toys await her.

"Don'tcha forget dis!" Mamme Mel shouts to him from her spot in the trailer's doorway, the paperwork in her hands.

"Oh, right, can't forget that. Be right there," an elated Gary says as he closes the crate. "I'll be right back, baby girl," he tells Persephone, giving the truck door a gentle slam then returning to the trailer to fetch the dog's papers.

For the first time in weeks Gary doesn't feel the urge to leave anyone dead and stinking—on the land or in the water, for the matter at hand.

He takes three steps and stops when Eloy shouts at him. "Ain't no coon takin' nunna my bitches!" Eloy's words are still hanging in the air when Gary's ears fill with the din of a gong being struck by a mallet. The lights go out for a second as Gary struggles to regain his orientation. This is followed by a wet crunching and an unearthly screech.

It's just like night when the IED went off in Nuristan all those years ago, except those Taliban lunatics were screaming Allahu Akbar at the tops of their lungs, Gary's instincts tell him, but he's about to discover they're wrong. Sweat and salt burn his eyes when he opens them, and he wipes his brow with a free hand. The liquid is sticky, and the coppery scent of blood pulls him from his stupor. I'm fucking bleeding? Gary wonders. That motherfucker hit me in the head with something?

Then he sees Eloy twitching on the ground in front of him and big Mamme Mel running to her son's aid. The woman is moving faster than Gary thought she could, with the little pus-face dog at her heels, yipping away. The key ring in her hand jingles with each bounding step. What happened to him? Gary wonders. His question is answered with a step forward. The barrel of an aluminum baseball bat is embedded in Eloy's face.

"Look at whatcha done to mah boy!" The woman screams. The man's lower jaw is dislocated, the mandible bent and twisted. If he had possessed any teeth, they would've been scattered around him. Instead, a pink froth of snot and blood discerns the seal between flesh and metal.

Bent over on her hands and knees with her housecoat riding up her bare ass, Mamme Mel coddles her son's broken face, still holding her keys. Peanut, the little fucked up dog, stops yipping but the other dogs in the sheds let it out with abandon. It's deafening. Gary slowly steps away from the pair, toward the trailer, while reaching behind his back. A few steps later he withdraws the Desert Eagle, keeping his eyes on the old woman the whole time.

Something he regrets doing almost immediately.

Behind the woman, the little dog is standing on its hind legs. Its front paws are spread out, one to either ass cheek. Her backside is riddled with dripping, pustulant sores. They surround and infest her exposed vulva and labia, swollen with infection. Swabs of toilet tissue are stuck to the inflamed lips.

The image reminds Gary of a spoiled roast beef sub, complete with curdled cheese protruding from between the flaps of meat, that he bought by accident from a vending machine back home in Georgetown.

A thick, matted cake of dried blood, shit, and hair covers where her taint and ass crack should be. Trailing out of a hole in the center of this mass is a lime green, thinned out turd, and Peanut is gobbling it up with glee. The little dog's tongue wipes it clean, before continuing to lap at the blisters and sores surrounding the woman's sagging and flapping vaginal lips.

Gary kicks the dog to the side. "No!" He commands the animal. Peanut ignores him and runs back to its master's exposed genitalia, tongue licking away at the pus-oozing boils.

No no no no no no no no fucking no... the word runs through his brain on repeat at light speed until Gary snaps.

WHAT IN THE EVERLOVING FUCK IS GOING ON HERE?

He aims the giant pistol at Mamme Mel's back around the vicinity of her heart, and squeezes the trigger. The report of the weapon sends gouts of blood squirting out of the exit wound in her chest. The splatter covers Eloy with a second coat of hemoglobin-infused paint. Gary hears the clinking of metal as the woman drops the key ring and slumps to the side, collapsing on her son's ruined face. His body kicks as she smothers him, but it doesn't stop the dog from digging into her ass for more.

Dead and stinking...

Gary has seen enough. He ignores Peanut this time and walks away, but not before grabbing the woman's key ring and taking the papers off the trailer's porch where the Bonney matron dropped them.

Near the sheds, he catches movement from the corner of a blood covered eye, telling him he's not alone. It's pitch dark without the lights of the trailer and truck illuminating the area. Gary decides it's better to handle this professionally. Unsure if it's a dog or another human, he stuffs the papers into his back pocket and returns to the F-150.

And what is my profession?

He opens the door to the cab and sees little Persephone wagging her tail and whining, happy to see her new human. Gary lets her sniff and lick his fingers. "That's a good girl. I'll be right back," he tells her as he places the paperwork on the seat next to the crate. "Be right back little girl. Daddy's got work to do." He blows her a kiss and shuts the door.

And said work amounts to dealing out death to some redneck motherfuckers who deserve it.

In the truck's bed is a locked case. It's long with no markings indicating what is inside. Gary unlocks the case with a key and opens it. Inside is his weapon of choice for close-up jobs, an SKO-12 semiautomatic shotgun. He loads it with a twenty-five-round drum magazine filled with two dozen shells packed with number four buckshot. At point-blank range the pellets will eat flesh and bone.

He wipes the blood from his brow, grabs a headlamp and slips it onto his head, then closes the case. The glow of the headlamp provides him with a good view of everything around him.

Time to die, motherfuckers.

A quick jog later Gary makes his way across the road and over the little footbridge to the sheds and barn where the other dogs are housed. Or so he believes. What Gary McCarthy is about to discover on this property will change him forever.

Behind the first shed, the headlamp illuminates a trail leading around the metal hovels. The constant barking from the dogs is deafening and emanates from all of the sheds, not any one in particular. Gary notes the stream runs under the backside of each shed—a practice done to keep salted food cool.

Now why would they need to do this? Gary thinks, not understanding how much he's going to regret asking himself this question. Hearing some commotion from within, he slides open the door to the closest shed and is greeted by a blast of hot air. The sweet stench of rotting meat and the sounds of sex greet him.

Chained to the floor on some sort of support is a large dog, and from the coat markings it looks to be a German Shepherd. The animal squeals in agony. Behind it, a naked man, covered in filth, is busy moaning and humping away at the dog's hind section.

He's fucking a dog? Already nauseous from the surrounding smells and a blow to the head, Gary loses the contents of his stomach and projectile vomits onto the wall. Bile and bits of finely masticated chicken nuggets and fried potatoes splash onto the man's backside. Without missing a hump the naked man turns around, revealing an insane, devilish grin on his face. He has one more tooth than Mamme Mel.

The man raping the dog speaks. "Spota be white? Spota say what? Spota—"

The hitman wipes off his lips and nose. He doesn't talk. Talking is for movies and dead men. There is no hesitation. Gary strikes the freak across the temple with the barrel of the SKO-12, ending the discussion. There is no discussion, Gary reminds himself, only action. The hillbilly drops to the ground and Gary steps on his neck. A wet crunch resonates from underneath Gary's boot. Blood froths and bubbles out of the freak's mouth and nose as he twitches. After one more convulsion his body evacuates, shitting all over the floor. The Army vet wrinkles his lip in disgust, steps back and kicks the body. A fecal streak marks the path as the dead man rolls off the floor and into the stream. Gary smiles at his work.

Dead and stinking in the water.

The Army vet goes to help the trapped dog. Part of him fears he may have to put the animal down. He looks for the restraints holding the dog in place. He unbuckles a leather strap and quickly steps back, shock and disgust working in tandem to repel him.

"You've got to be fucking kidding," Gary says, throwing a hand to his face and covering his mouth. He grabs the dog's tail and pulls. The head pops back, hollow and empty. The coat tears away from the animal's legs and comes off the body with ease, followed by a wailing screech and a sudden realization for the hitman.

This isn't a dog.

Chained to the floor and mutilated is a mustachioed man with thick, black hair and a bronze complexion. Gary isn't one hundred percent sure of his precise nationality, but he's certain of one thing, the guy is in a world of fucking hurt. His hands are missing, and the bloody stumps of his wrists are duct taped into the front paws of the dog pelt. Whoever had removed his hands, also amputated his legs from the knees down and sewed the stumps into the hindquarters of the pelt. They hadn't done a professional job. Bloody clots encircle the makeshift surgical points and a yellow mucus substance oozes through the fur.

"Help... us... please... help... us," the man manages to say, his words slurred and barely louder than a whisper. But Gary can hear a clear accent. Is he Afghan?

"Us?" Gary asks the imprisoned man.

"My... rider.... help... Allah...," he manages to say until his words trail off to labored breathing. The man passes out, his head hanging between his shoulders. Drool mixed with blood drips from his mouth. Gary resolves there's nothing he can do for this man.

I can still help someone, all the same. His thoughts are epiphanic as it all becomes clear. The dying man before him owns the rideshare car in the driveway and had a passenger with them. This person is likely somewhere on the property, probably in one of the sheds.

Ain't this a hoot, Gary thinks. After being wounded in the war, he never thought he'd see a day come where he'd be interested in saving a person's life. Yet here he is, putting together a makeshift plan to do just that.

He may not be able to save this man, but his passenger? This remains to be seen. Gary resolves he can only try. This day, or night, it seemed to him, was fast becoming a day of firsts. The hitman backs out of the shed cautiously, keeping the weapon level and his eyes open for any more surprise attacks.

He opens the door to a chorus of snarls, barks, and rattling cages. A first glance through shed number two tells Gary it's filled with a half dozen dogs in crates. They appear to be healthy. The two larger dogs in bigger crates are busy gnawing on bones resembling tibia. He flashes the light at another crate full of puppies, one gnawing on the remnants of a human hand. It's now become obvious, to Gary at least, how the Bonneys are feeding their breeding pack.

They're fucked up, but hey, at least they're not cannibals.

Gary moves on to shed number three.

The fetid stink of rotting meat overpowers the farm's skunky aroma. Other than the stink, at first glance, this one is mostly a bust. It's empty of living things, no barking dogs or people in duress. The origin of the shed's ambient stench is swinging from long hooks attached to the ceiling—pieces of carcasses.

Human parts and pieces.

Gary grimaces at the sight before his headlamp reveals a treasure in the corner, a pile of things. They're personal effects, and judging from their appearance, they aren't things in the Bonney aesthetic. Flip flops, women's clothing, sneakers, men's clothing. On top of the stack are two cell phones. Gary picks them up and notes both are powered down.

"Why the fuck not?" he says, and turns them on. In moments, both phones buzz to life with a cacophony of alerts from missed calls and text messages. He ignores the buzzing and chirping, puts the phones in his pocket, and moves on to shed number four.

As he nears the next building, Gary hears the sounds of a panicked scuffle from within the structure. He checks the SKO-12 to ensure the weapon is ready to rock and roll, and adjusts the headlamp to illuminate as much of his line of sight as possible. Gary aims the SKO-12 and slides the door open.

The Bonney farm does not disappoint, as Gary has learned from more than one instance on this night. The property is fast becoming a smorgasbord of backwoods inbred fuckery.

The hitman had expected something fucked up, and he gets it. A pair of bipedal dog-men are humping away at either end of a bound, naked woman. Gary aims the shotgun at the back of the closest dog-man's head, and squeezes off a single round from the SKO-12. The roar of the shotgun silences the barking dogs, while the blast removes the dog-man's head with a couple dozen pellets of number four buckshot from a 12-gauge shell. Pieces of skull, cartilage, flesh, hair, and brain splatter the ceiling, creating dripping stalactites of crimson goo.

A fountain of blood erupts from the stump of the dog-man's neck and covers the woman and other dog-man in a crimson spray littered with bits and pieces of head. The standing corpse slumps down to the floor and the stream of blood turns into an expanding puddle surrounding the body.

An inhuman screech of rage comes from the other dog-man. He leaps over the woman. The dog-man's dick, an all too human cock, is sticking out of a canine penile sheath, flapping around like a propeller. Through the dog-man-thing's gaping maw, Gary can see human eyes staring back at him from behind the teeth.

These redneck motherfuckers are wearing dog suits? Gary's mind does not want to accept what is going on with the Bonneys. His body shakes, his heart rate rises, his palms sweat. The Army vet's entire being wants to remove them from his presence, delete them from existence.

The shotgun obliges.

The hitman unleashes a barrage of shotgun shells at the man in the dog suit. The kick of the weapon pushes Gary back, out of the shed as the SKO-12 burps out a half dozen shells, creating a moving wall of ball bearings. Fire shoots out a foot from the barrel, lighting up the interior of the shed. Instantly, hundreds of impacts turn the costumed target into a gooey mass resembling a multi-family sized portion of steak tartare.

Then, for the first time since shit went down with the swinging of a baseball bat, the farm is quiet.

The bits and pieces of flesh, bone, and internal organs hover in midair, then fall. With a wet slap the matter covers the prone woman in a sheen of gory goop. Gary stands and stares at the bloody mess, breathing as deep and slow as he can to reduce his heart rate and slow his anxiety. His mind is still trying to rationalize what he has encountered at this farm on this night when his burner phone rings, ruining the moment's peaceful bliss.

This is not the time for this shit, Gary thinks before fishing the phone out of his pocket. He connects the call and doesn't wait for his client to speak. "What did I tell you about using these burners? Right now I'm not in a good place, so this better be important," he says.

"Well hello to you, too, Mac. You'll be happy to know I've regained contact with the mark and everything should be back on for tomorrow."

"Is that so?"

"Yes. It looks like the mark's at one of the ski lodges right now, so you might have to do some wilderness work to get it done."

Ski lodge in the middle of summer? he thinks before replying, "Enough, I'm in the middle of something. Call me tomorrow with the location, I don't care where they are now."

"Copy that."

"What did you say?" Gary's tone turns colder.

"I said copy that, you know, like soldiers say on radios when they're in the field."

"Are you prior service?"

"No. But I thou—"

"Then don't say that again." Gary hangs the up, then crushes the phone with his heel. Fucking amateurs, he thinks as he kicks and scatters the phone's pieces and shakes his head. He doesn't have time for this bullshit, and has a victim to save. Gary steps back into the shed and reaches down to the woman lying on the floor. He can hear her labored breathing, confirming she's at least still alive.

"Hey, are you with me?" he asks the woman as he touches her shoulder. She's shivering, shaking. The dogs restart their incessant barking. He speaks louder, so she can hear him over the dogs, but tries to maintain a kind tone. It's difficult for him to do, considering the circumstances. "Hey, it's okay. I'm Gary, I'm going to rescue you." The woman moves, covers her face with her hands and folds herself into a fetal position. "Okay, you stay here, I'm going to get you some clothes and something to clean up with. Nobody's going to hurt you now. They're all—"

A screeching wail erupts from behind Gary, and it drives the barking dogs into a frenzy. He spins around to see Mamme Mel, a giant bloodstain covering the front of her housecoat, charging at him with Eloy's ball bat grasped in both hands, raised over her head.

"Fuck ya, moolie!" she screams. "I'mma gonna hang yer balls on da porch!"

"Oh, would you just fuckin' die already?" Gary says, breaking his silence rule as he raises the SKO-12. He squeezes the trigger and unloads a trio of shells at the Bonney matron before she can reach him. The first burst of buckshot hits her in the chest, erupting into a bloody red flower exposing the bones of her sternum and upper rib cage.

It only slows her down.

The second and third shell loads hit the large woman on the left side of her body. She violently jerks to the side and something black splashes out of the impact points, covering the grass. Hypovolemic shock takes over her body. The baseball bat tumbles out of the woman's hands as she twists and falls from the force of the buckshot. Mamme Mel tumbles and rolls in the rain and blood-soaked grass, sliding to a stop, ass first, at Gary's feet. Sticking out from between her ass cheeks, coated in runny shit, the hindquarters of a little dog lay limp.

"Poor little Peanut," Gary laments for the pug mix before going to the previous shed and gathering the woman's clothes and a blanket. Unsure of which garments are hers, he grabs the whole pile. She's sitting up in a fetal position when he returns, her forehead on her knees. "Here you go. Do you know if there are any more of these hillbillies?" The woman shakes her head. "I think I got them all. Okay, then I'm good with giving you some privacy to get dressed. I'm going back to my truck. Come over when you are ready and we'll, well, we'll get out of here and call the cops. Sound like a plan?" She nods in response. "All right. I think one of these is your phone, too. You need me, holla. I'll be right over there." He points to the truck and leaves her to clean up.

Back at the F-150, Gary stores the SKO-12 before he checks on Persephone. The puppy's eyes light up when she sees her new human. His heart swells at the sight of her. He reaches into the crate and scratches the little dog's head. She licks at his hand and Gary allows himself to laugh for the first time in a month. Their bond is secure.

On the seat next to the crate is the mission briefing for his current job. Gary leans over and grabs it; he can't have the police finding a contract sitting out in the open. The contents spill out onto the truck's floorboards. "Are you fucking shitting me? Goddamnit!" Gary says as the picture of his mark stares back at him. He stands, motionless, gathering his thoughts until the puppy whines and paws at the crate. Gary picks up the papers and stuffs them back into the folder. "It's okay, girl. It's okay," he says to the dog. No, it's not, he tells himself, then closes the truck's door.

The woman is walking to him. She's now dressed and has the blanket wrapped around her. Gary stands in front of the truck, his arms crossed.

"I can't tell you how much... oh God, this... all this. I don't know. Who are you?" She shakes her head and starts crying.

"My friends call me Mac."

"I'm... I'm Wendy."

"Of course you are," Gary replies. "What brought you to this shithole if you don't mind me asking? I'm assuming it's for the same reason I came, to get a dog?"

"Yes... I came here to get a dog to protect me from my husband."

"Now why would you want to do that?" Gary asks.

"He's been trying to kill me for over a year. Getting rid of me gives him the free time to fuck his whores without splitting the bill."

"Do you have proof?"

She nods.

"Okay, then if you do, why don't you go to the authorities?"

"It isn't that easy, sir. He owns the police down here. Corruption is rampant in Cortland County. You ain't in Syracuse anymore, honey."

"Thank God I'm not, I'm from Georgetown, so go Hoyas, hah?" They laugh in unison. "It's good to know that after this with witnesses, you have an easy and convenient way to talk to them now, don't you?" She nods. "Hop in and we'll get you to a hospital and call someone who can take care of this for you." He opens the F-150's passenger door wide, almost folding it backward on the hinges before walking to the driver's side. He hops up into the cab and pulls the door shut.

"I can't reach the door handle," Wendy says, reaching out of the cab. Then she notices the folder on the dashboard. The picture of Gary's mark has slid back out. She stops breathing for a moment before asking, "Why do you have a picture of me in your truck?"

"Yeah, I know," Gary says. His right-hand slips behind his back and withdraws the Desert Eagle 50AE holstered there. Startled, Wendy moves but it's too late.

He doesn't speak. Speaking is for movie villains and dead men. He is neither. He only squeezes the trigger.

The automatic handgun fires a .50 bullet at just over fifteen hundred feet per second. It strikes Wendy in the face and travels through her cranium before her ears register the roar of the weapon. The woman's head splits in two, well, more like half of it is disintegrated by the impact. The other side still has a stupid fucking "what the fuck is going on" look on its eye and half a lip while cranial fluid and blood slip out the bone cavity. The whole scene resembles a raw oyster in a half-shell, covered with cocktail sauce. Wendy tumbles out of the open door.

Behind him, in her crate, Persephone softly whimpers. "It's okay, girl, we're done here." Gary places the pistol on the seat, starts the truck's engine. He jerks it into reverse, and physics closes the passenger door for him.

The soothing whine of the puppy behind him settles Gary's anxiety ridden nerves. Within a few more moments, he forgets the night's stress. In an hour he knows he'll be in his hotel with Persephone, and tomorrow he'll be getting home early from this job. He waits until he's a few miles from the Bonney farm to make the call. The burner phone rings and the employer answers. Gary doesn't wait for him to speak.

"It's done."

"Whattaya mean it's done? I was just about to call you and tell you we lost contact again."

"Cos I smashed her phone. The news will be all over this, and not on account of me, so you better cover your ass. We'll stay on the line until the transfer comes through."

"Whattaya mean the news will be all over this? Mac? What are you talking about?"

"The transfer, Dennis. Now."

"All right already. But you gotta tell me what is going on." The alert comes across Gary's primary phone for a six-digit deposit in his Bank of the Bahamas account. Gary disconnects the call. He waits until Dennis calls back to smash the burner on the steering wheel, then throws the pieces out the window.

"I don't have to tell you jack or shit, motherfucker," the hitman announces as the window raises back up. Behind him, secure in her crate, Persephone sighs before letting out a little yip, as if to acknowledge her new master's words. Gary reaches behind with his right arm, and scratches the puppy's head. She licks his hand in response and something wet and cold grazes his wrist. Gary turns around and sees a boogery, gray lump on the pup's snout. Realizing it's some of the mark's brains, he freezes in momentary disgust. Before he can act, the dog's tongue snakes out and pulls the cranial matter into her mouth. The dog gobbles down the morsel with glee. Gary snorts a chuckle and feels his muscles relax as the stress of the day leaves his body. "That's right, little girl," Gary McCarthy says to Persephone. "Let's go home."

THE STAFF

THE OFFER

Sitting upon a hill in North Yorkshire, England, overlooking the North Atlantic, is Whitby Manor. Inside the manor house, within the confines of an office, a pair of people haggle over an employment offer.

"Thank you for arriving on such short notice." A stodgy old butler shuffles through the papers in his hands.

"The air travel was a little crazy because of the Holiday."

"Ah, yes, Thanksgiving in America can be so, I'm told. I've never been there myself. You come rather specialized, Miss..." He pushes his round spectacles back up the bridge of his nose, "Ms. Wells?"

"Yes, Wells, Stephanie Wells. I do, as a matter of fact, come specialized," the applicant replies to the man's assertion, "and that's what I don't get it. I can't see how my expertise is applicable to the position you are looking to fill."

"You let us be the judge of that, please," he smiles, "Here, at Whitby Manor, we pride ourselves on our staff. As a result, we are particular about those we bring into the fold. As you will soon see, you'll be rewarded rather handsomely in return for your services." He pushes a swatch of paper across the desk. Stephanie picks it up. The number written down takes her breath away. She throws a hand to her lips and gasps.

"This... this can't be right."

"Oh, I can assure you, the figure is correct. You do have a community you look after, no?"

"But sir, I-"

"It isn't enough, is that the issue? I understand. This is by no means an entry level position. Please, forgive my ignorance. We live in a new era of equal rights, after all." The butler retrieves the swatch from Stephanie's hand and scratches out the previous offer. He ponders for a moment, then writes a new, larger figure down. After seeing this, she shakes her head in protest.

"Am I on a reality television show? Are you the host?"

"No, Ms. Wells, I'm afraid not."

"Then what's the meaning of all this?"

"What do you mean?"

"Why are you willing to pay me so much for this job?"

"Why, indeed," the butler says, adjusts his glasses, and lifts Stephanie's resume with a liver-spotted, wrinkled hand. "You are Stephanie M. Wells, yes?"

She nods.

"You have an RN from St. Joseph's and Upstate University Hospitals, as well as being a graduate of SUNY ESF's botany program. After graduation, you returned to the rural community you grew up in, Whitney Falls, located upstate in the Adirondacks. There you settled into a comfortable role assisting the locals. Your work as a midwife has fetched quite a positive referral list. Those you've tended to have nothing but good things to say. You are a member of the PEACE council, among other volunteer organizations in the neighboring, larger communities. In a manner of speaking, you are the perfect candidate for the position, Ms. Wells."

"Yes. It's all there on my resume. Please, pardon me for interrupting again, sir. But you paid a recruiter to seek me out?"

"Yes."

"And you want to hire me to be your, um, doorwoman?"

"Yes."

"You're going to pay me a quarter million dollars to do so. Open and close the front door? No catch?"

"Yes. That's it. No catch. Except on the door itself."

"Well, of course."

"Yes. It's a functioning door, or rather gate."

"I'll be required to stand there? Open it and close it as needed?"

"Yes. During your shift, which is the overnight shift. You will have a watchhouse to cover you from the elements."

"Of course it is. Luckily for you I'm a night owl."

"We were aware of this before offering you the position."

"Do I need to wear one of those stuffy, long jackets? You know, the kind that doormen wear in big cities?"

"No, that won't be necessary. We prefer your typical choice of dress, it tends to blend well with the aesthetic we've established here at Whitby Manor." She did find it odd that the staff she encountered wore what could be considered casual dress. Now she knew why. "You may even bring your cat, if you like. The wee beastie will have plenty of fun hunting these venerable halls, catching all sorts of vermin, I'm sure."

"What makes you think I have a cat?"

"Its hair is all over your clothing, ma'am. And your hands have scratches on them."

"Good to see you're observant."

"I'm a butler, it's my job to be observant."

"The scratches, they're actually from his teeth. Bacchus was declawed by his previous owner."

"What a cruel thing to do to an animal."

"What's happened has happened," she shrugs her shoulders, "He more than makes up for the disability, my little fat Jim Morrison. There is nothing wee about him. What became of the previous doorperson, if I may ask?"

"Father Juan Phillipe?" The butler crosses himself as he speaks the man's name, "I regret he passed away in his sleep a fortnight ago, at the ripe old age of, what was the Father?" He taps his temple with a finger. "Ninety-seven I think? He was really,

really old, which is why we were delighted to discover you so quickly. I'm almost embarrassed to say we were unprepared for his demise. You are a relief, of that I can assure you."

"I'm not here looking for lasting employment."

"Of course you aren't. Father Juan Phillipe wasn't, either. Until he had a change of faith, one could say, delivered to him in a wheelbarrow."

"What was in the wheelbarrow that changed his mind?"

"You'll learn soon enough," the butler ignores her question, "Ms. Wells, that Whitby Manor isn't your typical country estate. It's a bit off, some would say. As is natural with such peculiarities, there comes certain responsibilities which we, the manor staff, are charged with maintaining. And one of them is who we do, and don't invite, onto the property. This is where you come in as the door... person. You could say you are the first line of defense."

"Your first line of defense? Against what, may I ask? And about that wheelbarrow? Thanksgiving turkeys?"

"I regret that unless you take the position, I cannot divulge this information."

"Of course not," Stephanie giggles, "you can't be serious? This really is a reality TV show. I think I see a camera on the bookshelf over there."

"I assure you this is no ruse, ma'am, I don't know what more I can say to sway you from that belief. I think it's better I leave you alone with your thoughts. It's our wish you accept our generous offer. And if you don't, well, the search will go on. What more can I say? Good day, Ms. Wells." The butler exits the parlor, leaving Stephanie without saying another word.

THE ACCEPTANCE(S)

"I can't believe I'm signing this." Stephanie told the butler as she spelled her name on the contract. Her eyes shifted to the salary and she shook her head, still not believing the amount they were paying her.

"I can. As I told you, Ms. Wells, filling this position was of the highest importance to this manor house. We are so pleased to have you and Bacchus on the staff."

"Me and Bacchus?"

"Why of course, Ms. Wells. Familiars are sentient beings and deserve as much consideration as their human companions. Now, before we, um," he paused and smiled for the first time Stephanie could recall, "forget, here is Bacchus's contract. You will note he, too, is being handsomely rewarded." Stephanie took the contract and glanced over it.

"This is too much. You're paying my cat six figures? To sit around and lick his balls? Because that's all he does. Really. That's it. He eats, sleeps, shits where he likes, and licks his balls."

"And your point is, Ms. Wells?" He motioned to the pen. An 'X' was placed on the paper, indicating where Bacchus's guardian might sign, validating the contract. Stephanie signed the paper. A chonker of a tuxedo cat, Bacchus weighed in at a good twenty-five pounds and stood at least two feet at the shoulder. He slinked between his mistress's legs and meowed at her feet. She signed her name on the cat's contract and pushed both papers across the desk to the butler.

"Why do I feel like I've just sold our souls to the devil?" Bacchus mewed, again.

"In a manner of speaking, Ms. Wells, you have. Except, as you will soon learn, it is quite the opposite."

"The opposite of what?"

The butler ignored her last question and continued on. "Now that you've signed the contract, you are under an NDA, which prevents you, or your cat, from speaking about this property's secrets, I suppose I can tell you."

"Tell me what? What this is all about, why you are paying me so much Goddamn money to be a door woman?"

"Yes. Repeat after me."

"Okay."

"No."

"What?"

"No, don't say what, I said No."

"Wha-" He raised a finger, she stopped and corrected herself, "No?"

"More affirmative, please. NO!"

"What?"

"NO! Say no, like you mean it, Ms. Wells!"

Still mewling around her feet, Bacchus stood, dug his declawed toes into Stephaine's thigh, and roared in response to the butler, as if to mimic the stodgy old man's words. She pushed the cat down and screamed, "No!"

"Yes! That's what I want to hear! NO!'

"NO!" Stephanie repeated. The butler grinned.

"That's the only word you need to say when the Master arrives at the door."

"The Master?" Stephanie asked.

"Yes."

"The Master of what?"

"Why, the Master of Whitby Manor, of course. He is not welcome here, and when he arrives at the entrance, and asks for entry, all you are to say to him," the butler paused, swallowed, and took a deep breath, "is no."

"No?" Stephanie reiterated.

"Yes, Ms. Wells. No. That is what we are paying you a small fortune for. To say one word. No."

"No it is, then." Stephanie Wells said, "If you'll excuse me, I have to get settled in."

"But of course, we are pleased to have you aboard, Ms. Wells. Blessed Be, that's the correct term to use when saying goodbye to a witch such as yourself?"

"Wiccans will say that, as well as merry we meet, and merry we part. But not all witches. A simple goodbye works for me."

"Well, then goodbye it will be. Please, forgive my ignorance, the staff is more than happy to have one with your knowledge and skills on the payroll. We're so used to the Father's Catholicism. But we will learn your ways soon enough. Oh, and one more thing before you go."

"Yes?"

"This habit you have of looking people in the eye when you talk to them, you need to not do that while at your post. Especially while at your post. That is all."

Stephanie nodded and smiled in response. She then excused herself from the butler's office, with Bacchus following on her heels.

THE FIRST INCIDENT

It was near the witching hour of the first full moon after Stephanie Wells started her new job, when the man first came. A loud rattling startled Stephanie from her book. Sitting within the doorman's shack next to Whitby Manor's main gate, she lifted her eyes to the mirror, and saw nothing but the wrought iron of the security fence in the reflection. She set the novel down, looked out the window, and was surprised to see a tall man standing before the gate, shaking it.

The full moon cast a spotlight down on him. He wore long, crimson robes. His white hair shone in the moonlight. A long, gray mustache traced his lips and hung down his chin. She turned back to the mirror and did not see the man on its surface.

"Huh. What do we have here?" She whispered to herself.

"Hello! Let me in!" The robed man declared. Stephanie stood and exited the guard house. She approached the visitor, making sure to keep a fair distance between herself and the fence.

"And you are?" Stephanie asked the man standing in front of Whitby Manor's gate, giving him a quick once over before remembering what the butler said about eye contact, and dropped her eyes to stare at his feet. His boots were those of a cavalryman or horseman.

"Your boss." The man said.

"Is that so?"

"That is so." The man replied.

"The last I checked my boss was a stuffy old butler, and you do not resemble him in any manner, well, you are old, but you aren't him. So, let me ask this, sir. How can I help you?"

"You could open this gate for me and invite me in, to start."

"Oh, really?"

"Really."

"How about..." Stephanie paused for a brief moment, then a single word came to mind. "No?"

"No?"

"That's correct," Stephanie made sure to not affirm his statement with the word *YES*, out of fear it may have an adverse effect. "I said, no."

"I might traverse the length of this fence and find another entrance with someone less obtrusive standing in my way."

"I regret this is the only entrance you will find. But you should know that, after all you say this is your property."

"You're a wise one. Much more so than the old priest. For a good seventy-five years we'd meet at this very spot and we'd end up on our knees hailing Mary until the sun came up."

"So you're aware I can't let you in."

"I am."

"So why bother?"

"It's in my nature to do so. If you invite me in, it will all be over and we can all go about our business."

"No."

The man sighed.

"The answer is still no." Stephanie said.

"I wonder where they recruited you from. You're clearly American, I don't hear the King's U's after your Oh's. Was it some backwater town in West Virginia? Maybe. I don't hear a twang in your voice, and you don't sound like the Swedish Chef, that leaves the south and Midwest out, so you have to be from the northeastern seaboard."

"You fancy yourself to be pretty smart, don't you."

"When you get to my age, you tend to get pretty smart. I figured out what parish old Father Juan came from right away, some hut village in the Philippines full of uneducated savages. I showed up the next night with all their heads in a wheelbarrow, ready to shrink. I regret it had the opposite of my desired effect on him.”

“Let me guess, all it did was enforce his convictions to remain at his post.” This threat of violence against the residents she promised to protect caught Stephanie off guard. “I don’t think you’d have such an easy time with my people,” she revealed.

“Oh, I’m not too sure about that, missy, or whatever your name might be.”

“Missy? I like it. We’ll take it.”

“You know if you give your true name I will find your village and devastated it.”

“No, I only know the power of true names and what they can achieve.”

“I went to the Devil’s School to learn my magic.”

“I dip from the well of the elements.”

“Witch.”

“Now we’ve resorted to calling me names. But this is a title I’ll gladly accept.”

“I’ll curse you and rip your kin to shreds.”

“Yep, you can do all of that. But you know what I find to be hilarious?” Stephanie said, holding back a belly laugh.

“What can be so funny in the face of certain doom, witch?”

“None of that will help you get past this gate without my permission.”

“Look me in the eye and say that!”

“Um. How about… no. Nope. Uh uh.” Stephanie shook her head as she grunted, “Neigh. Nein. Neit. Ho. Non. Might I continue with *No* in every conceivable language I speak for you to get the point?"

"I'll be back. Maybe tomorrow, maybe next month, or the month after, Miss Witch, but I'll be back." The man said, and faded into a mist, before her eyes.

"I guess he did learn a thing or two from the Devil School." The cloud floated away on the breeze, away from the gate.

THE SECOND INCIDENT

Another month passed before anyone approached Stephanie's gate. During this time she started to believe this to be a waste of her time. This lasted until the next full moon, after the passing of the witching hour. Like clockwork.

Garlic bulbs, strung through strips of witchwood, hung from the iron gate of Whitby Manor. In the guardhouse, Stephanie and Bacchus waited for the night to fall and the moon to rise. A broom with a head of whicker bristles, tied to the shaft with a leather strap, rested along the corner.

Bacchus sensed the arrival of the intruder before Stephanie could see him. He came as a striking young man with a long mop of black tresses and groomed facial hair, emerging from the darkness, he stood before the gate of Whitby Manor.

Bacchus, sitting on Stephanie's lap, mewed when the man appeared, stepping out of the shadows of the darkness.

He resembled a younger version of her visitor from the month before. His attire changed from the previous visit, he now wore an elegant and expensive suit, indicative of a man of high social status. Stephanie checked the mirror, and sure enough, the man cast no reflection. "Here we go, again." Stephanie said before exiting the Guard house to intercept him.

"You, hoo, Miss Witchy poo!" The mustachioed man cackled as he spoke, "I'm back. What's that smell? Are you not feeling so fresh, my dear Missy, or should I say Stephanie?" He said, the garlic holding him back.

"I see you learned my name," Stephanie said, stepping out of the guard shack.

"Of course I did, Missy. Now why don't you open that gate and invite me in?"

"How about... no. I see you got a makeover?"

"How would you know? All you do is look at my feet."

"Are you kink shaming? How'd you get to be so young?"

"You could say I did it with a little help from your friends."

"My friends?"

"Didn't they tell you?"

"Didn't who tell me what?"

"Your employers. Ah, they didn't tell Father Juan, either. The look of surprise on his face when he saw his flock come to visit him from the neck up."

"I'm sure it surprised him. So what wasn't I told?"

"If you must know, I found the little village you used to protect, Missy."

"Oh, did you, now?"

"I did." He produced a satchel from behind his back and threw it at the gate. It bounced off the iron and landed on the gravel covered road. "If you open the gate you might be able to fetch it. Find out what's inside."

"I can wait until morning when I get off shift and you are long gone to open it."

"Can you now?"

"I can, and I will, now get out of here and let me get back to my book. For the record, I planted more garlic in my portion of the garden. It will bloom next month and be waiting for you."

"Of course you did, Missy. And Father Juan filled that guard booth with crucifixes and holy sacrament," the man pointed to the shack. "It held me back, but it didn't stop me from trying. Here's the thing you don't get. It wasn't the priest, or the priests before him, it may not be you, witch. But some time, somehow, some way, I will come home, whether you or any other member of my staff likes to think otherwise. Now open that Goddamn gate and let me in before I wipe everyone in your bloodline off the face of this earth." His eyes glowed a deep red, and he opened his mouth, revealing a jagged maw of pointed teeth.

"No." Was all Stephanie said. It's all she needed to say. The single word of refusal held the demon at bay. "Not now, not tomorrow, not the next day or month. As long as I live, I will stand here and tell you the same thing. No. No. No. You got that? For the last time and every time hereafter! No!"

She shot forward a hand and opened it. On her palm, a tattoo of a pentacle, blue from the woad used to ink it, stared the man down. He dropped to his knees, and started speaking in Latin. Stephanie recognized some of it from her theology classes. He was reciting the Bible, verbatim.

Bacchus pulled the satchel to the gate with a monstrous paw. Leaving her hand and palm extended to the man, Stephanie pulled the bag through the slats of iron. She opened it to reveal horrors she never thought she'd behold.

The overstuffed satchel spilled its contents out. Stapled to the money she gave them, the faces of the residents of Whitney Falls stared back at her through eyeless slits. The man wasn't kidding when he said he found her people. How he did so, Stephanie didn't know. But she wanted to find out. She dropped the satchel and went back to her shack. Behind her, the man stopped his Biblical monologue in Latin.

"Father Juan had a similar response. Except he broke into prayer and sniveled when he got back in the booth. Seventy-some-odd years of that gets old really quick."

"I don't pray." Stephanie said, closed the door of the shack behind her, and ignored his pleas to invite him onto the property the rest of the night. She didn't weep for her loved ones. She didn't quit her post. Instead, Stephanie Wells schemed.

Outside, the man disappeared, replaced by a large, snarling wolf. After howling through the night, the beast ran off into the darkness before dawn.

•

In a month's time, Stephanie knew this man would return. When this day came, he would understand she lived by a clear motto. What goes out comes back. Stephanie set about putting together a plan for revenge. This would require the cooperative services of the Manor's staff. Some unorthodox house cleaning was in order. She presented it to the butler the next morning.

"Brilliant!" He replied. He and Stephanie knew sometimes the gods, they work in mysterious ways. And one of those ways is using you as karma's weapon. In other words, payback can often be...

A witch.

PAYBACK

As the full moon waned, and the witching hour passed, Stephanie Wells, her cat at her side and broom in hand, stood inside the gate of Whitby Manor. They waited for the man this time, confident in the power of the fresh garlic bulbs braided into the wrought iron rails.

The man was punctual, if anything. When he stepped out of the shadows into the light of the moon, Stephanie noted he looked to have gained a few years from the wrinkles on his brow. His hair showed a bit more salt and pepper than his last visit. A revelation came to mind.

He hadn't fed since gorging himself on Whitney Falls.

"Hello, Miss Stephanie! I'm back. Did you miss me? I know you're ready to open that gate and invite me in."

"No. I am not. In fact, I think after this night, things are going to change."

"Is that so?"

"That's so."

"If you open the door, I will let you live, let you go back to your little dirt-eating village in the mountains."

"You killed every person I ever loved. What makes you think I trust you, let alone, what makes you think I want to go back there? If you need to know, Whitby Manor is my home now." Stephanie said. The man wasn't paying any attention to Stephanie. Instead, his attention focused on something behind her.

"What are they doing? Raking the lawn at night?"

"Not exactly."

"What do you mean not exactly?" The man asked.

"You see, I was hired for my skills as a witch. The Manor staff understood, finally, after three tries, that a Priest of Christ wasn't the way to deal with you."

"What do you mean?" The man showed fear in lieu of bravado for the first time Stephanie could remember. What she failed to share with the man was her aptitude, and it scared the bejeezus out of him.

In the month between his visits, Stephanie laughed at the ease it took for her to track down the man's lair. Quick research of the Manor's property records led her to a half-dozen locations in and surrounding London. She found it odd the records make no mention of the estate's Lord, whom she assumed to be the man claiming to own Whitby Manor.

The first property turned out to be a bust, as did the other three in neighboring communities. But when she arrived at the location on Piccadilly street, a posh mansion, Stephanie knew the man rested underneath its walls. Behind the building's stoop, a pair of doors covered the stairs leading to the basement. After opening the doors, Stephanie let Bacchus loose, sending him ahead as a scout. The familiar discovered the man's resting place, a giant box of earth, and returned to his mistress with the information.

Stephanie smiled. A new game was afoot, and the man wouldn't like its outcome.

"What are they doing?"

"Real magic from the well, not the parlor tricks you learned in Sorcery 101 at the Devil's School. They're sweeping you away, you son of a bitch, like the trash you are." Stephanie said, the words seething off her tongue.

The man roared in defiance, opening his gaping maw once again, snarling as he did. She opened her palm and thrust it forward at the man. He became enamored with the pentacle, again, and fell back to his knees, fumbling into prayer, as he did the month before.

"That's right, demon, pray. It's all you'll have left to do after tonight." Stephanie grasped her broom, and joined the housekeepers in their task.

•

Inside the basement of 138 Piccadilly Street in London, a dusty fog filled the air. A cadre of housekeepers worked, their faces covered with masks, like their lives depended on it.

"Hurry, hurry ladies, sweep, sweep it out, all of it! Out the door before the sun rises and the Master returns!" The butler told the maids as they swept the dirt out of the basement of the mansion. A trio of groundskeepers shoveled the dirt out of the crate onto the floor.

"That's the last of it, sir!" One of the men said as he dumped his spade's load.

"Good. Now, gentle fellows, kindly remove the box! We can't take any chances! Hurry, hurry!" The butler ordered. The team of workers converged on the basement's exit. "Now, all of you, go to the top floor and sweep all the way down, and we'll be done with this wretched affair."

"Yessir," the maids and groundsmen replied in unison before entering the manse's foyer, their brooms in hand.

•

The man fled from Whitby Manor, this time turning into a fluttering colony of bats, shortly before sunrise. Stephanie smiled, knowing what the coming daylight would bring. She held her broom with one hand while the other flipped the bats a middle finger. Moments later the butler and his bus, filled with maids and gardeners, returned to the Manor, after fulfilling their task in this endeavor.

SEVERANCE

"I do believe we've reached the end of our arrangement, Ms. Wells." The butler said. "I'm delighted to hand you this severance package. To say this has been a wonderful experience working with you is an understatement. Your expertise has led to a new era at Whitby Manor." Stephanie took the check. The amount on it was staggering. Still, she accepted it with grace.

"Please, don't hesitate to reach back out to me for assistance if he ever, well, you know."

"We won't expect another visit from the Master for some time, at least not in my lifetime, I don't think. If ever. Without the soil of his homeland, he's powerless, and trapped on this island. He's hiding now, vulnerable and aging by the day."

"Yes. And before long he will wither away into nothing but a bedtime story to scare little children into behaving."

"Isn't that the truth." The butler confessed. "Thank you so much, from the bottom of our, um, hearts."

"It's been my pleasure, Mr. Harker. We'll be seeing you." Stephanie Wells replied, and alongside her familiar, departed Whitby Manor.

CONCRETE HARVEST

1

Waxing to full, a Hunter's Moon illuminated the sprawl of New York City's boroughs. Silent on its watch, the cyclopean sentinel hovered over the metropolis, bleeding crimson from Rayleigh, scattering while clouds drifted past the enormous lunar illusion. Under this umbral glow, Rose McEntire sat atop her apartment building in Flatbush, her feet hanging off the ledge.

The brisk wind blew her curly, black locks about in a chaotic pattern while her legs dangled into the abyss. Lying back onto the roof's tarred surface, basking in the cool late autumn night's light, she talked to her mother on the phone. The light of the device cast a glow across her face, changing the hue of her gray eyes to an emerald green.

Rose made the fateful decision to miss her hometown's annual Second Harvest Festival, something she and her sister rarely did, and was listening to her mother's candid admonishment at the revelation.

"There's always something with your work. Are you sure you can't make it? Ever since you took that awful job in Manhattan," Peggy McEntire's voice, laden with concern, resonated from the phone's speaker as her daughter listened to the dejection in her tone. "That place is full of dig—"

"Mum! I can take care of myself."

"That's the problem, Rosie! I swear it's been like pulling teeth to get you home for anything. And last year you said you wouldn't miss it ever again."

"No, Mum," Rose replied. "I'm sorry. You know I can't miss this meeting. It's an important dinner for work. The designer from down south is coming. So are the buyers from the store in Fenton."

"It's only a four-hour drive."

"Upstate, but going back, I'll be stuck at the tunnel for at least two more hours."

"But it's the harvest feast—"

"And the posh dinner we'll have at The River Rat will suffice as a replacement, Mum. Jesus, I'll make sure I have salt potatoes and corn on the cob," Rose's rebuttals came before her mother could take another breath. "It's okay, Mum."

The McEntire matriarch sighed and paused before responding, giving her daughter a moment of concern. "But you haven't missed one since before I can remember."

"Not since I turned twenty-one and you allowed Erin and I to participate like it was drinking wine or beer."

"You and your sister were too young until then, needed to grow up some before you had your share."

"Which we did, and missing a year won't hurt. It isn't the first time, and it won't be the last."

"I saw a gray hair on you last year. You know what causes them?"

"Mum!"

"You're right, you're right. Just do me a favor, if things don't go as planned, don't take the subway home. I—we—know what comes out on nights like this. And don't forget a cathedral is always good sanct—"

"For feck's sake, Mum! Yes, I'll make sure I take an Uber and not the train to fecking church. Your guess is as good as mine when it comes to what might be lurking in the subway tunnels late at night."

"Are you sure an Uber is safe? I've heard stories about women being murdered or kidnap—"

"Mum. Really?" Rose's knack for interrupting her mother during discussions of this sort shined. Rose hated doing it, she often felt she did it too much, making her the outspoken problem child. She recalled the stern looks her father would give her when Rose would do this in his presence. The thought of him brought a smile to the young woman's face. "You are talking to your husband's daughter. I wish someone would try to kill, let alone kidnap or assault me."

"That be the truth. You're as stubborn as he be, too."

"And as tenacious," Rose growled after snapping her reply.

Her mother laughed in response.

"I'm sorry I interrupted you so much. I love you, Mum."

"It's okay. Love you, too, me little poison flower." Peggy McEntire's adoration of her youngest child danced on her words.

Rose smiled and closed the call.

Outside, the crisp autumn air blew and briefly hid the smells of the city behind the brisk aroma of dying leaves carried on the wind. It reminded Rose of home.

2

Dressed appropriately for the coming holiday, the waitstaff of The River Rat bustled about the restaurant's tight front-end. Each wore all black, their faces painted in the white and black harlequin style of Brandon Lee's Eric Draven, also known as *The Crow*. The River Rat sat within view of the Hudson from Riverside Park. To the uneducated, one might think the eatery's name stemmed from it being so close to the toxic river's rat-infested waters, but, no.

Rather, the establishment's name heralded from those who vacationed on the Saint Lawrence River on the border of New York and Canada. Filled with as many tables as possible, the staff could barely slip past the chairs of their hungry patrons. Booked solid every night, the gourmet bistro specialized in regional cuisine.

Inside, Edie Moyers, the designer from Hickory, and Bill Rosenblatt, the buyer from Donahue's furniture store in Fenton, New York, sat with Rose McEntire, reviewing the menu. The trio killed time perusing the entrees while soft music from the 1980s played, adding to the ambience. Rose found the era's music to be one of the best ever. Everything about The River Rat appealed to her, and for good reason. The place reminded her of home.

"I'm getting beef spiedies. What about you?" Rose said, not asking either of her companions in particular.

"They have haddock here in New York City?" Edie asked. "Like real haddock, not cod or flounder. I haven't had it since the last time I went up to Fenton."

"Yes, Edie. Real haddock," Rose replied, "and cooked in cornmeal like it's supposed to be."

"And served with those little salt potatoes and butter?" Edie's eyes grew large with excitement as she swiped errant strands of her long red hair out of her mouth

"And Salt potatoes, and creamy coleslaw," Rose concurred. "And this place? It even serves me favorite to wash it all down with."

"What's that?"

"Byrne Dairy chocolate milk."

"You're shitting me."

"Nope, not shitting. They serve Genny Cream Ale, too. And they have half-moons for dessert. Real half-moons, ya know. The cakes, not that cookie they call a half-moon down here."

"Damn, okay," Edie said. "I've got to use the ladies room; I'll be right back." The young woman excused herself and walked away.

"She does look vibrant, a classic red-head like Raquel Welch. You know she's going through a divorce?" Bill gazed up from his menu and spoke. His reputation as a lecherous womanizer preceded him but, that night, Bill seemed reserved.

"So I've heard," Rose replied. "Didn't she try to commit suicide or something like that, too, after her father died?"

"Yeah. I guess she failed. If you're going to fail at something, that would probably be my pick. I wonder if she's still single or if she just left him after surviving?"

"Don't get any ideas. Edie's got a reputation now," Rose said, then recognized the familiar chords and chorus of Hall & Oates' "Maneater" playing. *How appropriate,* she thought, and giggled.

"Ha! Don't you worry about that, Rosie. She's out of my league for sure. Plus, I'm way too old. But a man is allowed to dream a little, isn't he?" Bill said.

He's not wrong, Rose acknowledged silently. *Middle age crept up on him overnight,* she thought. Bill's once black mop of hair was receding on his forehead and highlighted by salt and pepper. "That he is," she said aloud.

"All jokes aside, she's got a good eye for this business. We're lucky to have her on board."

"That she does," Rose admitted and sipped on her glass of ice water. "Plus, she knows the right times to open her mouth."

"Yet another good skill to have in this business," Bill added. He saw Edie exit the lavatory and navigate the crowded dining floor to their table. "Shh, here she comes," he said as Edie reached her seat.

"What did I miss?"

"Oh, just us commenting on how big your mouth is," Rose admitted. She relished the opportunity to make the off-hand comment. She also knew Edie would be oblivious to its implications.

"It is pretty big, isn't it? Well, I'm famished," Edie said. "So right now it's big enough to devour all of this place's haddock."

Of course it is, Rose thought and smirked.

"That is, of course, if your eyes aren't bigger than your belly," Bill added.

Rose found the buyer's anachronistic clichés, the tools he used to secure big sales, oddly appropriate for the situation.

"Well, I can't go in blind now, can I? Gotta see the fish to eat the fish!" Edie replied.

The trio guffawed at her quip. The arrival of their waitress, a young woman whose badge declared her name to be Brie, ended this exchange, much to Rose's delight.

It could be the woman's scent, or her body language, or her attitude, but Rose knew one thing:

she didn't care for Edie. In hindsight, the youngest McEntire child wasn't afraid to admit...

She never did like the red-headed stepchild of a bitch.

3

Rose took a swig of her Genny Screamer, the pet name of the Genesee Cream Ale, and downed it like a champ. Her dinner guests laughed as she slammed the can back on the table. A frothy mustache remained on her lip. She licked it off and burped out a, "Hello."

"My, what a deep voice you have," Bill joked.

"All the better to speak with," Rose replied with a chuckle.

"So, Halloween is tomorrow," Bill stated. His dinner, a plate of Cornell BBQ chicken with Utica greens, steamed in front of him. He took a bite of the breast.

Rose swore he moaned as he chewed. "It is," Rose spoke up from her beef-spiedie skewers over rice.

"Scary," Edie added, dipping a fork full of fried haddock into a dish of tartar sauce.

"Did they ever catch that serial killer in your hometown?" Bill asked Rose.

"The Foothills Slasher? No."

"Aren't you afraid to go home?" Edie inquired.

"No, in fact I'd be home this weekend if not for this dinner meeting."

"Really?" Bill questioned Rose.

"Really," she affirmed.

"You know, where I live isn't much different from where you guys are from. Down in the Carolinas, and in the Appalachians, they've got lots of legends and stuff like that," Edie said. "Skunk Apes and Bigfoots, Mothmen, witches, and my favorite, Sin Eaters."

"Sin Eaters?" Bill asked.

"Yeah, they take demons and afflictions out of people, and absorb them into themselves, before vomiting them back up."

"Sounds gross," the buyer made a sourpuss and shook his head in disgust.

"It is," Edie said.

"I heard there were dinosaurs at the turkey farm in Fenton," Bill added.

"Right up there with the aliens in Happy Valley?" Rose quipped back.

Bill laughed in response.

"Other than serial killers, do you have any myths from where you grew up, Rose? It's kinda appropriate for where we're sitting, dontcha think?" Edie asked.

"I do. Well, sort of. We're in the woods of upstate New York so there's lots of legends. The local tribes have their monsters, like *Ne-On-Yar-He*, the snow serpent who eats wayward men." Rose winked at Bill. "The Headless Horseman is one of ours, too. And me Pa calls the bogeyman the Digger Do."

"Bogeyman? Isn't it the boogeyman?" Bill inquired.

"Bogeyman is the correct way to say it. It comes from English and Welsh legends, the Bogeyman was a goblin, a boggart," Rose said. "You might have heard of the Puca in Irish myth?"

"No, not really. But tell me, how do you get Digger Do out of that?" Edie asked.

"It's kind of like how we get Peggy from Margaret, and you can ask me mum about that, cos she is one. But the Digger Do isn't exactly a bogeyman."

"No? Then what is it?"

"It's the un—"

A piercing screech rose from under the music, filling the restaurant. As if rehearsed, everyone stopped whatever they may be doing in unison. The din of silverware and glass answered. Then, a brief moment of silence followed as no one moved.

"What the hell?" Bill mouthed.

The trio stared at each other until murmurs grumbled from the other patrons. Edie's head twisted left and right, seeking an answer to the sudden clamor.

A thud resonated throughout the house, breaking the silence. Another woman screamed and, within moments, it grew into a chorus as others joined.

"What the heck is that?" he motioned to a disheveled man carrying a bouquet of roses standing in front of the restaurant's bay window. Blood covered his face and dripped down his chest, making him unrecognizable. With his free hand, the man wiped his face off with a sleeve.

"Oh my," Edie said as her eyes grew wide.

Jesus Christ, you look like an anime character, Rose thought, *Sailor Moon anyone?*

"Why in the fuck are you here?" Edie declared.

"You know him?" Bill asked.

"It's Bryan, Bryan Moyers," Edie admitted.

Rose's jaw dropped in unison with Bill's at the revelation.

"You—your husband?" Bill's question came out in a stutter.

"My ex-husband."

"How did he get here?" Rose asked. "You're over six-hundred miles from home."

"Not to mention he looks like hell," Bill added. Bill's comment made Rose laugh out loud.

"You know what, Bill, you have a knack for pointing out the painfully obvious," Rose quipped.

Another chuckle built up inside her, but the man, Bryan, revealing the cause of the commotion, threw himself at the bay window, and shocked it out of her in the form of another burp. He drove his body into glass with all his force, creating another loud thud. The leaded glass again held firm and he bounced off it. He stood back for a moment, then charged into the window again with the speed of an NFL linebacker hungry to destroy the quarterback. His head struck the glass and the skin on his forehead split open. A crimson imprint of his wrinkled brow remained on the glass. It snapped him back and he stood before the window, staring forward.

"Eeeeee!" he screeched, pointing at the window. *"Deeee!"* Then he ran into it again, once again head

butting the glass. More blood splashed off his face, leaving splotches on the glass.

At first the patrons inside The River Rat reacted with curious stares and mumbles. After the third time, when they could see the bone of his skull behind the ripped skin, guests with weak constitutions gasped and fainted. The doors opened and diners flooded into the street, fleeing the scene, running to their parked cars or nearby parking garages.

"Let's go, don't let him see me!" Edie said and her companions agreed.

Bill pulled a wad of cash out of his suit jacket and placed it on the table.

"I hope three hundred covers the dinner and tip," he quipped and a moment later, Rose, Bill, and Edie joined the exodus and exited the building.

Hiding in the mob, they used the bodies to obscure Edie from Bryan's view.

"I can drive you both home," Bill said.

"Oh, thank God!" Edie said. "I'm so grateful and this is so fucked up. I'm staying at the Hyatt Place in Midtown. There's a bar, we can continue this there if you want."

"That's not far away. What a great idea," Bill replied. "Let's go, ladies!"

"Are you sure?" Rose asked.

"Yes. You can Uber from there or take a cab. Come on!" Bill motioned the women to his BMW.

They left as the crowd dissipated. Rose could see Bryan standing in the street, staring at them as they drove off, down Riverside Park, away from The River Rat and the fracas.

4

The bar at the Hyatt Midtown on 36th Street was empty except for the bartender, Rose, Bill, and Edie. Rose and Bill talked about the night's chaos while Edie sat at the end of the bar, on her phone with her attorney.

Fifteen minutes in, Rose couldn't hear their discussion, and she didn't care. She also knew Edie would spew all she spoke about with them soon as the call ended.

"I need to get back to my room," Bill said, and finished drinking his beer. "All this excitement has been too much for me. Do you need a ride home?"

"No, thank you, Bill," Rose replied. "I'm gonna stay here with Edie for a bit. I'll take an Uber when I'm ready. Thank you for getting us out of that mess."

"It was my pleasure." Bill tiptoed over to Edie and tapped her on the shoulder.

She glanced back and Bill mouthed 'good-bye' and waved.

She nodded and waved back, then muted her phone.

"Thank you for everything, Bill," Edie said and unmuted the call, returning to the conversation.

"Yes, yes. I'm still here. Sorry..." she turned her head and went back to her call.

Bill waved to Rose one more time and exited the bar.

"I'll have another Jameson and ginger," Rose told the bartender, a tall, balding man with blue eyes whose name badge read Charles.

He didn't respond. Instead, he grasped a rock glass and filled it with ice. The Irish whiskey followed, then the ginger ale, and lime.

Rose smiled as he set it before her, "Thanks."

"Not a problem," Charles replied.

"So, are we a Charles or a Chaz or a Chuck?"

"We're a Charles."

"Fair enough," Rose said.

"So, you were at the place on Riverside with the zombie guy?"

"Zombie guy?" Rose's curiosity piqued.

"Yeah, that's what the news is calling him. The talking heads are saying it was some Halloween Devil's Night prank."

"Yeah, I saw it all. It's appropriate. They caught him, right?"

"Nope. He disappeared in the crowd."

This can't be good, Rose thought. When they left, he was standing there bleeding from throwing himself into the window, staring at them. Her head darted left and right. Isolated within the hotel, there were no windows. *Could he have tracked us here? Did he know what hotel Edie was staying in?* The questions ran through Rose's mind at lightspeed.

A few moments later when her call ended, Edie joined Rose at the bar. Her facial expressions betrayed her concern, at least to the bartender.

Rose knew better. "What did they say?" Rose asked.

"One second," Edie held a finger up to Rose. "Bartender, I need another gin and tonic."

His name is Charles, Rose thought.

"So, from what Bracken, my lawyer, says, a warrant is out for his arrest. That's about all they can do. I'm also under the impression the cops didn't catch him back there. So..." she paused for effect while Charles placed her drink on the bar. She sipped it, then continued, "He's still fucking out there."

"I'm well aware. You've been through a lot in the last couple years. How's it feel to be riding a shit snowball downhill?"

"What do you mean?"

"Well, with your father passing, then the, um... suicide attempt, and now your divorce? And all this happens when you've gotten a promotion. I can't imagine the stress you're going through."

"Stress? You have no idea. Without my job to focus on I'd be in the ground, I'm sure. But I'm not and now you know why I like these so much." Edie raised her glass and toasted Rose.

"Slainte!" Rose declared, and the women finished their drinks. "Well, I'm going to call my Uber and go home. It helps living down here. Well, in Brooklyn, but you know."

"Yes, I do! I can't wait to see you again, Rose!" Edie said and blew her a kiss.

"Same here. I'm certain you'll see me soon!" Rose replied and mentally added, *Sooner than later.*

"Hey, one thing before you go."

"What's that?"

"You never did say what that Digger Do thing was. I mean, we were so rudely interrupted," Edie said.

"The Digger Do? It's how me pa says Dearg Due, the Irish word for what other people call vampires," Rose replied.

"You mean like Dracula?"

Rose nodded as she stood from her stool at the bar.

"Oh, isn't that cute. Bartender! I'll take another one," Edie said as Rose left and let the glass doors close behind her.

"His name is Charles," Rose said after the mechanism clicked. She felt a bit of relief by verbally expressing this thought. A toothy smile covered her face as the elevator doors beckoned and as a mental addendum formed in her head, *You asshole.*

5

The gibbous moon reached its zenith as Rose watched 36th Street in Hell's Kitchen from her perch. Obscured from onlookers by signage for a health insurance company and the Metropolitan Food Bank, her viewpoint gave her easy access to the street, or a nearby parking garage. She waited for the inevitable. Anyone walking from Riverside to

Midtown would pass this way. If Bryan Moyers followed them, at roughly three miles an hour walking speed, he would be coming this way shortly. Her intuition proved to be correct when Rose smelled him. This put her on alert, and she cocked her head down the alley.

A few moments later, she spotted him shambling down the sidewalk, his white shirt stained black from the drying blood. He still grasped the tattered remains of the rose bouquet in his hand.

Good. Now where is she?

Bryan stood still at the entrance to the alley.

Rose could hear his labored breathing from her hiding spot. His fetid stench permeated the air. It tickled Rose's nostrils and she wondered, rhetorically, *Is he dead or close to it?*

"Bryan, why did you follow me?" Rose heard Edie say.

The woman was out of eyesight, but Rose could tell she was outside the alley near him. She shifted in place to get a better perspective.

"EeeeeDeeee!" Bryan half mumbled, half roared, and held the roses out in front of him. Edie stepped into view, stopping before her ex-husband. He repeated himself, shaking the roses as he spoke. She didn't move.

"Keep those fucking things away from me! It's too late for that, Bryan. It's too late for all of that. And you know what? Come to think of it, I never wanted to be with you in the first place. My fucking father made me marry you because your family had clout. And what has that gotten me? Not a Goddamn thing! I should have killed you after I killed him when I had the chance, but no, I didn't. Well, after the stunt you pulled tonight, guess what?" She slapped the roses out of his hand. The flowers flew about in chaos, falling to the sidewalk. Before the last stalk landed, Edie reached forward with incredible speed and grabbed Bryan by the neck.

Rose watched as Edie lifted her ex as easily as one would pick up a drink.

"I'm free of both of you now, you sons of bitches!" Edie bellowed and threw Bryan into the alley.

His body flew under Rose's hiding spot and collided headfirst with a dumpster. The thud of a two-hundred-pound man hitting quarter-inch thick steel was followed by a sickening snap. Rose knew Bryan's neck broke on the impact. If he was near death before, he certainly was up close and personal with the Grim Reaper now.

Edie sulked down the alley and stood before Bryan's body.

"Finally, fucking finally, you bastard," Edie said and kicked his arm. It flopped back to his side.

Rose took advantage of the moment and, without a sound, dropped down from her perch, landing a few yards behind Edie, blocking the woman's exit from the alley.

"Digger... Do," Rose growled.

Startled, Edie heard the voice, but didn't turn around.

"My, what a deep voice you have," Edie said.

"The better to greet you with, Digger Do," Rose replied.

Edie turned around.

The shadows cast by the moon's light obscured Rose. She stepped forward and placed a hand on either wall of the alley.

"My, what big hands you have," Edie said.

"All the better to hold you with, Digger Do," Rose replied and took another step forward. Still hidden in the darkness, the crimson moonlight shone on Rose's eyes, and they came to life, burning a brilliant amber in the night.

"My, what big eyes you have," Edie said.

"The better to see you with, Digger Do," Rose replied and took another step forward, exposing her full form. Rose knew Edie expected to see a waif of a girl. Rose did, indeed, stand in the alley, but it wasn't the Rose who Edie knew. Instead, a half-human/half-wolf amalgam towered before her, nearly seven feet tall with a canine head and a maw filled with fangs and pointed teeth. Swirling tattoos of spirals and knots in a bright blue covered the creature's black fur. The woman-beast howled.

"My, what a big mouth you have!" Edie declared.

"The best to eat you with, Digger Do," the Rose-thing replied.

Edie screamed back in defiance and charged. She threw a punch and immediately regretted doing so.

Rose caught Edie's arm with a ham-fist paw and lifted her to eye level.

Edie thrashed about in Rose's vice grip, kicking and screaming. But the incredible strength she exhibited on the street had disappeared.

"Holy ground, Digger Do," Rose said and turned her head. The cross of Metropolitan Community Church glowed softly in the night behind her.

Edie fell into prayer, "I believe in God, the Father almighty, Creator of heaven and earth, and in Jesus Christ, his only Son, our Lord, who was conceived by the Holy Spirit..."

Ignoring the prayers, Rose held Edie up, and with her free paw, extended a claw and sliced the woman's belly open. Entrails spilled out, glistening in the moonlight.

Edie didn't stop praying, "...born of the Virgin Mary, suffered under Pontius Pilate, was crucified, died and was buried; He descended into hell; on the third day He rose again from the dead..." Most of Edie's blood evacuated her body with her guts. It was obvious her lungs were still in there, and somehow her diaphragm still worked, allowing Edie's prayer to continue, "He ascended into heaven, and is seated at the right hand of God the Father almighty; from there he will come to judge the living and the dead..."

Rose let Edie finish her prayer before finishing her work.

"I believe in the Holy Spirit, the holy catholic Church, the communion of Saints, the forgiveness of sins, the resurrection of the body, and life everlasting."

"Amen. Nothing I hate more than a shit licking Digger Do," Rose finished for her, and bit Edie's head off at the neck.

The head bounced in the alley and landed next to Bryan's corpse. No more blood coursed through

Edie's veins and, as a result, the act seemed anti-climactic.

Rose dropped her body next to his and licked her snout and paw clean of viscera and gore. Satisfied with the results of her hunt, Rose leapt up the fire escapes to the top of the building. With the moon behind her, she howled long and proud...

6

Inside her flat in Flatbush, Rose McEntire slept soundly, late into the morning of Halloween, until her cell phone rang. Waking her from her slumber, she fumbled about the blankets, looking for the intrusive device. The caller ID indicated Bill Rosenblat. She knew why he was calling and decided to play along. She put the phone on speaker.

"Hello, Rosie? It's Bill. Happy Halloween."

"Yes, I know it's Bill. Happy Halloween to you, too. What's up?"

"Just so ya know, the police might be calling to ask you some questions about last night?"

"Oh, why's that?"

"Bryan was found dead in an alley in Hell's Kitchen and Edie is missing."

"Are you shitting me?"

"Nope. I just got off the phone with the detectives. I guess they said you left right after I did?"

"Yeah, I did; took an Uber home. And thanks for waking me up." Rose pulled the sheets back and stood up.

"So, yeah, it's weird. Why'd she just disappear like that? And how his body was found, just weird. You think she… you know…?"

Bill's voice faded off and Rose went to her bathroom for her morning piss. "What? You think she might've killed him?"

"Who knows?"

"Well, thanks for the heads up. I don't want to talk to you while I'm on the bowl. It's not right, Bill."

"Yeah, I'm with ya there. Let me know what happens when you talk to the police."

"I will. Goodbye, Mr. Rosenblat," Rose said.

"Goodbye, Miss Rosie!" Bill replied.

Rose disconnected the call. She sat on the toilet, pissed, and pondered the previous night's events. "What a night," Rose wondered aloud. "Looks like I better make sure everything is cleaned up before I talk to the detectives." Rose wiped and moved to the sink to wash her face. The warm water woke her up more and rinsed the crusties from her eyes. She opened the shower curtain and grabbed a towel from the rack on the wall. "Ya know what? I can't wait to call me Mum. She's gonna be proud of me, tracking down a bottom feeding Digger Do all on my own for the Harvest," Rose said to Edie Moyer's headless, desiccated corpse hanging in the stand-up shower next to her. The dead woman's head rested on the floor of the stall by the drain, staring up at Rose

McEntire with lifeless eyes. "It's called the Hunter's Moon for a reason, ya know."

THOMAS R CLARK

GIANTS

1

Chaos resonated off wooded hills and fire burned, casting a smokey haze over the crimson embers of dusk. Sitting on the porch of The Syracuse Grand Hotel smoking a cigar, Johnny Lee Earle could hear the screams and gunshots, spoiling the serenity of the crisp fall night. Somewhere, a wolf howled in the wilderness, providing an eerie soundtrack to the violence.

A retired Union Cavalry Captain, Earle knew a battle of some sort ensued. He could see flames on the horizon and taste the smoke. The veteran in him recalled seeing this image as he marched with General Sherman as they righteously burned down Georgia and forced the rebels to submit.

Earle didn't come here to reminisce. His bones ached from travel. For a day he followed the Erie Canal from nearby Palmyra, on the orders of his Mormon brethren in Utah. The Twelve, the Mormon Church's leading body, heard of a miraculous discovery in the hills of New York and needed to understand more. Johnny Lee saw evidence of the rumors tacked on telegraph poles throughout the area.

"The Petrified Giant of Cardiff!" Placards declared, encouraging those who saw the sign to travel to the farm and see the wonder for themselves.

"*Has a petrified man from some biblical age been discovered in Cardiff? Or is it a fake?*" the telegram said. Earle's orders from the Twelve were simple. If it were determined to be a fake, leave it be and return home. But, if the giant is authentic, from the word of the Lord God ...

"*Take the asset by any means necessary.*"

Johnny Lee came here to investigate, to be the eyes and ears of the Twelve, to ascertain the mystery behind the curtain, and verify the claims. Proof of a Biblical giant helped validate the doctrine of the Mormon Church in North America.

The Twelve were no fools. Fifty dollars helped secure the deal. Much more came to the table after he completed the job. And thus Johnny Lee came to Syracuse. Other than the handsome stipend, he wanted proof of God for his own personal reasons. After witnessing the horrors of war, he now doubted God existed. And so, if not for the Twelve, then for himself, Johnny Lee came to answer the questions for all involved.

War. Johnny Lee shook his head in disgust. He took a toke on the cigar and turned his attention to the glow of the fire raging nearby. The clamor, the hoots, and hollering, it all brought him back to the war. He recognized them as Rebel yells. Whoever made the ruckus didn't know the War of Rebellion ended a couple of years ago.

A horse, being pushed to full gallop by its rider, roared past the hotel, and into the neighboring corral. Johnny Lee's own horse rested in the confines of the Salina Corral. He watched the rider sneak out the back a few moments later, and onto the deck of the Hotel.

"We don't serve your kind here," the overweight hotel doorman said while placing his hand up in a 'stop' motion, "plus, can't you read? No shoes, no service!" These words, spoken with disgust, caught Johnny Lee's ears and his attention. Sure enough, the doorman spoke to the rider, a dark-haired woman who wore the clothing of a typical resident. The distress on the woman's face betrayed the fear coursing through her body.

Johnny noted a long tear in the fabric of her shirt, exposing her back. Streaks of blood covered her arm. Mud and something black stained her cotton skirt. She wore no shoes, but what caught Johnny Lee off guard were the spiral tattoos, stained blue, covering her back.

A warbled Rebel yell echoed down the street. Johnny Lee saw the fear cover her face. She turned, and ran into the dark of the stable, blending with the horses and shadows.

Not long after, when the man missing half his jaw came looking for the girl, Johnny Lee Earle felt it prudent he not reveal where the young woman ran off to. The cowboy made this an easy task to accomplish. Johnny Lee feigned ignorance and an inability to understand the man's speech. Losing half your jaw is as good a catalyst as any for a speech impediment.

"Dib ube seeb abe wib cumb trube thibs wabes?" He wore the grey long coat of a Confederate veteran of the War of Rebellion. Johnny Lee saw this often, the veterans of the war coming north, looking for work.

Or trouble.

"Pardon me?" Johnny Lee said from the comfort of his chair on the porch of the Syracuse Grand Hotel. He put his hand up to his ear, "come again?"

"Ibe seb, dib ube seeb abe wib?" The man's frustration grew. Johnny Lee could see it glaring in his eyes.

"No, I haven't seen nothing. Sorry." He tipped the brim of his hat at the man, revealing the crossed sabers of the Union Cavalry.

"Ub courb yube dibn't," the rebel muttered. He fidgeted with his gun belt. The pistol wanted to fall out, but something restrained it from succumbing to gravity. Johnny Lee saw the Hotel doorman step forward. The fat fuck opened his mouth to speak until he saw the former Union soldier staring him down.

"Wub ub up ube?" The Confederate asked the portly doorman.

"What did you say?" The doorman responded. Johnny Lee continued to stare at him. He could see the sweat bead on the doorman's brow. He blinked his eyes far too much.

"Dib yube seeb a wib cumb dibs wabe?" The half-jawed veteran's frustration communicating started showing. He put his hand on his pistol.

"Did I see a what?" Johnny Lee saw the doorman's eyes moved and blinked in a pattern as if the fat bastard were attempting to tell him something. The blinks were dots, the moving eyes were dashes. Morse code. Eye-eye-blink, blink-blink-eye, eye-blink. Over and over.

Gun.

Johnny Lee pulled his service revolver, a Navy Colt out of its scabbard, and pointed it at the half-jawed man in the street.

"I wouldn't do that, were I you, Johnny Reb," Johnny Lee declared, his eyes never leaving the doorman. Then he cocked the trigger back with his thumb, "we have an understanding, yes?" The cowboy grabbed the reins of his horse with both hands and turned the beast around.

"Yube beb. Goob nibe!" The cowboy rode off at full gallop and everything returned to normal. The doorman slinked back into his position by the door. Johnny Lee holstered his pistol. He sat back down and retrieved his smoldering cigar from the ashtray.

A few minutes later Johnny Lee watched the tattooed woman sneak out of the stable with her horse. She clasped her chest in relief, showing appreciation for what Johnny Lee did for her.

"Ma'am," Johnny Lee replied, nodded, and tipped his hat. The woman smiled back and wiped a tear from her cheek. Without any words, she mounted the animal and ran off, away from the half-jawed man.

2

A forest canopy of trees covers the rolling hillsides. With the brisk air of early autumn, it is colored in a bright myriad of shades- orange, yellow, red, and green. A misty fog, the last remnant of an earlier rainfall, lingers about, clinging to the foliage. And in the middle of all of it, a throng of people gathered together, traipsing down a muddy trail stomped into the red clay.

A line of pedestrians, wagons, and horses spread down the crude path cut into the woods as far as the eye could see. Hundreds of pilgrims came from Syracuse in the north or Binghamton to the south. Just as many came from as far east as Albany, and more from Rochester and Buffalo to the west. Each with fifty cents in their hand. This would purchase a ticket for a wagon ride to an archeological location, to catch a glimpse of the petrified man of Cardiff.

Johnny Lee Earle, sitting atop his horse, approached the end of the line. A half dozen weathered cowboys on horseback preceded him, a grim reminder of the catalysts for Earle's loss of faith. One of them turned his head to give Johnny Lee a once over. He wore the long riding jacket of a Confederate cavalryman, Johnny Lee couldn't be sure, but these men were likely the friends of the half-jawed freak from the night before. He didn't see the man, something Johnny Lee felt grateful for. Johnny Lee killed more than his share of the cowboy's peers during the war. Earle tipped his hat in response, revealing the crossed sabers of his Union Cavalryman's hat. The cowboy nodded and went back to minding his own business.

From his viewpoint, near the top of the hill, Johnny Lee could see a staging area where visitors were being loaded onto a wagon. He hadn't seen a sight as remarkable since Howe opened up his cave to the public back before the war against the south. Johnny Lee remembered his folks taking him as a child to see a wedding at the Howe caves. He struck the distracting memory from his head. He didn't come here to reminisce. Johnny Lee focused on the task at hand, patiently waiting in line.

He wasn't at the end of the line for long. More pilgrims extended the line behind Johnny Lee. First, a family of negroes found their place next to him. A mother, father, and a trio of children, all boys. The wife, an attractive woman with a welcoming smile, and her husband a large muscular man. Barefoot, their clothing barely rags, but each held a pair of silver quarter dollar coins to see the curiosity below.

Then a single horse wagon with a middle-aged couple pulled in behind. He couldn't help but overhear their conversation. It occupied him and gave him pause to laugh.

"I don't know, Arthur. I know the paper said it's the petrified body of a giant from the bible, you know, with two rows of teeth. But then I heard

Joyce, at the church meeting. She said her Indian squaw friend, Mary Shint-wana'bar, at the market, says it's the remains of one of their heathen Stone Coats," The woman said to the man with the gusto of a skilled orator, Johnny Lee mused. "And they're cannibals who devour the flesh of evil men!" This made Johnny Lee giggle. Country life certainly bred a superstitious lot.

"That's all bullshit, woman, and you know it. For one, Margaret, you're going to believe the word of a redskin named Shits-with-a-bear? Does she shit in the woods, like a bear, too? For the love of sweet Jesus, I can't believe you're making me spend a dollar of my hard-earned money on this... this whatever it is."

"The remains of a giant from the Bible, praise the Lord. One of the fallen angels called the Nephilim." She replied. "And don't you be taking the Lord's name in vain, Arthur Warden! There are children present! What did I tell you about using those words?"

"I, I..." The matron slapped her husband. The blow knocked his hat forward onto his nose. The crack gave Johnny Lee pause, and he turned back to look. Johnny Lee saw Margaret, a frumpy matron, in a blue dress and white bonnet, scowl. Gray, curly hair stuck out from underneath the cloth. Mr. Warden, middle-aged, balding under his wide-brimmed hat, looked away in embarrassment. The discussion also attracted the attention of the cowboys. The one Johnny Lee nodded to spoke up.

"They're only coons, Ma'am," the cowboy said and spat on the ground. "It's not like he cussed in front of human children," a look of shock covered Margaret's face.

"Excuse me, sir?" Mrs. Warden admonished the cowboy. "I'll have you know our son died fighting those traitorous Johnny Rebs, so these poor negro children could live free!" Behind him, Johnny Lee could hear uncomfortable grumbles come from the cowboys.

"Is that so?" The cowboy said.

"Yes, it is so." She replied. He tipped his hat to the family and turned around.

"Margaret, maybe it's best we don't antagonize these nice gentlemen," Arthur interjected.

"This man is rude! Are you saying our son died for nothing? You should be ashamed of yourself!"

"It's okay, Ma'am. The children have heard worse." The father of the children cut into the conversation, bowing his head in humility. "And I'm sorry about your son."

Johnny Lee could feel something creeping up his spine. He looked around and saw the cowboys ahead of him were all focused on the interaction between the two families.

"Don't be. He died fighting for the right thing. Didn't he, Arthur." One of the cowboys spit on the ground and grunted.

"Yes, Margaret, he did. And we're mighty proud of him. I'm Arthur Warden, please forgive my language. You use words for so long, they often become a habit. What's your name?" He asked the father.

"Washington. Bill Washington. And this is my wife, Celia and our boys: George, John, and Joseph."

"Well, Bill Washington," Arthur said, "why don't you and your Mrs. hop in the back of our wagon and ride it to the bottom of the hill?"

"It's what our son would want," Margaret added.

"Thank you, sir... Ma'am. Thank you very much." Bill Washington bowed his head each time he said 'Thank You'. Another cowboy spit out a wad of tobacco, it sank into the mud with a wet plop.

The cowboys ceased to pay any further attention and focused on riding ahead to the attraction. The line moved forward, and Johnny Lee urged his horse down the trail. They arrived to find one wagon mostly filled. The cowboys filled the seats. Johnny Lee could swear they didn't stop staring at him the entire time.

When Earle finally made it to the front, where the farmer's house stood, he dismounted. Across the field, he could see the trail leading to the barn. A boy tethered his horse and another led Johnny Lee to a seat on an open wagon. The mud came up to ankles, and had he not been wearing the boots of a cavalryman, he may have lost his footgear. He saw the Washingtons didn't need to worry about the goop. None of them wore shoes.

A bumpy ride through the farmer's field followed. Margaret and Arthur sat across from him, next to the barefoot Washington brood. A bumpy ride across the field brought them to a canvas tent behind a barn, blocking the outside view of something underneath. A steward helped the patrons out of the wagon and led them in a single file under the tent. An usher stood at the entrance.

"You'll have five minutes to view the body," The usher, a young man in overalls and a straw hat, declared, and brought them inside. Inside the tent, minimal lighting worked overtime. What Johnny Lee saw, still partially buried in the ground, gave him pause.

A remarkable sight, indeed, he thought.

A large man, made of stone, lay in the ground. If he stood, the man would have been of giant proportions, towering over those present. Johnny Lee presumed the giant would stand at least twelve feet high. He found the face to be surprisingly familiar. He scratched his beard, trying to place it.

"Praise Jesus. He's got six fingers on his hand. It's a Nephilim." Bill Washington fell to his knees, reciting the Lord's prayer.

"Would you look at that, Margaret," Arthur Warden spoke up. "He's got a giant pecker!" The Washington boys giggled, their mother shot them an evil glare, and all three of them straightened up. Johnny Lee snickered, too, as he watched Mrs. Warden slap her husband in the back of the head. He spoke the truth, despite being vulgar.

"Watch your language, this is a sacred burial site!"

"Yes, dear," the dejected husband relented.

"Hey, that looks like Abraham Lincoln a little, doesn't it?" Arthur Warden noted. Johnny Lee couldn't tell in the dim light, but he might be right.

"Maybe if Lincoln were five thousand years old," the usher said. "Time's up people, please exit to your right and you will be returned to the top of the property. Thank you for witnessing the most exciting archeological find in history!"

Before Johnny Lee could get a good solid look at the body and face, the usher escorted them out of the tent. A flyby viewing and Johnny Lee Earle couldn't ascertain the Cardiff Giant to be the real deal or a hoax. As Johnny Lee, the Washingtons, Wardens, and all the others shuffled away, he knew one certainty.

He'd have to come back later...

3

The late October night in upstate New York possesses a bite as sharp as any predator. It's not cold enough to snow, but the cold chills the bones enough to remind you piles were coming. The darkness, in conjunction with the trees of the rolling hills, created a lightless void filled with dense vegetation. A low hanging fog blotted out any other light lucky enough to have slipped through the trees from the moon and stars above. It made for difficult, if not impossible, passage.

Johnny Lee Earle, a lantern in one hand and a pickaxe in the other, discovered this as he attempted to make his way through the woods surrounding the Newell Farm. He planned to circumvent the property and sneak back into the tent and get a better glimpse of the alleged petrified man.

The plan turned to shit. Any hope of it coming to fruition collapsed with each step Johnny Lee took. Gnarled branches, spiked nettles, and needle tipped Buckthorn cut into him, tearing his clothes and making a general mess of the whole situation.

This isn't worth fifty dollars, for the love of God, Johnny Lee thought as another thorn sank into his flesh. He bled from over a dozen punctures and scrapes. Each pinch and cut made him think of Jesus and his Passion.

Why endure this for a faith he may not believe in anymore? He asked himself. All for a closer look at a hoax. *Yes. It needed to be done.* He needed to know.

He would inspect it up close, check the mouth, see if it possessed two rows of teeth. Check the hands, verify the number of fingers. If these panned out, he could confirm a Biblical Nephilim. It would be the greatest and most important archeological discovery of the 19th Century, lending credibility to the scriptures.

Provided an authentic lay in the pit, in the first place. Johnny Lee would know the answer soon.

Then he heard the screams. They were shrill, like a rabbit, but clearly human.

The gunshots followed, and more screams.

Johnny Lee didn't have to wonder what might be going on. He swung the pickaxe, cutting a desperate path through the vegetation. Branches cracked and broke as the heavy iron tool pulverized the wood.

Thorns and splinters flew in the air as he made his way out of the briar patch.

The sounds of violence increased, as did Earle's fury in cutting out a trail. His breath, hot and frequent, created a secondary fog encircling his head like a halo. Sweat beaded on his forehead, dripping into his eyes, stinging them. He dropped his lantern. It wasn't helping anyhow.

Within minutes Johnny Lee found himself standing in a clearing. The screams became loud, resonating sobs, and they came from down the hill. He ran as fast as his legs could take him to the sounds. And fell to the ground when fire brightened the night.

Johnny Lee couldn't believe his eyes.

Arthur Warden's wagon, tipped on its side, burned. The flames crackled and snapped, filling the trail with light. The team of horses both lie on the ground in a clump. Hanging from the wagon's axles were two immolated bodies.

Johnny Lee Earle's mind did not doubt their identities. As he watched the blue, yellow, and red flames tickle the blackened bodies. He hoped his lack of faith was a misgiving. He hated to know what secrets, if any, were held in an afterworld without faith. Yet, if his faith were true, and Heaven did exist, then Margaret and Arthur Warden were reunited with their son.

One certainty existed, the cowboys he encountered earlier in the day were responsible in some manner for this atrocity. They made him sick. Bastards like them stole Johnny Lee's faith, to begin with. And here they were, testing his resolve one more time.

It's like God meant it to be this way, he thought.

Johnny Lee saw the fire lit up the trail leading to the Newell farm and the Giant of Cardiff. The trees lining both sides of the backcountry path gave it the look of a tunnel in the flickering light of the flames. From down the trail, the sounds of snorting, galloping horses and men, hooting and whistling filled the night. Johnny Lee hugged the tree line and crept down the trail. He came to bend in the path. Beyond it, the source of the commotion revealed itself. Rounding the bend, sticking to the hedge, Johnny Lee Earle came upon a true vision of Hell.

A scene of carnage unfolded before him. Six men on horseback, Johnny Lee recognized them as the cowboys from earlier in the night, carried torches. Five of them each dragged a single body behind their horse. The sixth, the cowboy from earlier in the cavalry duster, carried a Virginia Battle Flag of the Confederacy. Each of them hooted and whistled in jubilation as they urged their horses on, running in circles, dragging the mangled bodies behind them.

Though he couldn't see their mutilated faces, based on their numbers and what he could make of their attire, he knew who ...

The Washingtons.

Sweet Jesus, Johnny Lee thought, *how could they have done this?* He should have seen it coming, the way they reacted to them in line. Johnny Lee knew many ex-cavalrymen from both the north and south transitioned to the migratory work of cattle herders when the war ended.

The men reined in their horses and brought them to a stop. Mud splashed off the beasts' hooves as they did. Johnny Lee saw the bodies of the Washingtons slide through the mud and slap into one another, unceremoniously.

"What is it Jed?" One of the cowboys said.

"Yeab Jeb, wub ib ib?" Johnny Lee heard the half-jawed Confederate distinct speech impediment.

"Shut the fuck up, Bobby Bill. We can't understand a fucking thing you say. And Leonard? Did you hear that?" The cowboy carrying the flag, Jed, clearly led the band of misfits. Johnny Lee held his hat down. How could they have not seen him coming through the woods and down the trail?

"Hear what?" A perplexed Leonard replied. Behind him lay the body of Celia Washington, still wearing most of her dress. The rebels ripped off one of her breasts and caved most of her pretty face into her skull.

The racket became audible for all to hear. Branches cracked and broke, unseen in the darkness of the woods.

"Who's out there?" Jed shouted, "You like what you see? It will happen to you and your family, too, if you open your mouth!" He cocked the hammer back on his pistol.

Johnny Lee listened to the man. He couldn't know Johnny Lee wasn't local, or he didn't have a family. The time came to stop hiding and come out of the darkness. He still had work to do.

A long, baleful howl erupted from the woodline.

"Holy Jesus, it can't be!" Leonard shouted. Johnny Lee looked to the woodline and couldn't believe his eyes. A haze of gray smoke cut through the fog near the edge of the clearing. Something darted out of the woods, moving faster than a human eye could follow.

A giant bestial thing followed them. It stood nearly ten feet high with a humanoid-lupine head, and covered in thick black fur. It leaped out of the woodline, the eyes glowed a fierce golden amber. The face looked nothing like the giant at the excavation site. A scowling caricature of agony, with distorted features not quite human and not quite...

Wolf?

Long, thick, black hair fell from its head and covered its shoulders. It flowed behind like a cape as the thing lumbered toward the cowboys, the impact of each step sending mud flying in all directions.

Johnny Lee closed his eyes, clasped his hands, and started to pray. He started by reciting the Lord's Prayer. The smell of death permeated the air, bleeding from each wound the creature inflicted on the cowboys.

"Our Father, who art in heaven..." He tried as hard as he might to keep his eyes closed, but shouts and screams would force an involuntary response, flickering his lids open. Images of violence, each more revolting than the last, filtered through.

"Hallowed be thy name..."

The cowboys' horses reared and kicked. The terrified men could do nothing to control the startled beasts. Torches were scattered about, landing in a circle around the men. Before Johnny Lee could complete the first line, all six cowboys were ejected from their mounts, landing in the mud.

"Thy Kingdom come..."

One cowboy landed wrong, breaking his neck on impact. The half-jawed idiot went down, too, trampled by his own horse, an errant hoof flattening his skull. The horses ran away in fear, down the trail, towards the praying Johnny Lee.

"Thy will be done..." Earle saw the horses coming and rolled into the tree line to avoid getting trampled. The Washington family followed behind the stampede, their tethers still attached to the saddles.

"On Earth as it is in Heaven..."

Johnny Lee's pickaxe, left on the trail, caught Bill Washington's ribcage and ripped his torso off. His broken, twisted arms stuck out from his broken shoulders. His head lolled to one side, giving Johnny Lee a clear view of the dead man's brain cavity.

"Give us this day our daily bread..."

Down the trail, in the clearing, the giant, wolfman thing set upon the cowboys. It opened its snout wide, revealing a double set of fangs in its gaping maw. A long, hairy arm grabbed a cowboy by his kicking leg, lifted the struggling, twisting man into the air and ate him in three mouthfuls. The first bite took a chunk out of the man's left side, leaving his head still attached and allowing him agonizing moments to scream in terror before the second chomp shut him the fuck up.

"And forgive us our trespassers ..."

Another cowboy stood up, regaining his consciousness after being dazed from his fall. The beast helped him up, and the cowboy did nothing but stand paralyzed in fear.

Then the creature tore the cowboy in half.

The monster opened its mouth, relishing in the gore and blood, licking its lips with a slug-like tongue.

"As we forgive those who trespass against us..."

"No! Oh no, you don't! No!" Jed screamed as Leonard helped him stand. Jed drew a revolver from a holster on his hip. Leonard held a double-barreled shotgun. Both men unloaded all of their ammunition on the giant. The bullets smashed into the giant thing's hide, creating little fires in the act. They did nothing to stop the creature's progress.

"Do not bring us into temptation..."

The thing casually cast an arm aside, and a clawed hand caught Leonard in his chest. Johnny Lee could hear all twelve of the man's ribs snap in unison. A stream of bloody vomit erupted from his mouth. Earle watched the cowboy fly through the air, leaving a banshee howl, and a trail of gore, in his wake. The man disappeared into the tree line with his cries.

"But rescue us from evil..."

Jed attempted to reload his pistol, dropping a handful of bullets to the ground in the act. He bent over to retrieve one and the giant snatched him up by the long coat's tail. It held him high in the air. Jed fought and squirmed, trying to escape from the jacket's confines. The thing hung Jed over the creature's gaping maw, planning a second helping of asshole for the night's service.

Jed slipped out of the coat. He fell almost fifteen feet into the mud and rolled.

"Fuck you!" Jed screamed at the giant in defiance.

"For the Kingdom and the power and the glory are ours forever..." Johnny Lee's prayer continued.

The giant wolfman thing responded by flicking the cowboy in the head with one of its clawed finger tips. It shut the cowboy up for good.

Jed's jaw flew in the opposite direction of the rest of him. A stream of blood poured out of the bottom of the former cavalry man's face. He collapsed on the muddy trail in a clump. The creature raised a foot over what remained of Jed's head. Johnny Lee brought his clenched fists to his eyes, to shield him from seeing the clawed foot step on Jed's head. Thankfully it sank into the muddy ground before popping.

"In the name of the Father, Son, and Holy Ghost..."

The beast thing looked his way and snorted. Certain this ... thing to be a Nephelhim of lore, and thus a validation of his faith, Johnny Lee Earle refused to move. The enormous thing roared and walked up the trail toward Johnny Lee. He pinched his eyes closed, finishing his prayer.

"Amen." Johnny Lee let out an exasperated sigh of relief when he finished and said nothing more.

He watched the creature bound back into the woodline, following Leonard's trajectory. Crashing limbs and broken branches gave way to a brief screech of terror, stifled by a loud ripping sound from within the forest. His mind tried to tell Johnny Lee the crunching sound came from the creature walking. But reality told him Leonard became the main dish of the evening.

Silence hung in the foggy air for an eternity... until a victorious howl tore through the late autumn night.

Then the crashing of trees and brush returned in earnest. Johnny Lee laid motionless, breathing through his mouth so as to be as quiet as possible. He held his eyes closed as long as he could, opening them only revealed the corpse of Bill Washington, somehow still able to stare into his soul without a face.

He heard the steps of the giant thing grow closer. He could hear its labored breathing grow louder with each passing moment. Johnny closed his eyes again, knowing the end would soon come.

It didn't.

Instead, he heard the distinct clopping of hooves in the dirt and mud. A horse snorted. He opened his eyes.

The young woman from the night before stood before him, naked, with long dark hair and blue spiral tattoos covering most of her body. She mounted the horse. Tied to its mane by their hair, what remained of the men's heads screamed in silence.

"It's over, sir," she said, "thank you for yesterday."

"You're much obliged, ma'am," Johnny Lee said, his voice shaking as he spoke. He didn't make eye contact with her, or look at her nakedness, no Godly man would do such a thing. Instead, he stared back at the decapitated heads.

"The god provides," she said, and rode away.

God does indeed, provide, Johnny thought. He didn't move after she left. Above him, the moon grew smaller in size as frost covered his body, but he dared not move, out of fear the creature would come back to finish the job. Then the sun's glow came upon the eastern horizon, and Johnny Lee knew he needed to move.

He stood, a thin sheen of ice cracking off his clothing. He walked down the trail as the sun grew in the sky. Down the trail, past the farmhouse, he saw a group of people. Near the barn, a group of men lifted a large object, covered with a sheet, into one of the wagons. The wagon sank when it took the load. A team of eight horses pulled the heavy load away from the barn. The men all followed.

Johnny Lee slinked through the woodline, avoiding attention. A few minutes later he found himself under the tent, staring at an empty dig site. They took the giant away.

Inside the pit, Johnny Lee noticed a piece of gypsum laying on the dirt, the same color as the Cardiff Giant. The giant beast he witnessed this was not. They couldn't be the same thing. Johnny Lee surmised the beast he encountered to be authentic, an avenger of evil deeds, nature's executioner. A shapeshifting Nephilim, living in secret amongst men, without any shadow of a doubt. A God-fearing man had nothing to fear from her, or it.

Johnny Lee Earle's unquestioning faith in the Lord God couldn't be firmer.

This Cardiff Giant, on the other hand, he knew to be a fallacy to make money. Johnny Lee now possessed all he needed to report to the Twelve.

Giants stood in Cardiff, but this one fell under the category of a hoax.

And that's all need be said to the Mormon high council, or anyone else.

Amen.

LEAVING THE BEAVER

1

THEN...

A soundtrack of fiddles, with hand drums keeping time bounces across the waters of the Saint Lawrence River. Fires from torches light up the island the music resonates from, casting flickering shadows through leafy branches in the late summer night. Behind the trees, a throng of women dance in a pagan ritual under the full Harvest Moon.

The esoteric dancers are skyclad but for the beaver pelts and skulls covering their nakedness and obscuring their identities. They move with the beat of the music, as a unit around a central point. A hooded, nude man with a raging erection, stands bound to a post at this epicenter. He is complacent in his role at this ritual.

The music grows in intensity, triggering a transformation in the dancers' movements. The steps evolve into chaotic extensions of their sexuality. Each dancer caresses the man's engorged phallus as they pass him by, until the last woman in the line. She stops in place, along with the music. As the last notes ring out, the other dancers place sconces on the torches, blackening them. The only sound is of the river's waves breaking on the rocks surrounding the island.

Under nothing but the light of the moon, and before her sisters, the last dancer thrusts her exposed pelvis at the restrained man's groin. She rides him, taking his cock into herself as the dancers chant in time with her bucking. The man arches his back and thrusts back at her in his climax. Then she steps away, allowing his semi-flaccid penis to pop out of her vagina. Fluids drip from them as their combined juices glisten along his exposed member under the moon's light.

A chain reaction of whispers spreads through those in attendance until the last dancer opens her mouth and speaks.

"Castor Dea," she whispers once.

"Castor Dea! Castor Dea!" The attendees follow her lead in unison. "Castor Dea! Castor Dea! Castor Dea! Castor Dea!"

The waves breaking on the shore grow in intensity. This is replaced by the sound of something cracking branches in the wood line.

Something huge...

"Castor Dea! Castor Dea!" Tree trunks break and fall. Leaves flitter to the ground. The footsteps of an unseen behemoth crush vegetation and shake the ground. Hidden in the darkness, the great beast roars...

2

ODAY...

Alone in an outhouse, Brie sits on the cistern's cushy seat with her shorts pulled up, clutching a purse. Not having to use the shitter for anything but a privacy escape for the moment, she gathers her thoughts about the day. The scent of pine shavings, used as litter, fills the structure. It's better than the alternative stench in the cesspool below.

The reality is setting in. She's at a Labor Day party at a camp on a private island in the Thousand Islands, on the border between New York and Canada. She's a few margaritas in, and knows she needs to take her meds before the alcohol clouds her judgment and she forgets. Brie opens her handbag.

The prescription bottles within the purse stare back at her. She calls them her tittie skittles. Onc bottle holds Spironolactone to cut down on testosterone. The other is Estradiol, to boost her estrogen. They've become a regular thing since she started her transitional journey. Without the cocktail, she'd feel like a raving lunatic trapped in the throes of hormonal swings.

The bottle reminds Brie of a night, six months ago, when Katie first saw them in the medicine cabinet.

"What's this for? MS or epilepsy or something?" she asked, pointing out the bottle on the lighted shelf.

"Yes-" Brie stopped, and in a moment of clarity and self-respect, she spouted out, "No. I'm trans, okay? These are my hormones. It's who I am." She shrugged her shoulders, and fearing the worst, Brie chewed her lip, doing her best to stop from shaking. In lieu of rejecting her, Katie smiled, hugged Brie and kissed her for the first time.

The memory of the relief in her acceptance, by a woman she'd grown feelings for since they met, floods her with dopamine. And now? Six months later? As a couple, they're at an end of summer clambake at Katie's family camp on a private island in the St. Lawrence, and Brie can't believe it is happening.

Before Katie I was struggling to be accepted by society, my family, everything. Brie thought, But since I met her, it's all different.

When Katie asked her to come to her family's island for their annual Labor Day weekend clambake, Brie couldn't say no. All day she'd been having the time of her life, finally feeling accepted in spite of generational prejudices.

Everything she ever hoped for: to be accepted for who she is, and to be in love, Brie now possessed. She felt it empowering, in some manner, leaving behind the anxieties she felt haunted by. Her dysphoria from being born with male genitalia, the prejudices of society at large, and the fear of being killed for wanting to be yourself. All of it manageable because of the reciprocal love and respect Katie and Brie now shared.

Love, Brie decided, is the most powerful instrument for change to ever exist. Love, indeed, brought Brie and Katie to Beaver Island.

3

Transportation to the island required a ferry. In this case, they used a modified pontoon boat, from the mainland on the American side of the river, to Beaver Island. Katie's grandfather, Richard, a large bald man in a baby-blue polo shirt, drove the boat. He didn't say much during the ride, which suited Brie fine. Conversation was the last thing on her mind. Instead, she held Katie's hand and enjoyed the crisp wind blowing across her body as they skimmed across the surface of the seaway river.

Half-way to the island, Richard was forced to detour when a cadre of cigar-shaped speedboats shot down the river, leaving swirling wakes behind them. Richard gave them the finger, and turned the boat, allowing its pontoons to cut into the waves created by the speedsters.

"Hold on, it's going to be choppy for a minute," Katie said, the boat bucked as they cut through the waves. It reminded Brie of a bumpy country road, and a few splashes covered the boat's passengers in a spray of river water. Soon as it started, the water was calm, and in no time the island came into view.

Jimmy, Katie's Uncle, greeted them at the dock, aiding Richard in mooring the boat. He helped both women off the boat. At the end of the dock stood Jimmy's young twin daughters, staring at Katie and Brie, and pointing. They looked cute in their matching pink jumpers, white t-shirts, and pigtails.

"Gretchen! Heather! It's rude to point like that!" They heard a woman's voice bellow.

"That's my Aunt Millicent, we call her Aunt Milli," Katie told Brie. They watched the girls drop their arms, giggling, and run up the path to the island's cottage. As soon as they disappeared from sight, their mother came into view.

"The nuts don't fall from the tree, hah?" Brie asked, noting Katie's Aunt. She looked to be only a couple years older than Katie, a striking, beautiful woman.

"Sexy. It's in our genes. It attracted you, now didn't it?" Katie slapped Brie on the ass and kissed her. Milli walked down to the dock, kissed her husband on the cheek, and smiled.

"So this is the Sabrina we've all heard so much about," Milli said.

"Yes, it is," Katie replied.

"Call me Brie, please."

"Why, of course. I won't lie, Katie may have told you we were so disappointed when she came out of the closet, but not for reasons you might think. We're happy she's-"

"Gay?" Katie interrupted her aunt. The tone in her voice betrayed her irritation with this revelation.

"No, we're happy you are happy," Milli continued, "but I guess in another era the words were synonymous, so..."

"Buttons," Katie finished the cliche for her aunt.

"Mom and Kirstine, I'm sorry," Milli apologized, "Katie's mother, my sister Kirstine, everyone in the family, they can't wait to meet you. We always knew she was gay, but when she met you, we found hope!"

"Hope?" Brie questioned.

"You're a first for us, so we don't really know how to-" Brie noticed Katie stare down her aunt, purse her lips, and shake her head. Millicent got the point and shut up.

"Is Aunt Jamie here?" Katie asked.

"Not yet. Oh, and before I forget, I regret to inform you she's coming home empty handed."

"Of course she is. Damn girl can't ever make up her mind. Jamie is my age. No one expected Gramma to have another baby, but soon as Kirstine got pregnant with me, so did Gramma."

"It happens," Brie said.

"Ayup, it sure does," Katie agreed.

Up next came an introduction to Mom and Gramma. The family matrons sat in lawn chairs near the water's edge, enjoying their morning Bloody Maries. For older women, both had striking profiles. Brie felt out of place on an island full of women who could be supermodels.

"Aren't you the cutest little thing!" Linda, the aforementioned Gramma, said. Her accent reminded Brie of the way Katherine Hepburn would talk in the old black and white movies with Carey Grant. Katie ran over and gave her grandmother a peck on the cheek.

"What am I? Chopped wood?" Kirstine said, and turned her head to greet them.

Brie's jaw dropped in terror. Ragged scars crisscrossed the right side of Kirstine's face. Half of her nose was missing, giving Katie's mother a skullish visage.

Oh my God. Brie kept her thoughts to herself. She threw a hand to her mouth and gasped aloud.

"You didn't tell her?" Kirstine said, her eyes sullen. Half of her face was able to express her emotions, and it did. She cast an unhappy glare at her daughter.

"No, I didn't have the chance. I'm sorry, Mom."

"What happened?" Brie asked, ""I'm sorry if I was rude."

"No, no. You weren't rude. It's from a boating accident, happened shortly before Katie was born. I was water skiing. The boat stopped and I was dragged into the prop on the outboard motor by the undertow."

"Yeah," Katie interjected, "she's lucky to be alive."

"You're damn right she is, after what she pulled," Linda added, rolling her eyes.

"I'm so sorry!" Brie said, consoling the woman.

"It's okay, honey, you didn't do it. He did," Kirstine cocked a thumb at her husband, standing up by the steamers, prepping them for the day's feast. Linda burst out loud in a guffaw.

"If you want people to think that," Linda slurred her words out, raised her Bloody Mary, and took a long draught of the drink, "a whole lot of fuckery went on to lead us to this moment."

"Yes, you are right, I can't say that it was Noah's fault. He didn't know... what would happen."

"Stop blaming him. You knew damn well what would happen," Linda scolded her, "the goddess wasn't pleased with your shenanigans, and you know it."

"Goddess? Is that what you call the river? Like this is some sort of new age feminist thing?" Brie asked, and remembered being worried she might have run into a gaggle of TERFs. Fortunately, she didn't see any Harry Potter decor on the island thus far, to her relief.

"You could say that," Kirstine replied.

"I'll take your bags," Jimmy said, his voice a monotone drawl, "Follow me. You two are staying in the cabin."

"The cabin?" Brie remarked, "Sounds foreboding. Is it in the woods?" She laughed at her pop culture quip, but no one else did.

"We're on an island," Jimmy said, reflecting no emotion and ruining Brie's joke.

"Don't pay him any mind," Katie said, poking Brie in the side, "Be thankful he's taking your bags."

"Where's yours?" Brie asked Katie.

"I have clothes here, everything I need. Makes it convenient when I come home."

"I bet it does." The trio walked up the path, past the main residence on the island. Brie noticed the ground sounded different, like a hollow wall. She stopped, and stomped on the path. A dull thud answered.

"The island isn't really an island. Beaver Island grew on the remains of a beaver dam," Jimmy said.

"That's neat. Are there many islands like this?"

"I hope not," Jimmy replied.

"Don't pay uncle Jimmy any attention, babe," Katie added, "Isn't that right, uncle Jimmy?"

"Yes, don't pay me no attention, none at all." The man sounded defeated, and he hung his head as he spoke. And though Jimmy's behavior seemed odd, Brie found herself distracted and mesmerized by what Katie described as a camp. A compound might be a better word it.

A large bungalow stretched over to the boathouse and docks, looming over one side, while on the other, a stunning white gazebo sat alone in a quiet corner of the island. Near the cabin stood a large pavilion, in the process of being decorated and prepped by staff for the annual end of summer feast. A band, it looked like a country band to her, stood on a stage preparing to do a sound check.

This is how the pretty people live, she thought to herself, and came to an epiphany: ME! I'm one of the pretty people, now. Her body flooded with dopamine from the elation of acceptance. Brie couldn't believe it.

And the food? Brie's jaw dropped. She expected a grill and a pot to steam in, not a full-on catered affair.

It starts with the food and all the top shelf booze you'd want. She saw a sno-cone machine serving colorful, flavored balls of ice. A taco bar to rival most any taqueria. And a hot dog cart, burning the Hoffman's wieners into twisted, shriveled shells of their former selves. All of this for the kids who weren't yet fans of clams in their various forms of preparation.

A spread of typical cold salads could be found, of both the pasta and vegetable varieties. Boiled salt potatoes with drawn butter and Grandma Brown's baked beans completed the side dishes.

Steamed, raw, baked, and deep fried of the New York variety - Littlenecks, mahoganies and cherry stones. Unlike the full bellied clams in New England, these varieties of Atlantic hardshells are smaller. Dipped in drawn butter or cocktail sauce, Brie loved clams, and most seafood. The clambake felt like culinary heaven.

And Brie felt at home.

4

Though Brie finds acceptance, she still suffers from imposter syndrome as she washes down her hormonal cocktail with a swig of bottled water. Taking a moment longer to compose herself, Brie finally stands up and pushes the outhouse door open. And she nearly jumps out of her skin.

Jimmy is standing in front of the outhouse, staring forward with the same blank expression he, grandpa Richard, and brother-in-law Noah all share.

"Oh, Jesus, Jimmy, you startled me," Brie exclaims as she steps out of the commode and past him.

"It was the got dam beaver, I tell ya!" Jimmy says, his face a grimace of pain, then he steps into the outhouse, and closes the door behind.

"What?" Brie asks, not understanding his rant. Has he been drunk? she wonders, or are these guys the Stepford Husbands?

Music comes to life, as the band starts its first set. The Custom Traylor Park, a regional country cover band with a couple good original songs, is on stage.

"Come on! Let's go down there!" Katie shouts, running to catch up with her girlfriend, "My mom owns the recording label they signed a contract with. This band is the next big thing, you'll see!"

"Oh, really?" Brie quips back. Modern country music is Brie's least favorite musical genre, and the band on stage has a few years' experience playing pop rock with a twang, regardless of the singer's sex.

"Really," Katie affirms, and the couple embraces. The warm scent of vanilla in Katie's hair turns Brie on. She holds her girlfriend tight.

"Then I'll take your word for it," Brie says, and kisses Katie, long and deep.

5

A river of tequila flows by the gallon. Guided by a bartender from a train of pitchers filled with a fruity margarita mix, Brie and Katie drink their fill, plus some. After finishing their last round of the potent mixed-drink, Katie leaves the throng of dancers to procure the couple more alcohol. Both Brie and Katie prefer tequila's buzz. Despite its intoxicating effects on her body, Brie believed she could still think clearly, and thus keep herself out of trouble. This, of course, is a delusion. If anything, the excess tequila made Brie promiscuous and horny. Currently, or while in moderation, it helped her stomach the music playing. At the moment, Brie could tell she'd drank more than she should've.

Complete with a steel guitar and a fiddle player, The Custom Traylor Band, named after their lead singer, meets all the requirements for a country band. The songs the band plays meet all of the required lyrical content, including references to Jesus, guns, America, cheating blondes, and Honky Tonks.

"This one's called "Down At the Traylor Park!" the band's lead singer and front man, a black guy named David Traylor, announces on the mic. Trapped on the dance floor with other party attendees, dancing to the show, Brie finds herself cheering. The band comes to life on the cue, with a fiddle player, a pretty blonde woman, taking center stage next to the band's vocalist.

"She's hot, wooo!" An attractive woman dancing next to Brie says, and nudges her with an elbow. Brie smiles and nods in return. She realizes the woman is checking her out, "You're not so bad yourself." Brie blushes, not sure how to answer this compliment. She decides to keep it simple.

"Thanks!" Brie replies, aware booze can give her promiscuous thoughts, and the butterflies filling her belly are not helping her. She looks through the dancers for Katie, and can't see her. Their dancing becomes less focused on the music, and more intimate, starring each other in the eye as their bodies move to the music.

The woman puts her arms on Brie's shoulders, clasping her fingers behind Brie's neck. A jolt of electricity tingles down Brie's spine while the woman's thumbs tickle the base of her skull.

Is she doing this on purpose, Brie ponders as a tickle of euphoria spreads through her spinal column.

"What's your name?"

"Brie. And you?"

"My name's Jamie. You here with anyone today, Brie?" the woman asks, and leans forward to kiss her dancing partner. Brie, feeling the tequila, stops dancing and allows the woman to kiss her. She stops before their lips meet, "hey, wait, aren't you my niece's date?"

Her niece's date? Brie repeats in her head, then she realizes who this woman is. Katie's Aunt Jamie.

"I am. You must be Katie."

"I am. Did you know, they blame her mother for us being gay?"

"What?"

"My mother and sisters, they all blame Kirstine for Katie, and me, being gay. I know that's ridiculous and insulting, but they do."

"But why?" This talk was nothing new to Brie, she'd dealt with it her whole life. Now, knowing Katie, too, endured family prejudices, she found herself more in love with the woman.

"Kirstine fucked up the ritual, according to legend. It was before I was born so I don't know if it's true or not. And now look at what her daughter's brought for her offering," Brie prepares for a trans or homophobic insult, but gets none, instead, Jamie smiles and licks her lips before saying, "You are absolutely gorgeous."

"Thank you?" Brie responds to the compliment, unsure of what else to say.

"Shouldn't you be dancing with her?" The woman's tone comes across as scornful. The sudden shift in Jamie's demeanor makes Brie uncomfortable.

"I was, but she needed to get us drinks. See, there she is over there, by the bar." Brie points to Katie, who is talking to another woman. Blinking her eyes, Brie realizes it's Jamie, the woman she is talking to. Brie shakes her head, and looks around.

There is no Jamie, in fact, she's dancing by herself, with no partner.

But she was just here, with me. Brie thinks, how did she...

She looks again, focusing as best as she can. Brie feels a pit drop into her. It's clearly Jamie talking to Katie at the bar. Mentally blocking out the music, Brie walks off the dance floor and away from the party.

Stumbling up a small hill, Brie sees the twin girls in their matching outfits, watching her. The girls stare, unmoving.

Isn't that creepy? Brie thinks.

"If I'm seeing things, I need to take a nap," Brie tells the girls. They don't respond. She continues to believe they are another hallucination, until a shouting man catches their attention.

"Got dam beavers!" They hear a man shouting from up the path. Behind the twins she sees their grandfather, Richard. He has a broom clutched in his hands. A fileting knife is duct taped to the end of the handle. His face is covered with sweat and frustration.

The twins run away, back toward the pavilion, leaving Brie alone with Richard and his makeshift weapon.

"You see the fawkin beaver come this way?" Richard asks, the words seething from his mouth. He thrusts the broom into the air.

"No," Brie replies, "I haven't seen any beavers."

"Maybe not yet you ain't, but you will before the night is through, believe you me."

"Okay?" Brie states more than asks, and Grampa Richard runs by, his makeshift spear in hand. She shakes her head, having seen enough crazy stuff for one afternoon. Staggering up the footpath, Brie sees a lawn chaise off to the side; with a sigh of comfort, she lays down on the chaise's pillow covering, closes her eyes, and passes out...

6

Laying on the chaise, Brie feels as if she's on a boat in a tempest. Hovering between the conscious and subconscious, her body sways in the dreamscape. The island is spinning and she can't stop it. An aroma of vanilla fills the air.

As her eyes flitter in and out of lucidity, Brie sees and hears things she cannot comprehend. A crowd of people, each of them distorted by fire light, has gathered around her, they are pointing fingers, their voices gasping in awe. A trio of weird sisters step forward, covered in black shawls. The clique separates, revealing a fourth dressed in white. They fall upon Brie's prone body, fondling and groping until reaching her groin.

"How are we supposed to use that? Look at it," A crone in black cackles as she speaks.

"You had one job! One job! And you blew it!" Says another hag clad as the night.

"Blew it? Shit! There's nothing there to blow," A third witch in ebony quips, "do you think that little blue pill might work?"

"We gave her the little blue pill!"

"Yeah, that's not a good sign."

"No, it isn't. We're fucked. Well, not fucked. But you know what I me-"

"Silence," The High Priestess interrupts, her white robes shimmer in the twilight. Her accent is odd, its cadence is somewhere between a New England Yankee and Midwestern drawl. "The goddess requires a sacrifice! She hungers for that which she craves most. It was your duty to bring the sacrifice here, as we all have done before you."

"And what about Jamie?" Brie hears a voice that is Katie's, but not quite, she's using the same accent as the older woman. "She didn't even bring anyone at all! Hell, she tried taking my betrothed."

Betrothed?

"I did nothing of the sort!" the witch contests.

"You lying sack of shit!"

"Enough of the bickering!" The hag interrupts, flailing her arms. "The goddess is not happy. She hungers. And we have nothing to offer her now, yet again!"

"We humored your 'feelings' as much as we could, for years, and accepted you for it." The crone adds.

"It was your idea to bring a trans partner with me in the first place, mom! 'They're still technically a man, I'm sure the goddess will be satisfied with the offering,' you said. Or do you forget? I swear Freud would feel right at home during this picnic."

Mom?

That means... this is all a ruse? The words are daggers in Brie's heart.

"Well, we didn't tell you to fall in love with... with... it!"

"With her, Brie is a she! And of course I've fallen in love with her. What did you expect? We were supposed to get married tonight!"

Married?

"There will be no marriage. The ritual, and ceremony are off," the High Priestess says, "We sent the band and guests home. When she wakes up, we'll decide what to do with... her."

Brie slips away into a technicolor void, and with her the memory of this vision fades.

•

ello? Hello? Brie? Hello?

H*ello? Hello? Brie? Hello?*
The words echo in Brie's throbbing head as the visions subside, swirling away as fast as they came into being. There's a disconnect between the muffled words and reality. Brie fights to open her eyes, and manages to accomplish the feat.

Wake up, Brie! Come on! We've got-

It works, her ears rumble and the words become clear.

"Brie! Come on! We've got to go!" It's dark outside, and Katie is hovering over her, a look of despair on her face until she sees Brie open her eyes.

"Katie? What time is it? Is everything alright?"

"Everything is fine, come on, we've got to go. I've got the boat ready."

"But I thought we were staying in the cabin tonight."

"Come on! They think we are fucking. It's our only chance to get away before..." Katie looks around, frantic.

Fucking? Brie thinks. Yes, I'd like to be fucking right now. Brie reaches up and caresses Katie's breast. "I'd like to fuck right now."

"So would I, and that's what they want us to be doing. Plans have changed. I never should have brought you here."

"What do you mean?" Brie questions her lover, More like what the fuck! I finally find a place where I feel I fit in and this happens? She thought. If she could roll her eyes, she would, but they weren't cooperating with her.

"There's no time, let's just go. I've got the boat ready. Come on."

"What about my bag? And purse!"

"Never mind about your bag."

"But my purse, it's got my meds in it and I need them, remember?"

"Can you get more when you get home?"

"Well, yeah, of course I can."

"Then that's what you're going to have to do 'cause we're running out of time." A flood light comes to life and splashes white light across the pavilion area.

Katie grabs Brie's hand and helps her up. Her knees wobble as she stands. The duo runs off to the boat house. Brie is not faring well. Her legs don't wish to cooperate with her brain for some reason. She stumbles and almost falls as they make their way to the dock. Katie helps her up.

"Jesus, am I still drunk?"

"I think you're drugged."

"What do you mean drugged? Like someone roofied me?"

"Well, yeah. I think so."

"But who would want to do that to me here?"

Katie doesn't answer her girlfriend, she instead assists her onto the pontoon boat.

"What's going on, Katie?"

"Just sit down, I'll explain everything once we're in our car and on the highway going back to Fenton." She turns the key in the ignition, and the pontoon boat's outboard motor comes to life. She backs it out, slowly, and lights come on all over the island. "Shit!" Katie exclaims.

Brie sees a throng of people running toward the boathouse with flashlights in hand, as Katie swings the bow around to starboard. Then she puts the boat into full drive, the nose rises up slightly off the surface of the river, and it skips away from the island. Behind them, Brie can hear the islanders, consisting of Katie's family, screaming and shouting. The sky turns red as a flare hangs overhead. Soon the boat's motor overpowers and drowns out their voices.

"So glad I tore the distributor caps off the other boat and it will take them forever to find them. They won't be able to follow us right away, but they will. That's if they even care. I'm not worried about them so much as I'm..."

"So much as you're what?" Brie asked, concerned with Katie's tone.

"Let's just say the mainland can't come too soon," Katie replies, her hands firmly on the boat's steering wheel. A mask of determination to get as far away from Beaver Island as possible covers her face.

•

On the shore, the family watches the boat drift away. Jimmy fires a flare into the sky, lighting up the river with crimson shadows. The twins, Heather and Gretchen, are standing side-by-side in their identical outfits, silently pointing in unison at the party barge, chugging away from the island.

"Girls! What did your mother tell you about pointing? It's not polite. Mind your manners." Jimmy scolds his children. The girls drop their arms and continue to stare across the river with their typical, blank expressions.

"Hurry, Richard, get the fishing boat started," Linda orders her husband.

"It's not turning over. I think Katie sabotaged the motor."

"Of course she did!"

"She is your granddaughter after all, Linda," He retorts.

"Wow. When did you grow your balls back?" Linda throws her arms in the air, "Now do you see, Kirstine? Your little ploy twenty-five years ago has led to this. Love. See what love gets you? I should have let you bleed to death that night, but I didn't. Why? Because I love you. Love's a fucking cunt."

Kirstine, standing next to her husband, ignores her mother's rant. Instead, she looks Noah in the eyes. Tears drip down both their cheeks.

"She's just like you, stubborn and thick headed," Noah says, his words are soft and consoling. Kirstine nods and embraces her husband. "I hope they get away," he whispers, and his wife clutches him in a bear hug.

"They will," Kirstine mumbles into his shoulder... and remembers.

7

*T*HEN...

"Castor Dea! Coaster Dea!" the dancers chanted as the great beaver stepped out from the woodline, her thick coat of fur shining black from being soaked in the river. She's as big as a fully grown bear, with a tail as long, her presence brought a silence upon her faithful. They didn't fear the creature, she didn't come here for them. The beast walked straight toward her sacrifice and offering...

The bound man.

Noah.

"No!" Kirstine, the last dancer, screamed and threw herself on the lawn between the man and the monster. She held the sacrificial knife in her fist, and with an outstretched arm pointed it at the giant beaver.

"What are you doing?" One of the other dancers shouted. It's her mother, Linda.

"Breaking the cycle, Mom, like we should have years ago," the last dancer replied.

"You don't understand, this whole island is built upon her dam, it's so old trees and grass grow on it! In order to stay here, we must pay her tithe, in return she sees to our prosperity. Everything we are, everything this family has is because of our devotion, don't you get it?"

"It's all bullshit, Mom. It's just a big fucking beaver, everything else would have happened anyways."

"It is our family's curse, going back to when my own grandparents first discovered this island and its blessings. He must offer the sacrifice for the tithe to be paid, he must! If he isn't, we will fall into poverty."

"I won't allow it, Noah doesn't deserve this."

The beaver opened her maw, and barked, exposing her curved incisors. Water and mucus dripped from her lips as the great beave charged, her eyes on the target behind Kirstine. The beast lumbered forward, moving much faster than you would think she'd be capable. Kirstine stood her ground and when the monster was close enough, she struck. The woman stabbed the gigantic beaver over, and over again in the side with the sacrificial knife. Blood spit out of the wounds, spraying Kirstine and the ground in a crimson sheen.

The beaver yowled in pain and lunged, twisting her great head as she did. She ignored the blade being stabbed into her thick pelt. And with a flick of her jaws, bit Kirstine in the head, putting an end to the assault.

The beaver skull and pelt she wore offered some protection, for which she felt grateful. It did not shield her one hundred percent.

The razor-sharp tooth still managed to cut a slice of flesh, bone, and cartilage off Kirstine's face. She fell to the ground, screaming in agony. Blood spurt out of the wound in an arc like a fountain.

Linda ran to her daughter, a towel in her hand. She covered the wound and motioned to the other dancers. Milli with her husband, Jimmy, ran to join her at Kirstine's side.

Behind them, the beaver goddess didn't wait. She took her sacrificial offering, and snipped off Noah's scrotum with almost surgical precision. He screeched like a baby rabbit in a cat's maw while the scent of vanilla filled the air, covering the stench of the blood cascading down his thighs. Then he passed out.

"Take her inside, we'll need to get her to the mainland. Tell them she hit a boat prop or something."

"What if she dies?" Millicent asked, "I mean things are pretty fucked up right now, but if she dies and we can't make the third aspect. Who knows what might happen."

"Aw, fuck, you're right," Linda said.

"You know I can hear you, right?" Kiristine says, the pain of the bite still present.

"Take her away, then come back for him," Linda ordered her daughter and son-in-law.

She watched as they carried her away, through her good eye, the other swollen closed by the bite. Kirstine saw the beaver, satisfied with their payment. The giant beast walked away, back down the path she blazed through the trees, to the sanctity of the river and her den, hidden below the island. Linda stayed with Noah, who now lay prone on the ground.

Kirstine noted her husband's cock, for a recently castrated, and currently unconscious man, still stood erect, a result of the E.D. drugs they'd fed him earlier. It didn't matter that he couldn't make anymore sperm, his cock was coated in it. As Milli and Jimmy carried her away, Kirstine watched as her mother mounted Noah, and fucked his semi-hard blood and semen covered cock.

8

*N*OW...

Brie and Katie sit in silence for a few minutes, listening to the hum of the outboard motor, the lights of the party barge guiding them across the river. The cool night breeze sobers Brie up some. Finally, tense and nervous from the hasty exit, she speaks.

"I still can't believe you tore the distributor caps off the engine of the other boat. You're a tough ass broad."

"You bet your ass I am. Wait till I tell you why."

"This better be a good story," Brie says.

"Oh, you better believe-"

The boat comes to a lurching stop, cutting off her sentence. The motor grumbles as water floods its intakes and the engine dies out. Katie falls over onto the seat, and Brie is thrown to the deck. The bow of the boat is underwater.

"Oh, shit. That isn't supposed to happen!" Katie exclaims, shaking in fear.

I can't swim! I'm going to fucking drown! Brie thinks, and panic sets in. A cooler, once near the bow, is floating in the river's water encroaching the barge's deck.

Brie grabs her bag and scrambles on all fours to the back of the party barge and the housing of its motor. Here, by the boat's stern, the women hold each other tight.

"She doesn't want us to leave!" Katie says, her voice shaking, "I never should have brought you here! Never! I'm so stupid!" Katie pounds her forehead with her palm.

"Huh? What doesn't want us to leave?" Brie asks, but Katie doesn't reply, she continues to smack herself. "Stop that!" Brie declares and holds Katie's wrist, preventing her from hitting herself anymore. "What's going on?"

"The goddess, she's out there, in the water, right now, I'm sure of it."

"Goddess?"

"Yes, goddess."

"But that's bullshit," Brie says, pushing Katie away from her. A distant roar of boats fills the waterway, echoing off the forested banks. Lights grow in brilliance as they move closer and closer with each passing second.

"What's that?" Brie asks, pointing to the lights.

"It looks like boat lights, and they're moving fast."

"And we're in their wake, aren't we?"

"Yeah, oh shit. We have to get the motor started and get out of their path." Katie runs to the wheel and turns the ignition. The motor smokes, sputters, and dies.

"What's wrong with it?" The lights illuminate the water of the river, casting a reflection of the tree line on the water.

"It's flooded." The motors of the speedboats grow in volume, filling the night with their thunderous roar.

"Well can you get it started?" The lights cast shadows across the bow of the party barge.

"I, I don't know!" She turns the key and it only clicks.

"It's the speedboats we saw this morning!" Brie notes.

"They're going back home in Alex Bay. This isn't good, Brie, not good at all. Their wakes might capsize us!"

"I get that." The lights of the boats fill the night with their brilliance.

"Grab a seat, they can be used as life preservers!"

The river erupts in a violent splash of water, blotting out the light. This is followed by a screeching cry as a speed boat strikes an invisible barrier, hidden in the darkness, and is deflected away from the pontoon boat. The speedboat careens bow over stern across the water and collides with another.

The boats, freshly fueled in nearby Clayton, explode on impact.

In the shadow of the fires, Brie sees something large- nearly the size of a boat -slink across the surface and dive into the water.

"What the fuck was that?"

"The goddess?"

"Oh no, Katie," Brie says, shaking her head, "I'm not buying that bullshit."

"But it was. You saw it for yourself. Now, if you don't mind, we need to get this boat started while she's distracted."

"Distracted?"

"Yeah, the drivers of those boats? They're giving us time to get away."

"I don't get what you mean. Get away from what?"

"Look!" Katie shakes her head in frustration and points out the speed boats' pilots, both of them alive and bobbing in the water's waves.

"We should help them," Brie confesses.

"No, we need to get the boat started so we can get away from her." Katie turns the ignition over again. It clicks twice, then the outboard motor of the pontoon boat smokes, before kicking into life and creating a boiling swell at the barge's stern.

As Katie drives the pontoon boat away from the wreckage of the speed boats, Brie watches the silhouettes of the pilots, protesting being abandoned in the river. One man thrashes before being pulled under the water by an unseen force. The other climbs on the wreckage of his boat, and Brie can hear his screaming fading as the distance between them grows.

A gigantic black shape launches out of the water, blocking the low hanging moon as it engulfs the shadow of the man.

The goddess? Brie wonders.

"Almost there!" Katie shouts. Brie sees the lights of the dock growing brighter, and can make out the other boats on the marina. The water is too shallow for her here, I hope!"

The boat is in jumping distance to the docks. Brie can hear the waves breaking on the nearby shore.

Until the boat stops.

A force pulls the stern backward and into the river. The pontoon boat's bow catapults up out of the water, ejecting Katie into the river behind them with a splash. Brie, already sitting in the boat's stern, is waist deep in the brackish water before she can move. As the boat lurches, she falls onto the outboard motor's housing. The rumble of the engine hums, and she can smell the burning gasoline and oil.

And something else.

Vanilla.

Brie looks into the water of the river and sees something she should not be seeing. In her peripheral, twenty feet away, Katie thrashes in the water, swimming to the shore, she is shouting at Brie to move, to get off the boat.

But Brie can't.

She's frozen in terror, locked in a stare down contest with a giant fucking beaver in the water. Eyes locked, without blinking, the woman and beast watch one another. The creature is massive, at least the size of the party barge, with massive paws, one on each pontoon, pushing the boat's stern into the water.

The goddess. Oh, my God, it's real, Brie's mind processes the information better than she thought it would.

The beaver's massive head rises out of the water. Its giant buck teeth glisten in the lights on the dock. It opens its mouth and grunts, snapping its mouth closed.

"Oh, fuck you! I've had enough of this buck-toothed bullshit!" Brie says, and pulls back on the outboard motor, resting under the beaver's chin. Still running at top speed, the prop digs into the beaver's thick coat around its neck. At first the animal is oblivious to what is going on, until the blades drill through her blubber and bite into her flesh. The goddess squeals in agony.

Is this the first time this thing has felt pain? Brie ponders as she holds the motor steady.

The froth of white water turns pink, then black. The creature convulses, and the boat shakes. The paws slip off the deck and the party barge slaps back onto the surface, one of the pontoons landing on the dock. Wood snaps and cracks, but it's drowned out by the screeching death throes of a giant beaver.

The Evinrude motor slices up the giant beaver's throat as the boat stabilizes. A spray of blood covers Brie and the deck. The beaver goddess's body twitches once more, then slips into the water of the St. Lawrence.

"Damn!" Brie says, wiping gore off her face.

Katie climbs out of the water onto the remains of the dock. Brie crawls over to her, through the wreckage. The couple embraces and stares at the starry sky above.

"Oh thank God you're okay. You weren't kidding," Brie says.

"About what?"

"The goddess. Holy shit."

"I don't think I'll be welcome at any future family reunions," Katie says. Brie laughs.

"So what exactly had they planned for me?"

"We were supposed to get married, have sex, you were supposed to get me knocked up, and the beaver goddess was supposed to eat your balls, like it's done with my grandfather, dad, and uncle."

"How was I supposed to get you pregnant? I can't get it up, even with a pill. And my balls? They're raisins right now. The beaver goddess would have been awfully disappointed."

"I know, I tried telling them, but my aunts, and my gramma, they watch so much PornHub they think they know everything."

"I love you, Katie. You know we can still get married."

"I know. I love you, too, Brie. Let's go before they fix the other boat."

"Good idea." The couple kisses, then walks away from the dock to their waiting vehicle. Brie looks behind them one last time, afraid she may see pursuing cultists or a pissed off giant beaver climbing out of the water. Instead, she sees only the moon reflecting off the river's rippling surface. To her it looks as if the current of the St. Lawrence is waving goodbye. Brie winks, and with her free hand she returns the gesture.

BAD, BAD BOGEYMAN

The Bogeyman was in deep dookie. It took one glance at Sebastian for you to understand the severity of the situation. The toddler was armed for teddy bear, bringing the wooden spoon and handi-wipes with him. You never knew what to expect with the Bogeyman. For this mission, they were the only necessities required. It was Sebastian's duty to ensure the Bogeyman got a good spanking for what he did. The handi-wipes were to clean up the mess after.

Naughty, naughty Bogeyman, taking my Mommy and Daddy away like you did! Sebastian mentally affirmed himself.

They fell asleep on the porch and the goblin struck, dragging them, unaware, into his faerie realm. The baby's feet scurried across the floor, resembling a miniature Fred Flinstone leaving the quarry as he bounced over the deck's wooden planks. Sebastian's feet and wheels propelled the child and his walkie to the entrance of the Bogeyman's lair. The location of this one-way dimensional portal changed multiple times during the course of a day. The spot depended on where the residents of the house were at any given time. Right now, at this moment, the Bogeyman's door was at the edge of the porch, obscured by the shadows of night.

During the day, this was a simple, walled corner at the end of the family's enclosed sunroom deck. But Sebastian, two weeks shy of his first birthday, knew as all young children know. When the sun set and the nightmares came to life, the rules changed. Adults forgot all of this as they learned to speak, hit puberty, grew and aged. This was a good thing. They'd be too scared to live the lives they do if they still knew the truth.

Nightmares were real.

And the Bogeyman tended them, molded them, nurtured them.

For centuries, civilized Man and Woman believed the cries of their young were in fear of being snatched away by the Bogeyman. They've been all wrong, all along. It was quite the opposite. The Bogeyman doesn't want the young children. He wants their parents for his nefarious pleasures deep within the goblin's faerie realm. And somehow, someway, Sebastian's crafty Bogeyman got away with it tonight. Or so he thought.

"I come getchu, Bogeyman!" The little boy declared, holding the spoon high in his tiny fist. It was obvious the Bogeyman grew a pair, snatching his parents away right in front of Sebastian. He deserved more than a spanking when Sebastian caught up with him. If he were Daddy, Sebastian would have taken his belt off and cracked it! But Sebastian didn't wear a belt. His jumper and pull-ups didn't require it.

The walkie carrying the toddler rolled at maximum velocity into the shadowed corner. The air shimmered as Sebastian, walkie and wooden spoon morphed, blending into the darkness. Within the time of a blinking eye, the toddler disappeared from this mortal world on a one-way mission...

•

Outside the world of men, between then and now, lies the Playground. It is a no-Man or Woman's Land faerie built on a foundation of the imaginations of children throughout the multiverses of reality. Within its recesses is an endless forest, growing through a jungle gym of infinite proportions. The ground is soft as fleece, to comfort falls from above. Mother's Milk flows from fountains. It is a place built on the joy and excitement, a haven to the young. Yet it stands deserted. There are no children running and playing. No one comes here you see, for it is home to the Bogeyman.

While in the Playground, reality is warped and curved. Here the toys of our world become implements of use. The young become old, and the old shirk, to be held captive by the Bogeyman to torment as he pleases. Once brought here, only blood will free those imprisoned by the ancient hobgoblin. And once blood is spilled, blood must remain.

Sebastian piloted his tank, guiding the metal machine's tracks. It made short work of anything in its path. Plowing over and through the swing sets, monkey bars, see-saws and other various playground implements, the machine was unstoppable. Nothing was immune to the treads of the tank. Inside the metal death machine, Sebastian, now an old man with gray, stringy hair, was strapped into the pilot's seat, hanging from a bungee cable. He held a long spear with a carved, spiked tip, helping to balance him in place as the tank rolled over everything it came in contact with. He giggled and cooed like a baby through the one tooth sticking out of his now ancient mouth.

"I'mma comin' fer ya, Bogeyman!" Sebastian said, shaking his fist in the air. Each syllable was accentuated by another, and another, crumbling bit of real estate. Behind the tank was a clear path, marking the exit from this pocket realm. Before him was a wall of dense vegetation, built to confuse and trap anyone who didn't belong here. It failed to hinder Sebastian. The world forgot who built it, the Sebastians of the multitudes. He was every bit as much a master here as the plane's primary denizen.

"You're bad, Bogeyman! Come out, come out wherever you are!" Sebastian shouted over the tank's speakers. The words echoed through the forest. The top hatch of the tank opened, and clanked to the side. Sebastian, clad in something resembling a red and white striped one piece swimming suit from the 19th century, climbed up out of it. He held his wooden spear, designed with one purpose. "Now, I'm going to close my eyes," each 'S' slipped and slurred around Sebastian's tongue and tooth. "I'mma gonna count to ten." He paused again, gathering his breath. "And then I'mma gonna find you!"

"One... two... three... four... five... six -" the last number rang out as something slapped its hand on the bow of the tank. Sebastian stopped counting and watched. It was a hand, stringy and black, sinewy. The arm it attached to was long, sending a shiver up Sebastian's spine. But what really got him, the part of the goblin being more terrifying to behold, was its face. The Bogeyman's features were Sebastian's own, as he now stood, old and withered.

Behind the goblin, on a leash tied to the creature's ankle, were a pair of babies. One boy and one girl, crawling about in the comfort of the soft ground. They wept and cried, but no sound came from them. The Bogeyman took their voices. The goblin spoke with them now.

"You failed in your duty. I have taken what is mine, fair and square." Banshee tones shifted with each word, sending a shiver up Sebastian's spine.

"I brought the wooden spoon for you, Bogeyman." the ancient toddler raised his wrinkly old arm, hoisting the spear high above his head. "Your tushy is about to get blistered." Sebastian was here to take names and drink sippy cups. He looked around. Nope. No sippy cups to be found. He didn't bother wasting any more time.

Sebastian threw the spear.

The point pierced the Bogeyman's chest. The impact dragged the goblin with it, pinning him to the wall of a jungle gym. Black liquid poured from the hole in the monster's chest. It writhed in agony, gore covered hands flailing and pulling at the wooden shaft. Sebastian jumped off the top of the tank. He landed on the plush ground without a sound. He walked over to the Bogeyman. Sebastian starred the goblin in the face for a moment. He reached into his pocket and pulled out the handi-wipes with one hand, and pulled the spear out of the monster with the other. The Bogeyman fell to the ground in a clump. Sebastian cleaned off the wood with the wet napkins.

"Do it. You know you have to do it. So just do it. There's only one way to keep them safe from me. You know it." The Bogeyman hissed in his sing song screech. Sebastian ignored him, instead, he focused on something else. He bent over, his hand fumbled about the Bogeyman's waist for a moment, then Sebastian withdrew his arm back. Within his grasp, Sebastian pulled the goblin's belt off his trousers. He folded the belt in half, held it between his hands and snapped it. There was a crack like thunder.

Sebastian meant business.

"You don't have to do this. You know what will happen. What has to happen if you do this." The goblin cried. Sebastian shrugged his shoulders.

"I know." Sebastian said, and wrapped the belt around the Bogeyman's neck before he could take another breath. He tightened it, squeezing the goblin's neck, choking the creature. He heard the neck bones snap and watched the goblin's head loll to one side.

The child-like effigies of Sebastian's parents were still tethered to the deceased Bogeyman's foot. They were next to it, clawing at the air as their cries went unheard, silenced by the death of the goblin. Their son stepped back from them and the Bogeyman's dead body. The tank welcomed him back. He climbed in through the hatch, settled back into the pilot's seat and turned the key to start the engine back up.

He watched. Outside, a wormhole opened at the entrance, it widened and expanded. A vortex captured and engulfed his infantile parents. It snapped and retracted to its swirling source, sending them back to their home in the world of Man.

·

Justin and Marie woke from their impromptu naps on the deck of their new home. The enclosed porch was a favorite hangout of the new family. Until today. Marie opened her eyes first. She saw their son, Sebastian, sitting in his walker, and nothing looked to be out of the ordinary.

Marie's thoughts were garbled and her heart rate elevated. She had a nightmare, but couldn't remember what it was. Then she smelled it.

Something rotten, a stink of excrement and it didn't smell right.

"Sebastian?" She said. Her son, just shy of his first birthday, was always responsive to her when she called. But not now, not today. She thought he might be asleep. "Sebastian?" She couldn't quite see his face in the dark of the shadows on the porch.

"Justin, wake up. I think something's wrong with Sebastian." She shook her husband, waking him, as she rose from the Adirondack chair she was sleeping in.

"What? What is it Marie? What time is it?"

"Oh no, no, no!" Marie screamed. She held her son in her arms, he wasn't cooing or making up words. He wasn't even alive. His face was blue, lifeless eyes stared, unblinking, into the night.

"Sebastian!" Justin cried in unison with his wife as they held their dead child in their arms.

•

From deep within the shadows, through the closing portal of darkness between the world of Man and the Playground, the new Bogeyman watched.

The goblin of nightmares wept.

Blood spilled.

Blood remained.

VALHALLA

THE BATTLE OF TYR

Near Sí Bheag and Sí Mhórin Hills in County Wicklow, Ireland, is a farm. Cattle grazes on the grasses of the serene landscape, while deep under this farmer's field, an archeology team is at work. Within a domed chamber, Billie Powell sits on the collapsible stool she brings to digs. Overweight with chronic back pain, the stool is a lifesaver for the technician.

Currently, she is sorting through a set of ground radar stills of the aforementioned hills, called Big Girl and Little Girl by the locals. To an untrained eye, the LiDAR and GPR print-outs might resemble pixilated gibberish. But to her, the team's ground radar expert, the series of photographs stand as their map to this lost tomb.

It's mostly dark under the mound. Glow sticks and head lamps serve as their primary source of illumination, but her ability to read these maps makes Billie the team's eyes in this subterranean labyrinth. The earthen walls are covered in moss and myriad fungi, and the team's UV lights leave fluorescent streaks in the lichen, giving the chamber an otherworldly aesthetic.

"I think I agree with our previous assessment, based on the size of the barrow mound," Tony Gillen, the dig's supervisor says.

"Look at these," Billie tells Tony and shines her headlamp on the LiDAR map. "See the pattern?"

"That's a Vegvísir," Tony admits.

"It is." Billie concurs, recognizing the lines and runes of the famous Norse compass. Her wife, an ocean away in Canada, wore one on a daily basis. She'd bought it for her on their honeymoon, a fjord cruise through Norway, going on five years ago, now. Billie missed Jennifer while away on digs, but they talked on video chat nightly.

"Remarkable. We knew this might be from the Viking age. There are other chambers. Look at the number of tunnels, six of them, each with an antechamber."

"One for each line of the compass. So this is just the burial room."

"Yes. And this grave tells us so much more. The body, its placement, including the large stone laying on the rib bones tell us they feared her coming back to life. It looks as if she was burned, too. See the carbon scoring?"

"Her? How can you tell?" Billie asks, wiping a lock of purple-dyed hair from her face.

"Yes, her. See her pelvic bones? They're rounded and wider than a male's." Tony shines his light on the exposed grave. Surrounded by an oval circlet of wrapped oak roots and vines, the skeleton is accompanied by the accouterments of a great warrior. There is a helmet, drinking horns, bejeweled silver and gold, and fragments of body armor; as well as a rusted ax head and sword blade.

"Whomever she was, she was a giant of a woman, so I'm betting they had a good reason to fear her, even though her bones look brittle, likely from cancer. But in her prime, she was a monster, for sure. I'm going to say nearly seven feet tall, based on the size of her femurs."

"Holy shit, that's a giant for sure." Billie says. "So another Abertacht? A vampire king, or rather Queen in this case?" One of the crew members snorts and grumbles something unintelligible at this statement. Billie isn't sure whom.

"They were revered, whoever they were, that's for sure. I doubt she was a real vampire; they are fairy tales. Whether or not she was a Queen remains to be seen, but I can say with confidence, this is the royal burial chamber we've been searching for, the first of many surprises we're going to discover today, I'm certain of it." Tony says. The darkness hides the smile of elation on his face, but the tone of his voice betrays the excitement of the moment.

"Okay, people, you heard Tony. Set the lamps up. Let's see if we can't find out who's so damn important they're buried here," Billie announces, and the team gets to work.

Tony shrugs his shoulders. "Judging from the runes carved on that stone, we're looking at the remains of Ivar Ragnarson, better known as Ivar the Boneless. And apparently he was, indeed, lacking a bone."

"I thought Ivar was a man, and he was buried near Hastings." Billie says.

"Well, she likely lived as a man, this wasn't uncommon in medieval Europe. As far as his—well, her—resting place, the legend says William the Conqueror defiled that grave, and until now, it seems, no one has known where Ivar was—" Tony's words are cut short.

Within seconds, chaos erupts and spreads through the chamber...

"Ui Ivair!" Someone, Billie thinks it's their security coordinator Theresa Butler, screams the Gaelic words. When the first blow strikes Tony in the shoulder, he doesn't expect it. Hell, no one does. It surprises the feck out of the old man and everyone present. Billie sees the attacker is, indeed, Terri Butler.

The transformation of one of their bodyguards into a raging ax murderer is the last thing Billie or anyone else for the matter might have on their archeology BINGO card on this day. Bones? Check. Pottery? Mark it off. Jewelry? Dab it! But the figurative BINGO cards go down when Terri starts screaming bloody murder, swinging an ax around like a whirling dervish. Most of the team makes haste to the mound's entrance.

They will regret this.

Instead of following her peers, Powell chooses to remain seated. Tony, however, turns to join them. It's a mistake he will regret for the seconds left of his life. He throws an arm up to deflect the next blow. The ax blade slices through Tony's wrist, lopping off the hand. His arm transforms into a spigot, spraying the surrounding area in a crimson sheen. Tony screeches, fear and the realization he's been dismembered, meeting in his mind.

Terri strikes again, quicker than the supervisor can move, making him the first to die. She chops away a number of times at his exposed back. Gillen spasms with each impact of steel on bone as blood, black in the shadows, sprays across Terri's face and upper body, decorating her in gory face paint. She's a visage of madness, and Billie freezes at the carnage unfolding before her.

Shoulders arching, Tony gasps, and spits out a lungful of blood onto Billie's lap. Powell screams while the supervisor slumps forward and face-plants at her feet. Terri stands behind his corpse with a maniacal grin on her face, the weapon's handle grasped firmly. Blood covers the ax blade and head, dripping to the floor.

What the feck snapped in her head? And why here? Billie ponders the answers to this thought for as long as her fear and sense of self-preservation allow. As things turn out, it isn't long. Before Billie can solve the riddle, Terri speaks the answer.

"This place wasn't meant to be found! You've defiled all we've protected for a millennium!" The murderer's words are greeted with screams pleading for mercy. Light flickers from down the passage in synchronization with the burping of automatic gunfire. Deafening thunder overcomes the wailing of the victims. The sounds distract Terri long enough for Billie to make a move to escape. Seizing the opportunity, Powell stuffs the pictures into her pocket, collapses the stool, and stands.

She throws the stool at Terri with all her might. Much to Billie's relief, the hard plastic strikes the ax murderer in the temple, dropping her to the ground. Billie gasps, then flees; disappearing into the darkness of the barrow. All she can think is I have to get out of here for Jennifer.

•

Above ground, a pair of support team members, two middle-aged men, Mr. Hughes and Mr. Osborne, sit on folding chairs, monitoring the radar and computers. They are too busy with their work to give any attention to the guards. Heather, Siobhan, and Erika stand in stoic silence, keeping guard outside the site's entrance, waiting for Terri's signal. Vigilant and alert, their hands resting on the hafts of their traditional axes, the trio remain patient. Mostly.

"You think we're even needed here?" Heather asks, breaking the silence.

"We can't take the chance. So we're here." Siobhan answers.

"The grave has been lost for-fecking-ever, Siobhan. It's a fecking myth at this point. Terri is daft." Erika counters, obviously irritated she has to be here.

"I have faith in Terri. She's our war chief for a reason." Siobhan says, knowing if this isn't the place, they'll go home and life carries on. However, if Terri finds out otherwise, she knows their time to strike will come, to honor their oaths and protect the secret hidden under this mound.

As the Norns would have it, they don't have to wait long.

"Uí Ívair!" the ancient battle cry of their sect, the Scions of Ivar, echoes out of the hole in the ground. near the dig entrance don't have time to react to the sound. The women see to this with their ax blades. Blood splashes on the technological devices as a couple heads roll onto the ground, their faces forever frozen in bewilderment.

They won't be the last scientists to wonder why their lives are being cut short on this day.

Professionals with years of combat experience between them, they get to work. The trio rappels into the barrow on the threaded, orange nylon lines used by the team to initially descend into the lost tomb. Strapped across their backs, automatic weapons rattle.

Heather Crovan is an Uzi girl, a result of her time in the Middle-East training with an Israeli Anti-Terrorism division. Siobhan Lewis prefers the .45 caliber calm provided by the Thompson handed down by her mother Moira, and her grandmother Skye before her and the days of The Troubles. Erika Harris, on another hand, loves the lightweight ease of her Black Mamba, the SIG MCX LVAW she acquired while working with the Russian military as an undercover operative in Ukraine a few years before.

As the women land in the tomb, they are greeted by a chaotic throng of terrified archaeologists and workers fleeing for their lives. Without hesitation they charge their weapons. The trio opens fire on the dig team with controlled and disciplined three-round bursts. The victims scream in terror, pleading for their lives as they realize what they believed to be an exit to safety is instead their death chamber. A menagerie of bullets ranging from 9mm to .45 caliber riddles them; painting the earthen works in their wake with blood, flesh and fragments of bone.

The gunfire ceases and is replaced by the whisper of the assailants' breathing. Acrid smoke fills the tomb, obscuring what little light illuminates it. The scent of sulfur tickles their nostrils.

A low moaning emits from the darkness. Siobhan points her Thompson in the general direction of the noise. The antique weapon burps to life with the fervor of a backfiring motorcycle, once again filling the barrow with thunder. When the clamor subsides, there's no more moaning to be heard.

"All clear." Siobhan says and slings the machine gun to her shoulder. The other two reply with the same words in tandem. Likewise, they sling their weapons and relax. The adrenaline coursing through their bodies begins to subside and the trio lapses into a calming state.

This lasts until the steps of someone approaching from the darkness causes the women to go on the alert. Their guns are cocked and pointed in the direction of the intruder before another breath is taken. To their relief, Terri is revealed in the light from their headlamps. She's sitting down, nursing a black eye. They lower their weapons.

"One of them got away." Terri says, wincing. "She caught me by surprise and went deeper into the tunnels. I don't know where she thinks she'll go." She smirks.

"Which one?" Heather asks.

"The fat dyke with purple hair." Terri replies.

"She's a bookworm and'll be easy to catch." Siobhan affirms.

"What are we waiting for?" Erika adds. "Let's go get her." She slaps the collapsing stock of her Black Mamba for effect.

"I'll stay here and guard the exit in case anyone noses about." Heather says, unslinging her Uzi.

"Or slips by." Siobhan adds.

Terri wipes blood from her ax blade, nods, and waves the others on. "Here little piggy! Come out, come out wherever you are!" She shouts. Weapons in hand, the foursome turns from the entrance and heads into the depths of the lost burial mound to finish the work they've dedicated their lives to keeping secret...

ODIN'S COURT

While a second, albeit briefer, round of gunfire echoes through the earthworks; Billie Powell pushes herself to run as fast as her circulatory system will allow her. Years of sedentary office work put on the pounds, and the results have left her in peril on this day. Stabbing pain shoots through her lower back, accompanied by cramping worse than any period she can recall. Her heart pounds in her chest and sweat soaks her hair and upper body.

Billie closes her eyes and visions of her wife flash through her mind. *Jennifer!* Seeing her again is all Billie wants at this moment. The gun shots have released a derby's stable of theories, trampling through Billie's mind. This flurry of thoughts, in conjunction with a lack of oxygen in her brain, has removed all reason from the academic. She is left with only the basic instinct of survival.

The first gut punch she receives is seeing her phone's lack of connectivity. This far under the mound, there is no way for a cellular signal to get through. Calling for help is out of the question. Now her phone is a thousand-dollar flashlight.

Guiding herself by the light of the screen, Billie quickly learns the barrow is a labyrinth. Navigating its earthen tunnels is a challenge and twice the darkness obscures a low ceiling. The second incident leaves a knot on her forehead when Billie's head grazes the stone and dirt while her attention is focused on the floor. Momentarily dazed from the glancing blow, the reality she may never leave this tomb finally settles in.

Eventually I'll come to the end of the tunnels. She mentally notes. Her pursuers are also cognizant of this reality. She can hear one of them taunting her.

"Here little piggy! Come out, come out wherever you are!" The voice is muffled by the tunnels.

Billie pulls the LiDAR map out of her pocket and shines her phone on it. Another room, larger than the burial chamber, is ahead. It appears to be the central hub, wherein other tunnels surrounding it circle around back toward the entrance. She pushes onward, putting as much time and space between her and the people who want her dead. An epiphany arises within Billie's mind, one she hadn't considered since Terri swung the ax at Tony.

I might get out of this alive and get home.

Ahead, down the length of the passageway, Billie notices something. *The wall is glowing?* A tendril—an oak root maybe?—softly emitting a blue-green light has pierced the wall. Billie touches it. A bit of the substance rubs off onto her fingertips. It's fungal, of that she's certain. Whether or not it's toxic she is unsure. Biology wasn't her strong point in college.

Gazing down the tunnel before her, Billie's eyes adjust to the lighting. Giant oak roots, glowing in the dark, are sewn through the earth of the barrow. It appears as if more and more of the bioluminescent roots are exposed going into the grand chamber, filling it with an eerie glow. The technician doesn't hesitate a bit and rushes in, hoping she will be able to find an exit to circumvent her pursuers.

"Holy shit." Billie whispers at the visual spectacle greeting her, one she never dreamed of. A room filled with amenities and walls covered in brightly colored murals on tapestries is unveiled. Spread out before her is a great dining table, surrounded by chairs. This takes up the most space in the chamber. She realizes she is at the head of the table, where a giant throne rests against the back wall, next to the tunnel she entered from. What appears to be Futhark runes mark the art and furniture. Decorated shields rest on easels behind the table, next to weapons racks filled with swords, spears, and axes.

Billie cannot believe what she sees. An undisturbed Viking era great hall, preserved under the earth for a thousand or more years. She knows enough about Norse mythology to see the story of Ragnarök displayed in the murals. Balder's fall from a mistletoe arrow. Skoll and Hati catching the sun and moon. Tyr fighting the Fenris wolf. Thor in his prophesied death battle with the Midgard Serpent. The fall of Asgaard as it burns from Surtur's flames.

A great sword, sheathed in a leather scabbard, rests across the throne's arms. It's huge, nearly as long as Billie is tall, but it's the only weapon she can find. With one hand holding the scabbard, she withdraws the broadsword from its sheath. Remarkably, the blade is well oiled and glistens, free of rust or pitting. It's lighter than the woman thought it would be, and though she has to use both hands, she can swing and poke the blade with ease. The runes along its blade tell her the sword's name, *Caladcholg.*

"The Hard Cleaver? Well this is something. I'm ready for you now, motherfeckers." She quietly says and hides behind a chair with her eyes on the tunnel entrance. With her attention focused on the blade and her new found confidence, Billie fails to notice the changes in light coming from the roots. It pulses, ever so slightly, not enough to be noticed, but enough to tell a stalwart observer the fungus is alive...

Standing watch by the burial chamber at the other end of the mound, Heather Crovan, too, fails to notice anything out of the ordinary. A single earbud rests in her right ear. Her Android is playing the infamous Burzum demos, and she bangs her head in time with the beats. She's too absorbed in the music to realize the changes going on in the earth.

The oak roots surrounding the grave are coming to life with a soft bioluminescent glow, and even less fanfare. She'd see all of this if she wasn't too busy admiring the oil glistening on her Uzi than the soft light entering into the grave, illuminating the bones of the interred.

With her mind distracted by the mundaneness of guard duty, she is oblivious to the activity occurring next to her. To compound her imminent problems, she fails to notice her head lamp's light is dimming. By the time Heather discovers her errors, about the point the lamp fades to black, she won't be able to do a damn thing about the outcome.

Except die.

•

"**W**hat's this?" Terri Butler says less to her friends and more to herself when she steps into the bio-illuminated chamber. Tree roots, glowing with a soft blue-green hue, are threaded throughout the walls. Their head lamps light up the room, and as Terri's eyes absorb the contents, her body fills with emotion. Murals depicting the Twilight of the Gods are laid out around the chamber. In its center is a long serving table and chairs. She and her companions know what this room represents.

"Odin's beard, it's Valhalla!" Siobhan says and falls to her knees.

"Skal!" Erika says, following suit. Together, they immediately start chanting in Norse.

"Tyr Vallha—"

"Get up, you fools." Terri smacks the back of Siobhan's head with the flat of her ax blade. "The dyke is in here with us, somewhere, remember?" They stand back up. "Now let's search this room, if she isn't here now, we should be able to find which path she took out. We can force her back to the entrance and—"

The rat-a-tat-tat of a submachine gun followed by a blood curdling screech echoes through the tunnels. It breaks Terri from handing out instructions and leaves her momentarily stunned. They know the voice behind the scream, and it's not the radar tech.

"Come on!" Terri orders, and the trio leave to seek their comrade in arms. Their goal is to aid her. *Their plan won't play out as they might wish.*

•

Sensing movement in the darkness from her peripheral, Heather ducks in time to feel something cut the air above her head. Years of para-military training keep her focused-on survival. She rolls away from the motion, disengaging the safety on the Uzi while in the act. Closing one eye, she stops her roll and braces herself back up with one knee.

The outline of a gigantic figure, softly glowing in the darkness, looms before her. *Is that a ghost?* She wonders for the briefest of moments. Then, without further hesitation, Heather flips the Uzi onto full-automatic, squeezes the trigger, and unloads 9mm hell. *Let's see if ghosts are immune to bullets!*

Fire bursts from the submachine gun's barrel, lighting up the tomb. She sees someone, not the radar tech, not her shield-sisters in *Uí Ívair*. It's a shape made of the very darkness itself, outlined in starlight. What it is, Heather knows not. She only stares at its enigma until her fate, long ago predetermined by the Norns, is cut.

"Hǫggva mann ok annan." A disembodied voice announces through the earbud. Heather shakes her head, seeking the source of the voice. The phrase is repeated, *"Hǫggva mann ok annan."* as something strikes from the void. It impacts Heather in the sternum, between her breasts. Whatever it is, it's silent and sharp, and followed by a soothing warmth covering her chest. All Heather Crovan can do from this point on is scream for her mother in response, as the figure engulfs her in its chilling darkness.

The words don't come out as intended.

VALHALLA

Huddling behind the ancient throne, Billie breathes through her mouth as quietly as possible. She shakes in fear of being discovered as she listens to Terri barking orders. The radar tech, however, is as surprised as Terri and company when she hears Heather's Uzi... and ultimate death rattle screech.

What happened to her? Billie ponders.

"Come on!" She hears Terri scream the order to her confederates. Peeking out from between slats in the throne's back, Billie watches the women exit the chamber. After a few moments, still grasping the great sword, she allows herself to move. Her body aches and sweat stings her eyes, reminding her she still has to find an exit without getting shot or dying from a heart-attack; or at least get close enough to the entrance, where she might get a signal.

Dragging the massive sword behind her, Billie traces her path back to the burial chamber. The glow-in-the-dark fungi covering the roots are more prominent than she recalls. It's almost as if they've all come to life, illuminating the entirety of the underground barrow. It's a relief to her, to see without using her cell phone's light and burning any more battery life away, and helps ensure she'll at least have power when the time comes.

The fungus mesmerizes Billie. She finds she can't stop staring at it as she walks. It takes concentration to maintain her path. This time, at least, she's able to avoid knocking her head on low ceilings.

Behind her, the sword's tip furrows the earth and makes a slithering sound as the metal scrapes through the dirt and stone. It reminds Billie of a serpent. The sword's name, *Caladcholg*, is one of legends. She doubts this is the actual mythological blade wielded by Fergus mac Róich, but finding it in such pristine condition makes her wonder if it is, indeed, magical—or at the very least made with some lost technology preventing the steel from rusting.

A cool breeze hits Billie in the face, an indication she is nearing the dig's hole in the ground. Holding the sword with one hand, she turns her phone on with the other. It lights up, but to her dismay, the phone is still out of cell service. Then something catches her eye. The Bluetooth. It shows a connection.

What is the Bluetooth connected to? She wonders, then tries to make an emergency call by dialing 999. An operator doesn't answer. Instead, the phone squeals aloud, the shrill noise echoes throughout the tunnels of the barrow. Billie drops both sword and phone as she attempts, in vain, to shut the device off.

Before she can, the squealing stops. Shaking, Billie retrieves the phone. Coming from the speaker she hears a vocal melody, sung in what sounds like Norse. She puts it to her ear, and feels her nape hairs raise. The walls of the tunnel, covered in the glowing fungi, pulse in time with the melody. The words she hears chill her.

"Þat mælti mín móðir."

The trio of armed women moves with military precision, playing hopscotch with one another, alternating positions as they make their way through the tunnels. Standing at the point, Siobhan stops and raises a fist. The others join her.

"Look at that shite, Terri." Siobhan says, and points the Thompson's barrel at the glowing fungi on the wall. "It's all over the place now."

"Ignore it." Terri says, "It's not hurting you. It's giving us extra light so be thankful. You feel that breeze? Be alert, we're near the burial chamber. Look for Heather and if you find her, tell me she's okay."

"What about Purple Hair?" Erika asks.

"What about her?" Terri sighs, then continues. "I can't believe I'm saying this. If you see the fat piece of shite, don't feck around. Let Barney the Butch find right the feck out."

The women enter the burial chamber and stop in their tracks. It's not the sudden reveal of a black light mural in the lights of the wall, depicting a mighty invasion of dragon ships. It's not the accompanying recreations of land victories of a great warrior king riding a chariot into battle. It's not the impressions of this king, a massive warrior, shown cleaving the enemies before him with a giant sword. No. It's the scene of carnage taken straight out of a scrapbook for Dante's Inferno. The display of carnography causes all three women to shiver in fear.

Heather Crovan, or what used to be Heather, is pinned, or rather crucified, to the wall with her arms outstretched in a Christ pose. At her feet someone stacked the bodies of the dead archeology team. Her sternum is opened and cracked with the ribs protruding outward. A slop of entrails is piled under her feet at the base of the pile of bodies, and the large intestine is still attached to something within her pelvis. The woman's remaining internal organs are exposed, but covered in a crimson sheen.

"Heather!" Terri shouts. But Heather doesn't answer. She's incapable of doing anything except rot at this point. Her tongue is lolling out of her gaping mouth, and her lifeless eyes shine in the darkness, covered with the glowing fungus. They stare at the darkness of the barrow... and into the souls of the living.

"Let's just get out of here." Erika says.

"Not with a survivor running loose." Terri reminds her friends.

"Then let's find her and go." Siobhan adds.

"Split up," Terri orders, "we're bound to find her, or at least herd her into another chamber. If we're lucky she's already dead from a heart-attack." A high pitch whine fills the chamber, emanating from the depths of the barrow.

"What the hell is that?" Erika says.

"I've got three guesses for you and the first two don't feckin' count." Siobhan answers.

"It's got to be the dyke bitch. Follow the noise!" Terri orders, and the trio runs off down the tunnel.

In their haste, the women fail to see the shadow-covered shape step out of the wall behind them. It hovers, watching until the trio disappears in the passageway, then the darkness fades, absorbed by the fungal light...

•

"*Þat mælti mín móðir.*" The poetic words are repeated by the phone's tinny speaker. They resonate with Billie while her hands shake out of control. Reaching down to secure the broadsword, she drops the phone, again. This time the screen cracks. Frustrated, she stands and hefts the blade up with both hands; holding it up like a baseball batter in the box, waiting for the next pitch.

In front of her, Billie watches as a starfield falls from the walls of the tunnel. It swirls into the void and fills the passageway with its eerie luminescence, creating a reflection of the tech in its light. It distorts her, much like the curved mirrors of a funhouse. The image buckles the dysmorphia Billie has experienced from her obesity. For the first time in a long time, she's enamored with her own body.

The reflection is of a stereotypical Valkyrie from legend, with brilliant shades of purple streaking from her hair. Silver chainmail and leather flaps cover her in a coat of impenetrable armor. She holds in her hand the same sword, *Caladcholg.*

That can't be me... can it?

The starlit passage encroaches, but Billie cannot move, she can only stare at her unearthly reflection. The darkness and light engulf her as the phone pulses and Billie hears the mysterious poem coming from the speaker, this time with more lyrics. She knows this poem though she's never heard it before, at least in this language.

"*Þat mælti mín móðir, at mér skyldi kaupa, fley ok fagrar árar, fara á brott með víkingum,*" As she raises the great sword before her, she repeats the stanzas. They are words the Irish woman's never spoken before, in a tongue not her own. Yet somehow, they feel familiar, and right. "*Standa upp í stafni, stýra dýrum knerri, halda svá til hafnar...*"

She stops singing when she hears a commotion growing in the tunnel. Within the span of a couple breaths, the source of the clamor comes into view. It's Terri and her murder pals, Heather and Erika. Softly, the radar tech repeats the poem's refrain. "*Hǫggva mann ok annan, hǫggva mann ok annan...*" She stands firm, the sword raised and ready to strike. The words chill her. Billie instinctively knows their meaning in English.

Hew many foe-men.

Memories she knows are not her own flood Billie Powell's brain. She smells the salt of the open sea, the putrid malodor of a battlefield, and a summer wind blowing across a field of grain. She feels the emotions attached to them. The exhilaration of battle. The anticipation of war. The fear of loss. The anxiety of responsibility. An amorous devotion to the gods. Each of them twists the hormonal cocktail coursing through her veins.

Other memories flood in, each more precise, starting with a young woman's fear at discovering her first blood and culminating with the coronation of a great leader and a mob of cheering spectators. Now she sees visions. Rivers, fjords, and glaciers with volcanoes spewing fire on the horizon. A great fleet of dragon ships blocking out the sea. A massive horde of warriors, armed with shields and axes, charging across a field. A king, with a crown nailed to his head and body crucified to a tree, his lungs pulled out of his back. Finally, she sees her own reflection, wasted and gaunt on a litter, a drinking horn in hand and a smile on her face.

These visions please Billie. Her heart rate lowers and the sweat cools her skin. The back pain and cramping leave. The radar tech stands up, holding the broadsword with one hand. She's Billie, but she's no longer Billie Powell, she's something—someone—more, filled with confidence and righteous rage.

Now, she is both Billie and Ivar... *and they wait in the darkness of the barrow's tunnel to express their displeasure with the heretics wandering about.*

•

Charging down the expanse of the barrow's passage, the trio of armed women are determined to end the shenanigans and call this a day. Their white skin glows from the bioluminescence of the fungi covering the walls. The women have a duty, to hide this tomb and the secrets within, and it won't be complete until Billie Powell, the last survivor of the dig team, is dealt with.

"I want her scalp." Terri orders her friends, rubbing her black eye with her free hand. "I owe that cunt for this." She points to the bruise with her ax blade.

"Don't you worry. You can take your time with her once she's caught. She can't be far. I mean, like where can she go? The only exit is where we came in." Erika says.

"I think the throne room is down this way." Siobhan points out.

"The end of her line." Erika adds.

"For certain." Terri says and flicks the edge of her ax with a thumb. "I'll go in first. I want to relish this like our ancestor buried here would've. You cover me with your guns." The duo nod in unison and raise their weapons, pointing them into the chamber. Terri advances slowly, her ax held low and ready to swing at the first person she sees.

The throne room is no different from when they found it. There is nothing amiss, and Terri can see no one else.

"Come out, come out, little piggy." The woman taunts. She isn't expecting an answer.

"*Heil ok sæl.*" A deep, thundering voice says. It seems to come from each of the tunnels connecting to the throne chamber. Erika and Siobhan spin around, pointing their weapons at random entrances.

"Is that you trying to scare us little piggy?" Terry responds, "why don't you just get this over with."

"Gnyðja mundu grísir, ef galtar hag vissi."

"Show yourself, you dyke bitch!" Terri screams.

"There!" Siobhan shouts and fires off a line of fire from her Thompson. Erika joins her and lets loose with her Black Mamba. The bullets divot and splinter the surfaces of the feasting table and shields on the far side of the room. The painted tapestries flutter from the impacts and the din of shells falling fills the chamber as smoke from the spent ammunition creates an almost impenetrable gray fog.

"Stand down!" Terri orders them. "There's no one there. Don't waste your ammo." A stillness fills the room.

It is short-lived.

"Hǫggva mann ok annan…RUS!" The last word is more of a growl than anything. It's low and guttural, and causes Terri's nape and spine to tingle with fear.

"Feck you!" Terri curses in response and brandishes her ax above her head, shaking it in frustration. "COME OUT AND FIGHT ME!" Siobhan and Erika give Terri Butler a preview of what the Norns have in store for her.

"Hǫggva mann ok annan! RUS! RUS!"

The passageway behind Siobhan and Erika comes to life in a brilliant light, so bright it blinds Terri and forces the woman to cover her eyes.

"RUS! RUS! TYR VALHALL!"

Erika screams first as the sword seemingly materializes from the light. She can do nothing as the steel pierces her breast, except fall into the blade. This results in her aiding the weapon in its goal of removing her from the equation. It slices through bone and muscle and exits her back before the wielder twists it and withdraws. The action carves a six-inch diameter hole through the woman where her heart should be.

Blood streams, then pours, from both sides of the wound until Erika Harris drops her Black Mamba, crumples to the floor from exsanguination, and dies.

Siobhan is quick to react, but not quick enough. She steps to the side and aims the Thompson at the source of the sword. As she squeezes the trigger, the blade slices the machine gun's barrel off near the ammo drum, cutting Siobhan's left arm off at the elbow. The weapon explodes, blowing off her right hand.

"*RUS! RUS!*" Her assailant chants. Gouts of blood stream out of both stumps, and in moments Siobhan Lewis succumbs to her wounds and joins Erika in the dirt, their lifeless eyes staring at one another.

Terri grabs the closest shield, one decorated with a pair of ravens—likely Huginn and Muninn, Odin's famed corvids— and screams, "ENOUGH OF THE GAMES! FIGHT ME!"

She will soon regret making this challenge as a shape steps out of the tunnel's light...

•

Billie Powell, possessed by the spirit of Ivar Ragnarson, sees their foe standing before them, weapons held ready for combat.

"How the little piglets would grunt if they knew how the old boar suffered." They say, then *"RUS! RUS! TYR VALHALL!"* They cry out, and charge at the heretic, *Caladcholg* held high. Their first blow meets the heretic's shield, chipping it, but the enemy stands their ground.

Good, they think, *a fight worthy of the glory of Asgaard!* Another swing of the sword is deflected by an ax handle, but not without slicing the weapon's head off. Billie/Ivar continue their assault, chopping the sword at the shield until it splinters to pieces, all the while singing their favorite poem.

"*My mother told me someday I will buy galley with good oars, sail to distant shores.*"

Caladcholg swings down and cleaves into Terri's shoulder, creating a 'V' notch. Terri cries out in pain, but Billie/Ivar ignore her pleas for mercy. There is no mercy for heretics.

"*Stand upon the prow, noble barque I steer, steady course to the haven.*"

The weight of her arm pulls the wound on her shoulder open wider, and blood erupts from the gash, coating the woman's side. She stands limp, unable to defend herself. Billie/Ivar doesn't care.

"*Hew many foe-men...*"

They continue to hack at Terri's body, finally disemboweling her with a broad swing across the heretic's midsection. She tries in vain to keep the intestines in her belly, but Terri Butler's entrails slip through her fingers and fall on the floor.

•

"*H*ǫggva *mann ok annan!*" Joining her entrails on the floor of Ivar the Boneless's hidden barrow, Terri Butler listens to the words closing the Viking era poem. They echo through her dying mind. Despite their best efforts to satisfy the oath she and her shield-sisters took to keep this place a secret, they have failed.

How is it you? Terri wonders with disdain for her enemy. She sees no ravens, no Valkyries. The All-Father does not stand over her in approval. In fact it's quite the opposite and this enrages her. *You are undeserving to wield the blade of Kings! I am a Scion of Ivar! I'm from a line of pure blo—*

These thoughts are interrupted and put to rest when a final swing of *Caladcholg* removes Terri Butler's head from her neck.

•

Eyes fluttering, Billie Powell awakes from a nightmare, only to find herself in a hellscape of dead bodies in the burial chamber. They're everywhere, shot, chopped, or otherwise splayed out. Much like a night after binge drinking, she knows what has happened, but parts are cloudy, almost as if her mind is filled with static when she tries piecing together the lost time.

Last thing I remember was that poem... she thinks and gazes about the chamber until something nearly stops her heart, almost as terrifying as the number of dead.

A shadowy figure gestures at her to follow it.

Without any other recourse, she does. There are no movements of aggression by the form, it only beckons, and points at the tomb's exit/entrance. Billie now understands. *It's time to leave.* She walks past the shape, and finds the rappelling lines and rope ladders are still attached.

Grasping a rung of the nearest ladder, Billie takes one last look back at the burial chamber. The shadow figure is gone, and the bioluminescence of the fungi is fading. Climbing out, she's relieved knowing she will see Jennifer again. She also knows what must be done, that her wife must move here, to Ireland. Billie is certain Jennifer will like it here, especially after she learns of the importance. After all, secrets must be kept.

Thus is the duty of the *Uí Ívair*.

HEARTS ALONE

1

Deep within the recesses of the cosmos, the gods watch over us. Their influence is unending. Through the ages, they've been muses to move the masses, once and forever devoted to their glory. High in the summer night sky, Venus, the goddess of love, known by many names throughout civilizations, observes the earth from her synchronous orbit around the sun. The twinkling planet focuses her attention on a campground next to a large inland lake in the North American continent. From within its rustic setting, she hears her names called.

The Queen of Heaven and of Earth watches, and listens...

•

"**Y**ou guys remember the last time we were in Canada? When we were going through the toll booth at the Peace Bridge? The border guard looked in the truck and said, *'I ain't ever seen a black cowboy, a white rapper and a pirate in one vehicle before,'*" Morgan said as he shuffled the deck of cards, "argh! I'm a pirate! Does that make me Captain Morgan? Where's the rum?"

Laughter erupted from the half dozen friends sitting at the picnic table with him. The group, a trio of couples, were on their yearly camping excursion to Fenton State Park on the shores of Lake Ontario. Euchre, their card game activity of choice for the friends, precipitated a night of shenanigans while drinking around a campfire. Four of them played the team game, the other two waited their turn to challenge the winners.

"Wasn't that up on the St Lawrence?" Eric, Morgan's partner in the card game and the aforementioned white rapper, asked, "you know, for the clam bake for the record company?" He sat next to his wife, Shelly, a frumpy blonde nurse who still wore scrubs while off duty.

"Yeah. The food was killer. Top shelf bar, too," Dave, the *black cowboy,* or more accurately country singer, added, "we didn't have to bother with customs 'cause we took the boat in."

"Imagine his shock if he knew the name of your band!" Dave's wife, Anna, a voluptuous woman with fiery red hair and a mouth that matched, added. She sat across from her husband as his partner in the card game. "The Custom Traylor Park!" They burst into laughter, again.

"Yeah, you're right on all accounts," Morgan affirmed. Next to him sat his fiancée, Amy, with her head down on the table.

"I'm surprised you didn't write a song about it," Morgan quipped at Dave.

"Maybe I have, and if I haven't, I'll have one written this weekend," Morgan flipped Dave the bird. He didn't miss a beat retorting, "that's why you play guitar in my band."

"Your band?" Morgan raised an eyebrow, "did I ever say how much I hate country music?"

"Our band, sorry. And yes, you have. Frequently. But it pays the bills," Dave conceded on both parts. The pair started the band, Custom Traylor Park, together, but Morgan's experience and true musical love lay rooted in playing heavy metal. A few years earlier, Custom Traylor Park gained regional success with a small radio hit, "Broadway Honky Tonk," and were still living off its laurels, playing the regional touring circuit.

"True," Morgan conceded, "I smoke so much weed I had to make a career move. Whoever would have predicted I would end up in a country band. I've become Willie fucking Nelson."

"Play nice, boys. It's only euchre," Anna interjected.

"Where's the dog?" Amy asked. Morgan's dog,

Fred, joined them on this camping trip, as he did on all others. The problem with Fred? The terrier and lab mix's fur, black as night, blended into the darkness. Quieter than a church mouse, he often wandered off. On more than one occasion the mutt made friends with neighboring campers.

"Flipper, come here boy!" Shouted Eric, which received a cross look from Morgan in return, "What?" Big E failed at hiding the grin his lips formed as he uttered his last quip. Morgan looked under the table. There lay the dog, curled up in a ball and sleeping at the groups' feet.

"There you are!" The dog opened an eye, stood up, and began licking his master's face. "Good boy, you're so quiet we thought we lost you."

"Stop making out with the dog!" Eric grimaced, "that's gross. He licks his balls."

"Oh shut up, you're a clown, with big red shoes with white soles and curly toes," Morgan retorted. "Ain't that right, Fred," the dog wagged his tail and moved out from under the table, "I think he wants to go for a walk, Amy, can you take him? I'm still in this game," Amy lifted her head off the table and nodded.

"Sure," she sighed, "Shelly, come with me? We'll take him up to the bathhouse with us, I've got to go anyway."

"Why not," Shelly answered. Amy got up from the table and followed Shelly to the screen house's exit. They unzipped the fly and the women went off with the dog into the late night shadows of the campground, guided by the light of the full moon.

2

“Jesus Christ! What the fuck?” Dave banged his knee on the table and shouted out in pain. “Oh fuck! Son of a bitch that hurts! Fred! Jesus!” Fred the dog returned unannounced, without the women. He placed his wet nose on Dave's hand, and scared the living shit out of him. A roar of laughter came from the others.

“Good boy, Fred. Come here!” Morgan praised his pet. He reached up and grabbed a pretzel from a bag on the table, “sit,” the dog did so, “good boy. Now shake,” Fred raised a black paw with a white stripe across its tip, and Morgan gave him the treat, “good boy!” The dog’s tail wagged as he crunched on the pretzel.

“That's a pretty good trick.” Dave said, rubbing his knee, “I don't know of any dogs who wouldn't take food from somebody. Plus that dog hates me.”

“Be nice, Dave,” Anna admonished her husband, “Fred loves you.”

“Yeah, yeah, yeah. I love him, too. Now watch,” Dave reached over to pet the dog, whose wagging tail fanned back and forth at breakneck speed until the singer touched him. Fred growled and stuck his tail down.

"Yeah, good boy," Dave removed his hand and the dog tailed went back to wagging, "See? Let's finish this. I want to sit by the fire and drink."

"Fine," Eric said. Morgan's partner in the game, threw his hand on the table, "Hearts, alone," before him on the table laid out a four point perfect hand, Both bauers, the queen, king, and ace of hearts. The queen slid out from the rest of the pack and spun on the table top.

"Ask and you shall receive. We're done whooping your asses, sure." Morgan said and threw the deck on the table.

"Now I want a victory drink." Eric said.

"Smartest thing you've said all night, Big E." Morgan returned and patted his friend on the back as they moved to the fire pit. Dave cracked a fresh beer open, he drank a big gulp and sighed. All remained serene until Morgan shit on the moment of peace, ripping out a loud crackling fart. The others laughed.

"Jesus Christ, man!" Eric stated, trying unsuccessfully to keep a straight face, "check your drawers!"

"I think I've got to take a dump," Morgan said, sitting up.

"Oh gee, thanks for sharing," Eric chortled.

"Come on Fred, time to go back to the bathroom," Morgan commanded his dog, "let's take a walk," he grabbed a flash light off the table and the pair took off toward the restrooms.

"Don't you go and get lost, too," Dave said.

"Very funny," Morgan replied as he and Fred disappeared into the darkness.

3

Anna waited for Morgan to disappear before making her move, one she waited to make since they got to the campground.

"Hey Dave, you think he's gone?" she asked.

"Yeah," her husband replied.

"The girls, too?" E chimed in, questioning as he scanned the area around the campsite.

"Looks like it," Dave said, "this is hot, do it quick, they'll be back soon." Anna stood up from her chair, as if on command, and walked over to Eric. She smirked at him and he smiled in return. Anna dropped to her knees in front of him. He wiggled his ass and pulled his Syracuse basketball shorts down, revealing his open fly boxers.

"I need your cock in my mouth, lover," she said to Eric as she reached into his boxers and freed his penis. Without hesitation she engulfed it in her mouth. Eric threw his head back in ecstasy and held her by her red hair.

"Yeah baby, suck his white dick," Anna's husband commanded from his chair as he watched his wife perform fellatio on their friend. "Mammy always told me when I was a boy to find a girl who gives good head, then you'll never get her pregnant."

Anna's head bobbed up and down in sync with Eric's moaning. It didn't take long for him to tense up and orgasm. She swallowed it all.

"Ah, my daily dose of your cum," she said, licking her lips and throwing him a seductive stare. The duo stood in unison, Eric pulled his shorts back up, and walked off to the side of the campsite to piss.

"Come here, Anna," Dave told her. She obeyed and walked back to him, "that was hot. Kiss me," he told her, and she did. A deep, long kiss, their lips and tongues interlocking until they could no longer hold their breaths. Finally she pulled back and broke the moment.

"I love you, baby," she said to her husband.

"I love you, too, baby," the singer replied.

"What about me?" Eric asked, returning to the fire.

"I just love your cock and your come," she answered.

"That's more than enough for me. Shelly hasn't sucked my cock in years," he replied, "it's like she's afraid of putting it in her mouth. But I can go down on her no problem."

"Well you don't have to worry about that anymore, do you?" Anna asked him. Dave reached a hand up behind her and rubbed her round ass, smiling.

"I guess not," Eric agreed, "they'll be back any

minute. Who needs a beer?"

"I do," Dave said and smacked his wife in the ass. She threw her hands behind her back and clasped her buttocks.

"Woo, baby, don't turn me on any more than I already am!" she declared.

4

It took a few minutes for Morgan and Fred to walk to the restroom. He could find no site or sound of Amy or Shelly. A swarm of bugs hovered near the flood light attached to the pitch of the building. He listened for the girls near the door of the women's room, and still heard nothing.

"They must have gone for a walk like Anna said, Fred," Morgan told the dog. He found the gentlemen's lavatory, the interior light illuminating as he opened the door. The bugs on the roof attacked the screen.

Fred followed him into the men's room and now the dog's clawed feet clicked on the cement and echoed through the small lavatory. Morgan found a stall, closed the door, dropped his shorts, sat down and proceeded to shit his brains out. He sighed in relief as he relieved himself.

The dog continued to wander about the lavatory. The clicking of his claws created a surreal sing song with the bugs crashing off the screens in the windows of the building. After a few moments of making sure his bowels were emptied, Morgan stood up, flushed and exited the stall. The toilet roared to life, a roll of thunder resonating through the lavatory.

He washed his hands at the sink, and gazed at his warped visage in the stainless steel mirror overlooking the basin. He looked down at the dog, splashing the four legged companion with the water from his hands. The dog sneezed and shook his head in response. They exited the building and stood for a moment under the light from the roof, Morgan thinking and staring off into the darkness.

"Wait a minute, Fido, sit," Morgan commanded the dog. The canine relaxed on to his haunches and gazed at his master, waiting for another command, "stay," the human continued and the dog decided to lay down on the grass next to him, "good boy."

"What are you staring at?" Amy said. Morgan jumped out of his skin, startled. His heart pounded in his chest as he looked over his shoulder to see Amy and Shelly walking toward him.

"Jesus Christ, Amy," Morgan chastised his girlfriend, "you scared the shit out of me."

"I guess so," Amy laughed in return. Shelly started a full belly laugh, herself.

"Man, you should see your face," she said to Morgan.

"I bet. You two are really funny. Where the fuck did you go off to?"

"There's a meteor shower, we were down by the waterfall watching it," Amy replied.

"There was a streak or two every minute. Beautiful. You should go grab a beer and come back down with us," she said.

"That's an idea," he answered and they headed back to the campsite, led by their dog companion. Their return to the camping area and fire came without fanfare from their friends.

•

"It's about time, kids," Dave taunted them.

"Oh Jesus, Urkle, would you be quiet?" Morgan replied.

"I will not. Look at you, a white man telling a black man what to do," Dave shot back, a smirk on his face. Morgan gave him the finger.

"Which ain't as bad as a white woman telling a black man what to do," Anna interjected. Her husband laughed.

"Ain't that the truth," he managed as he giggled.

Morgan, Amy and Shelly joined their friends at the fire, each sitting in a folding chair. Shelly gave Eric a peck on the forehead before sitting down.

"Love you, girl," he said.

"Love you, too, boy," she replied.

"Hey Amy, why don't you tell us something weird and creepy?" Anna asked, "we've got a campfire and it requires either Kumbaya or a scary story."

"Okay. Like what? Didn't Morgan bring his

guitar?" Amy questioned. He shot her an unapproving glance.

"I'm not playing tonight. It's too late. The ranger will bitch," he said, and sipped his beer.

"Well, that leaves Amy, and since you are the only witch I know," Anna stated, "or any of us know, scary story time falls on you."

"True. But I'm not in the mood for anything scary tonight."

"How about something sexy, then?" Anna asked, "if I can't be scared, how about you make me horny?"

"Aren't you always horny?" Dave asked his wife.

"Shush, you!" she told her husband.

"Well, I suppose I could. I do sex magic with Morgan all the time."

"You mean you light stinky incense and light candles?" he added.

"If you say so. I've never heard you complain before."

"And I'm not about to, but I thought you said love spells created stalkers."

"They do, but this is different, we're all married or together here. Okay, Anna, here's one. You see that star up there, the bright one?"

"Yes."

"It's not a star, it's a planet, Venus, and the Goddess of Love's home."

"Oh, sexy."

"All the gods you've ever heard of in mythology are all different personalities of God. So Venus is also Aphrodite, and Ishtar, and Inanna, and etcetera and so on. This spell invokes Ishtar, so we'll need the fire, it's her element. First, the pit will be our altar. We'll need the fire stick to use as a ritual blade," she picked up the poking stick, a stout tree limb about a yard in length and handed it to Anna, "when we're done, thrust the stick into the center of the fire."

"Like a big wooden dick?"

"Yes, that's exactly what it represents, putting a dick in a pussy."

"Oh baby, that's one hot vajayjay you got there!" Anna declared, pointing the stick at the fire. This brought a series of giggles from their friends.

"Okay, so repeat after me," Amy directed her friend.

"In Ishtar, Goddess of all things,
In the Lady of Heaven and Earth,
Ishtar the Queen of Heaven, the Goddess of the Universe,
In the One who has brought life by the Law of Love,
Thou hast brought us harmony and led us by the hand."

The pair created a back and forth sing song, as Amy recited the love spell and Anna repeated it. When the last word rang out, Anna stabbed the stick into the center of the fire pit. Embers crackled and flew into the air, creating a small fire devil in the center.

"Well that was exciting!" Anna shouted, "now it's time for me and Dave to go to our tent."

"Alrighty then!" Amy replied, "Morgan, grab your beer, let's go back to stream and watch the meteors. You coming, too, Shelly? Eric?"

"Naw, we're going to finish our beers and hit our

tent, too. Been a long day." Shelly replied. She took Eric by the hand and led him to their tent.

"Good night, guys," he said, the others replied the same in near unison.

"All good, then. You ready, Fred?" Morgan looked to his dog, the loyal hound sat by his side this whole time. The dog stood up on all fours and started making his way to the edge of the campsite.

"Well, wait for us, Fido," he yelled to the dog, grabbed Amy's hand and the trio trotted off to the nearby creek.

5

"Yeah baby! That's it fuck my pussy! Fuck me! Fuck, baby!" Dave bent Anna over a cooler at the edge of their air mattress, doggy style. She loved it. Her fingers clenched the nylon flooring in her ecstasy.

"You like that my cock in your pussy, baby?"

"Yes I do! I love it!" she gasped in response. He leaned forward and whispered into her ear.

"You want a cock in your mouth right now?" she grinned, twisted her head and nodded in approval. He grabbed her face.

"Yes!" she answered and sucked on Dave's fingers. He hopped off the air mattress and thrust his pelvis in her face. His rigid member tickled her lips.

"Sing to the BBM, baby," BBM was Dave's pet name for his penis, aka the *Big Black Microphone*. She smiled and engulfed it in her mouth. Anna bobbed on her husband's cock until her jaw got sore. She popped it out of her mouth, gasping for breath, drool dripping down her chin.

"That tastes different," Anna said after removing Dave's penis from her mouth. She looked at the member in the half light of the shadows and noticed a slime darker than the others. Blood, "looks like Aunt Flo is having a threesome with us, baby. No wonder I'm so horny."

"How about my cock in your ass?"

"Oh yeah, baby! Fill me up!"

He mounted her from behind, slowly entering her anus. He held it for a moment as she relaxed and adjusted to sodomy. Then he thrust forward, stimulating the rectal nerves. She cooed in pleasure and bucked back into him, signaling him to give it to her hard, so he did.

The humidity in the tent rose with each thrust. Sweat glistened on their bodies. Shadows swirled about them as they made love.

"Sing to me, baby. Sing to me," Anna asked her husband.

"How about a Sexy Spell Remix, by Dave's big black microphone?"

"Oh yeah!" she moaned as his thighs slapped against her backside, keeping time.

He wasted no time in replying, repeating the Sumerian love spell Amy cast earlier. Almost the same, his eidetic memory caught the words, but the artist in him changed the tune to a gospel rendition of "How Great Thou Art" with a liberal interpretation of the spell's words as the lyrics.

"In Anna, Goddess of all things," he pulled her hair and snapped her neck back. *"In Anna, the Lady of Heaven and Earth,"* she bucked her hips back as he thrust forward, the tip of penis plowing into her ass, stimulating nerves with an electrifying punch. In mid thrust he pulled out and re-entered her vagina, never missing a beat. *"In Anna the Queen of Heaven, the Goddess of the Universe,"* Dave arched his back, clenching his rectum as he held back his orgasm. *"In Anna who has brought life by the Law of Love,"* Anna gripped the fabric of the tent's floor in her hands as her own orgasm flooded her body. *"Thou hast brought us harmony and led us by the hand."*

He came on the last beat.

Husband and wife collapsed next to one another on the air mattress, spent from their love making, the sound of their labored breathing a lingering reminder of their coitus. They embraced each other in a post coitus silence, while their bodily fluids pooled between them.

•

Eric and Shelly lay on their air mattress, they heard Dave and Anna fucking in their tent, despite them trying to be discreet. Quiet, it turned out, wasn't an option in tents. Through the tent's opaque walls they saw the shadows of their friends in action. Eric and Shelly watched as the voyeurs this time. They'd shared a bed with Dave and Anna on more than one occasion.

"If the tent's a rockin', don't come a knocking," Eric joked to his wife.

"You can join them if you want," she told him, "I'm just tired, plus I have my rag."

"No, I don't want Morg and Amy to say something, 'cause you know they will." he replied.

"I don't see why they are so uptight. It's what we choose to do," an irritated Shelly stated.

"Whatever," he shrugged it off, "I'm good here with you, baby," Eric embraced Shelly, they kissed. He pinched her ass and she fondled his hardening phallus. He placed a hand on her shoulder and pushed down, signaling he wanted her to continue with a little more than a hand job. She followed his direction. Much to his surprise, she complied.

"Yeah, that's it," he said as she licked the tip of his organ. Shelly tickled the glans with her tongue, making him shiver. He put his hand on her head and pushed it down. Shelly swallowed her husband's penis to the base, and kept it there. She used her tongue to massage the shaft, driving Eric to an immediate orgasm. She pulled her mouth away and he didn't care. She blew him for the first time in years! He shivered and convulsed as sperm ejaculated from his rock hard cock.

"You like that, baby?" Shelly said, a seductress moving back up to the pillow. Snuggling back into the crook of his arm.

"Holy shit," he exclaimed, "yes, thank you."

They heard Dave singing to Anna, the slapping

of his pelvis on her thighs cracking through the darkness, keeping time for the tune.

"He's something else," she whispered, "that guy."

"Dave? Yeah, he is," Eric said. He hugged his wife and the two fell asleep.

6

Stars and planets lit the sky, no ambient city light to dim their shining glory. Falling pieces of debris streaked through the canopy of celestial objects. All of this became the perfect backdrop to the serene rolling waters of the stream, a pond's tributary leading to the nearby Lake Ontario.

Morgan and Amy sat upon a rock at the shore, holding one another; watching the meteorites and listening to the gentle sound of the brook. He sipped on a beer while she lit a cigarette and puffed on it, the exhaled smoke fogged the surrounding area.

"So quiet out here, beautiful, isn't it?" she asked her boyfriend, tapping the gray ash off the paper and tobacco fag.

"I can't argue that," he replied.

"I could live here, all my days, sitting here every evening, listening to the sounds of nature."

"You'd freeze your ass off come winter, dear," Morgan grabbed her tight, "it gets mighty cold and snowy up here."

"No shit, Sherlock," she jabbed him in the ribs with her elbow before resting her chin on his arms and sighing.

Fred sat up without warning and started growling, his attention on something in the direction of their campsite.

"What's his problem?" Amy asked.

"I have no idea. Relax killer, there's nothing out there," Morgan told his dog. But the mutt snarled and charged down the pathway, "Holy shit, dog! Fred! Get back here!"

They heard a blood curdling scream echo through the campground. It made Morgan think of a baby rabbit in the clutches of a cat. His nape hairs stood on end.

"What the fuck?" Morgan shouted. The scream was followed by another, and yet another, all shrill, raising the hair on his arms and nape. The burst into action and ran after the dog, back toward their campsite as another banshee shriek pierced the park's serenity.

7

"I have to pee," Anna said and sat up, breaking the moment, "I'll sneak behind the tent and squat, I don't feel like going to the bath house."

"Okay, baby. Don't be sneaking off to Shelly and Eric's tent, now," Dave told her.

"Naw, I'm pooped-out after that, plus my rag," she pulled a pair of loose shorts on and slid into a T-shirt and grabbed a wad of napkins and a tampon before unzipping the tent's fly and crawling out into the dark.

The flames of the fire lit up the site, shadows danced about, creating pockets of darkness. Anna did what she said she would. She crept behind the tent, dropped her shorts and squatted to urinate. Her bladder opened up and she relieved herself.

She wiped and the iron smell of fresh blood caught her attention. She looked at the napkins and saw they looked dark in the dim lighting. She stood up to get a better look at it. The napkins were bright red, with much more blood than she discharged during her time. Her hands, even, were stained crimson with blood. She looked down where she pissed. A puddle of blood glistened in the moonlight.

"Oh, this isn't good," she whispered. Anna returned to the tent and her husband. He snored, fast asleep. She shook him.

"Dave. Honey, wake up. Something is wrong."

"Huh? What?" he mumbled.

"Baby, you fucked me really hard. I'm bleeding bad. I didn't bring any pads, only plugs. I have to go ask Shelly if she has any."

"Okay babe. I'll be here, sleeping," he replied and rolled over. Anna stepped out of the tent and started making her way to Anna and Eric's tent. She took a couple steps and stopped in her tracks. Cramps wracked her midsection in pain.

"Ouch!" she cried out as the cramps built in

intensity. She stumbled forward and fell onto Eric and Shelly's tent, face first; her body bringing the tent down with her, snapping poles and tearing fabric.

"What the fuck?" Eric screamed as the tent collapsed on him and his wife, waking them from sleep. Together they pushed at the tent's nylon material, once a shelter, now a restricting net, entangling them.

"Help," Anna managed outside, her body wracked in pain. She wretched, blood soaked vomit erupting from her mouth. The pink gore sprayed the tent and surrounding area. At the same moment she shit herself. Liquid stool, streaked in bright red blood erupted from her rectum, squirting out from under her shorts, down the back of her legs.

Eric and Shelly managed to break free of the collapsed tent. Both were covered in bloody vomit and shit.

"Oh my God!" Shelly screamed, "Dave! Wake up! It's Anna!" They watched their friend writhing on the ground, blood now coming out of her eyes, ears and nose. Her crotch, stained red and dripping into a pool of crimson growing around her.

I'm bleeding out? She thought. Shelly ran to her side and fell into emergency room nurse mode.

The fly opened on Dave and Anna's tent. The singer stuck his head out to see what might be amiss and saw Shelly kneeling next to his wife. Anna lay on the ground, blood oozing from every open orifice.

Shelly, frantic, attempted to find a cause. Dave screamed and jumped out of the tent, buck naked, running to his wife's side. Air bubbles frothed in her mouth.

"Anna, are you with us? Anna?" Shelly asked. Her friend didn't reply, "let's get her off the ground," Shelly commanded. Eric and Dave bent over and helped Shelly pick Anna up. Tears covered Dave's face.

He mumbled unintelligible nonsense, the tongue of a man in the grasp of madness, in his wife's ear as they carried her over to the open screen house and placed her on the picnic table. Shelly unraveled two handfuls from the roll of paper towels on the table and placed them over Anna's ears.

"Here!" She handed a wad to her husband, "jam this in her crotch!" He did so. The white paper turned red as it soaked the blood up.

"Where the fuck are Morgan and Amy?" Dave threw his hands up in the air, left the screen house and went back into his tent to put on clothes.

"They went to the stream to watch the meteor shower," Shelly replied, "they should be back soon."

"Maybe one of us should go find them?" Eric inquired.

"No, they'll be back soon. I'm sure someone heard all the racket we've made," his wife added, "we need to watch her."

"Fuck!" Dave pulled on a pair of sweatpants and a t-shirt, then exited the tent. He stopped in his tracks.

The puddle of blood Anna left behind bubbled, resembling a boiling pot of black gravy, "Guys! Da fuck am I seeing here?" he pointed at the effervescing ground. They turned to look. Eric obscured Shelly's view.

"What is it?" she asked her husband.

"I don't know," he replied and stepped out, pushing Dave behind him.

"What do you mean, you don't know?" Shelly returned. Eric tilted his head and furled his brow, trying to understand.

The bubbling increased, each popping and splashing higher and higher until the ground itself rose with it. The pool shifted and oozed up, defying gravity, growing in height by the moment.

"Holy, fucking, shit," Eric said. He stepped back, shaking in fear. Eric stood in front of a five foot tall mound of bloody sludge resembling a chocolate fountain. He watched with the others as it transformed, *becoming* something.

A faceless head formed first, then the shoulders, and torso. Arms pulled out of the sides of the muck, the base split into two poles, the latter morphing into a pair of legs. The face started to form, becoming more familiar to those present with each shift in the wet mud.

Anna's face.

Eric grabbed a huge knife edged grill spatula from a plastic tote next to the screen house. His wife bought it from a kitchen party a few years before. The *Grill Commander*, a combination grill scraper, bottle opener and knife, with an eight inch long razor sharp blade. A full two feet long from the handle to the tip of its blade, the implement cut the air with a hiss when he swung it.

"I don't know what the fuck you are, but you are going down, bitch!" Eric challenged the golem, its back still turned to them. Eric charged it, the spatula held high overhead. He swung it down with all his might.

The simulacrum grabbed him by the groin in a steel grasp. Eric screamed, shrill and high pitched, hitting a soprano note not meant for men to sing. The back of the construct's head became the front, morphing before Eric's eyes. He saw its body did the same, mutating as he stood, unable to break free of the golem's grip.

The thing ripped the *Grill Commander* out of Eric's restrained hand with its free appendage, breaking his fingers in the process.

They snapped in chorus.

He screeched in further agony until his vocal cords shattered.

"No!" Shelly shrieked. Eric did try to move, but the golem held him fast by his destroyed testicles. Trapped and unable to escape his fate, husband and wife watched in horror as the spatula's knife edge swung down at his exposed neck in slow motion.

The blade passed through with no resistance.

Eric turned his head to look at his wife, and it slid off his severed neck into the dirt, bouncing in the dirt and grass a few times before coming to a stop. a fountain of blood pumped from the stump, coating everything near his corpse in a crimson paint.

The golem dropped the spatula and released its grip on Eric's headless body. The latter slumped to the ground in a pile, blood pouring out of the stump, pooling at the golem's feet. The simulacrum became more and more human as the blood absorbed into its body almost as quickly as it left Eric's.

Shelly couldn't move or speak, catatonic in fear

and shock. She heard a familiar growl, followed by mad barking.

Fred.

8

Morgan and Amy found Fred standing at the edge of the campsite, his ears and tail down, uncharacteristically snarling and snapping at apparently nothing. Amy stayed behind the dog, but Morgan continued into the campsite, the flashlight raised like a weapon. He realized quickly he wouldn't need it.

Morgan shot his gaze about the site around the fire, which burned high and bright. Palpitations jittered his head as it turned. Two of his friends were dead and in some form of desiccation.

Eric lay on the ground, or at least his body did. Blood covered the front of his basketball jersey, staining the white a crimson shade of pink. His head lay on the ground in front of the campfire. Dirt and pine quills were hanging from his lips and protruding tongue.

Dave stood in the screen house with Shelly. Both were disheveled from terror. A glimpse at Dave's wife, Anna told him why. She lay splayed on the picnic table, under the screen house, her legs spread eagle to either side. Blood still dripped from her extremities and pooled in the dirt and grass around the table.

Do mud pies made with blood taste better? Morgan dealt with stress with an internal monologue of dark humor. The guitarist couldn't move, the shock of seeing all of this froze him in place.

He shot his head around and watched as Amy started to scream and sob. Fred started howling and ran off, away from them into the darkness of the park, terrified. Amy ran to Shelly's side.

"What happened?" Amy asked her friend. Shelly didn't answer, instead she pointed in the direction of the bodies, "who did this? Shelly? Dave? Who did this?"

"No, no, no, no," Morgan muttered, snapping and shaking his head trying to remove the carnage from his vision and mind. But it hung there until the figure stepped out of the shadows of the tents. It resembled a thin Anna.

Covered in blood from head to foot, its face gaunt and black in the flickering light of the campfire, the thing moved into view. Shelly ran from the screen house to the campfire, screaming bloody murder as she did.

"What the fuck are you? You killed my husband!" Shelly grabbed the tree limb they used as a poking stick for the fire pit. Shelly threw it at the simulacrum with all her might.

The red, glowing tip of the makeshift spear streaked through the darkness, leaving a trail of sparking embers in its wake. The projectile struck it in the chest, and passed through unabated, and landed harmlessly on the grass behind it.

"Oh shit," Shelly said.

The thing took a step toward Shelly. She stumbled back and tripped on the pile of firewood, landing face first in the grass. Stunned, she pushed himself up, using a lawn chair for leverage.

"Shelly!" She heard Dave and Amy and Morgan scream in unison. The nurse turned around. The mud-pile doppelganger of her friend stood before her, far too close for comfort. She backed away and fell again, this time into a lawn chair.

It screeched and struck Shelly in between the eyes with a balled fist. Dave, Morg and Amy heard the crunch of Shelly's face breaking and the pop as the back of her skull blew out. The thing's fist plowed through the woman's head. Then the simulacrum pulled its arm back through. Bits of brain and bone, once belonging to Shelly, absorbed into the gory golem. It stood there, marveling at its arm, twitching its head as it twisted the arm to the left and right.

"Who the fuck are you?" Morgan challenged the thing, but it didn't answer him. Instead it sobbed. Within moments it built up to a cry of sheer terror, piercing Morgan's ears. Blood soaked hands, with long claws growing out from the fingernails, covered her face.

The naked thing shrieked, again.

Morgan threw his flashlight at the creature. It tumbled through the air and hit the simulacrum in the chest with a thud, sinking in the thing's chest, stopping midway through.

It looked down at the flash light and stepped forward.

Morgan became frozen in fear, his heart throbbing, about to explode. But it didn't seem to be concerned with him. It slowly walked toward the screen house.

Its arms snapped inward, the bloody hands grasped the flashlight and pulled it out from between its breasts. Blood spurted out, a fountain of brackish, black gore. Morgan backed away.

"Dave?" Amy called to her friend, who stared back, a blank expression covering his face. Morgan looked to his friends, painfully aware the simulacrum moved closer to them.

"Guys, we should be smart like the dog and run," he told them.

"Shut up for one second, please, Morg," Amy commanded him, "Dave, what happened?"

"Anna started bleeding from everywhere and, and," Dave began hyperventilating, he struggled to get the words out, unable to speak, gasping for air, until finally he burst, "that thing killed my wife!" he spit the words out as snot bubbled in his nose, "I made up words to your love spell and-"

"You what?" Amy interrupted Dave, "what spell?"

"I sang her the spell you the girls at the fire earlier. But I changed the words some."

"You did what? You've got to be fucking shitting me. That wasn't some bullshit spell I made up, I took that from the fucking Necronomicon."

"The what?" Dave's eyes bugged out.

"The Book of the Dead!"

"What? You mean the Evil Dead? Ain't no way I'm strapping a chainsaw onto my arm." Morgan asked.

"Not that Book of the Dead, the real one, the Sumerian seals translated by the Mad Arab." Amy corrected him.

"The Mad Arab?" Dave inquired.

"Never mind! You must have summoned the avatar of a fucking Sumerian god, and if I'm right, we're in a pissing match with Inanna."

"With who?" Dave asked.

"A death goddess!" Amy shouted out.

"What a dumb fuck!" Morgan added, "but I hate to say it, we should run the fuck away. Now!"

The avatar stood at the opening of the screen house now. Morgan deftly unzipped the opposite flap and pulled Amy along with him as he ran out. Dave stood there, paralyzed in fear, clenching his dead wife's hand.

"Dave! Come on!" Morgan shouted to his friend, but the singer wouldn't move. He stood his ground.

The avatar hissed and hopped on the picnic table, on top of Anna's corpse. Dave jumped back, let go of Anna's hand, and turned to run out of the tent. The thing moved faster than their eyes could register.

"Oh, fucking no, not on my watch!" Amy screamed. She ripped her pentagram out and wrapped it around her hand.

"Babe?" Morgan asked. She ignored him.

"*Nach i An Bhitseach í!*" she screamed in Gaelic, "*trasna ort féin!*"

The words caught the naked, shape-shifting golem's attention. It made eye contact with Amy and curled a lip menacingly. The stare down ended before it started. The avatar lost form, reverting to a muddy sludge, splashing over Anna's body on the table.

"What the fuck, Amy?" Morgan said, his voice shaking in terror, "what just happened?"

"I don't know? A blood avatar of some Sumerian god?" she told him candidly, maintaining eye contact with the creature.

"How the fuck do you know this?" Morgan asked, "and why haven't you ever told me?"

"You know I'm a witch," her tone dripped in sarcasm, "I'm supposed to know this shite. Who thinks to tell their other half, 'Oh, if you summon a Sumerian death Goddess it'll piss in the Cheerios of your camping trip!' I never thought I'd have to deal with one killing my best friends."

"I don't get it," Dave choked out.

"What don't you get? They're dead because you cast a love spell to the ultimate green monster. It picked you!" She chastised him. Dave sat with his head in his hands, weeping.

"Calm down now," Morgan piped in, "is it dead?"

"I don't know."

"*David Christopher Traylor?*" They all heard Anna speak her husband's name. But it couldn't be, Morgan said to himself, Anna bled to death before Amy and he found their way back to the campsite. Covered in gore, it pointed a finger at the singer.

Dave ran around the back of the screen house to the fire pit and found the poking stick. The tip still smoldered. He held it like a baseball bat, ready to swing at the thing that used to be his wife.

"Fuck you bitch," Dave defied the thing that used to be his wife. The singer swung the stick at his dead wife's head. It broke at the point of impact.

He stared back, dumbfounded.

Amy and Morgan watched the back of Dave's head blow out. A red fist erupted from the gaping hole. The fist held something, it squirmed and dropped on the ground with a wet slap.

His tongue.

The fist retracted and Dave's body collapsed to the ground.

"Now, if you don't mind," Amy started moving forward, toward the creature, her hand held forward, the silver pentacle shining in the moonlight.

"Are you crazy? She'll kill you!" Morgan grabbed Amy's shoulder. She pushed his hand away.

"Morgan, if you want to help," Amy directed him, "get a tire iron from the trunk of the car. Don't argue with me about it. Don't question why, just get the fucking thing and bring it to me," he broke away and started running to the car, pressing the trunk's release button on his key chain.

The trunk beeped and clicked open. He dug into it, throwing dirty clothes and bags about as he moved the floor panel to gain access to the spare tire and tools underneath. He found the multi- tool, cross of iron and snatched it out from on top of the spare. He turned and saw the bloody changeling continuing to menace them.

"It's not working, Amy!" Morgan screamed.

"Oh, yes it is," Amy replied, "now watch this," she raised her hands high above her head and made arcane gestures with her fingers. The avatar stood its ground before her, hissing in agony. It pulled a hand back to strike the witch.

"What am I doing with this tire iron?" Morgan interrupted.

"Hit her with it!" she directed.

"What?" I don't think I can do that," Morgan replied, sincerely.

"For Christ's sake! Hit the changeling!" she screamed at him.

He threw the tire iron at the creature, which was still mesmerized by Amy's necklace. It spun through the air and struck the creature in the chest, sinking in and impaling her. On impact the *fae* being screamed in agony, twisting in unnatural positions. Its arms snapped inward, the clawed hands grasped the tire iron and pulled it out from between its breasts. Blood spurted out, a fountain of brackish, black gore.

Still, the changeling avatar stood its ground before her, dropping the tire iron the ground, hissing in agony. It pulled a clawed hand back to strike the witch.

"Amy!" Morgan shouted in alarm. She didn't budge, but she did start chanting in Gaelic.

"Ár nAthair, atá ar neamh, Awr nyahher, ahtaw air nyav, Go naofar d'ainm, guh nayfer danim, Go dtaga do ríocht,guh doguh duh reeokht, Go ndéantar do thoil ar an talamh, guh nyayantur duh hell air on tahlu, Mar a dhéantar ar neamh. mar uh yayantar air nyav."

The words struck the avatar, an invisible force. It screeched and bent in agony with each syllable. It stepped back, one foot at a time, until it backed up to the fire pit. Amy spoke the same sing-song spell she evoked earlier, turning up the dread in her tone a notch.

"Ár nAthair, atá ar neamh, Awr nyahher, ahtaw air nyav!" The avatar hissed at Amy.

"Go naofar d'ainm, guh nayfer danim!" The changeling took a step forward, then cringed, throwing its hands up over its ears.

"Go dtaga do ríocht, guh doguh duh reeokht!" A leg stepped forward, shaking and quivering. Its foot stepped back down, and pulled back.

"Go ndéantar do thoil ar an talamh, guh nyayantur duh hell air on tahlu!" Now Amy stepped toward the avatar, her extended arm holding the pentacle by its leather thong. She thrust her arm forward and touched the avatar with the charm. It screamed in agony.

"Mar a dhéantar ar neamh. mar uh yayantar air nyav!"

The simulacrum fell backwards, into the fire. The blaze roared to life bright and high in an instant. Amy fell back, the heat of the flames singing her hair and eyebrows. Morgan threw his arms up to block the glare of the flames. The golem shrieked in agony as the flames increased.

A pile of alien bones, blackened and burning still remained in the fire. Wisps of smoke rose from the pit. The stench of burning hair and flesh lingered in the air.

Amy collapsed into Morgan's arms.

"Is it over?" Morgan asked.

"I think so," Amy replied.

They heard Fred barking in the distance. A flicker of light caught Morgan's attention, and he turned his head and saw the headlights of a vehicle driving toward them.

The park ranger isn't going to like this, he thought.

Morgan held Amy with one arm, his head turning to the sky. Venus, the Queen of Heaven and Earth, millions of miles away, shined in the heavens, and looked him back in the eye. Once a brilliant white, a crimson haze now covered her. Morgan didn't question her wardrobe change.

He knew the answer.

THE HAUNTING OF ROUTE 13

It's a brisk Halloween night in upstate New York. Trick or treating kids, dressed in myriad costumes crossing eras of pop culture, roam the streets of a small town. An early snowfall has covered the ground in a pristine white. Snow on Halloween is common in northern New York. The children have adapted accordingly, with winter attire hidden underneath their costumes. I fit right in with them on my sled as I come to a stop at an intersection past the canal bridge.

An attractive woman chaperones a throng of appropriately dressed kids, standing at a crosswalk across from me, and waits for the light to change.

Across the street, multiple signs in a cluster identify the local state highways. Route 31 is three miles to the south, Route 48 is four miles to the north, and the main street here in Sylvan Beach, a resort town on the eastern shore of Oneida Lake, has a curious designation.

"Am I standing by a cursed road on a snowy Halloween night?" I hear you ask, gazing at the white and black sign designating New York State Route 13. You're not talking to me in particular, but if you were, I'd fill you in with a load of bullshit. First, I'd agree with you. The United States of America is chock full of famous highways, with Route 66 topping the list.

This being said, yeah, you'd think a state highway featuring a perennial bad luck charm, in the number thirteen, would be somewhat infamous on a national level. But not the hundred and fifty-two miles making up NY 13. To anyone outside New York, Rt. 13 is nothing more than a back country highway. It cuts off New York's snout, bisecting the upstate region from the southern tier to the eastern shores of Lake Ontario.

To the locals living along its expanse? Well, it depends on who you talk to. The young couples who've moved into the country to escape city life, they'll tell you it's a busy road in a quiet place and to save your faerie tales of headless horsemen for the Catskills. The old timers? They'll tell you the road and the land around it are cursed.

Tonight I'll tell you the story of the cursed highway. It's a perfect story to tell on this All Hallow's Eve, the night where the veil between the dead and living is thin, and the spirits straddling both worlds can be seen in the shadows.

It's easy to see why some might believe there's a blight on this highway and the lands surrounding it. The highway runs through some of the most hilly terrain in the state. The black top twists and turns like a snake, and this leads to a staggering number of automobile accidents every year.

This says nothing of the poverty stricken communities the road meanders through. The major urban centers the highway travels near are some of the most economically depressed population centers in the state. Syracuse and Utica are rampant with crime, not to mention racial and social unrest.

Along its rural route, hamlets filled with dilapidated trailer parks line the road. It intersects small cities composed of crumbling brownfields and rustic villages, their main streets consisting of long dead businesses.

The residents, whose families have deep roots in the counties the highway traverses, are an eclectic lot. Many tend to be on the low end of the income scale, with less than a full high school education. Naturally, ignorance on this level leads to some hysteria, and what's easier to point the finger at than a road with the number thirteen.

A rational man will tell you not to worry about black cats crossing your path or roads with an unlucky number. But I've been riding down this road for an awful long time, and I can tell you a tale or two about Route 13. Why don't we start at the beginning?

"The beginning of what?" you might ask if we were actually speaking to one another, "The curse or the road?"

I like to answer this question with, "Both?"

Like many of the roads in New York, Route Thirteen started as a deer trail. Located in the southern tier of the state, in Chemung county, the highway wasn't built until 1924. But some say its curse dates back to the birth of a nation. And who am I to argue with that?

After the Revolutionary War ended and the United States won their independence from Britain, a great explosion of settlers, many of them veterans of the war, moved into the lands of what is now upstate New York. Towns and villages came to life almost overnight, displacing the native Iroquois who supported the British. The Senecas, Onondagas, Cayugas, and Mohawks allied themselves with the wrong side in the war. But it wasn't without some little victories, like kicking John Sullivan's ass.

Late in the summer of 1779, the army of General John Sullivan forced a march over four hundred and fifty miles of rough terrain to attack the Cayugas in alliance with Britain. The land fought Sullivan's men, with a devastating effect. They made it as far as what is Geneseo today, then retreated. Upon their arrival at Fort Reid, the army found themselves forced to euthanize their horses. On top of injuries sustained in their march, the summer mosquitos spread equine encephalitis through the herds. The soldiers slaughtered the sick animals and left them in massive, fetid piles, before retreating.

Legend has it the Cayugas, in an effort to scare off any further white invaders, lined the trails with the rotting heads and bleached skulls of the horses. Whether or not it achieved the effect the Cayuga's wished for remains to be seen. But from that day forward, the tribe has referred to this spot as the Valley of Horse's Heads.

The local settlers, horrified by the morbid display, believed the trail to be cursed, and avoided it at all costs. Then someone heard their neighbor sheltered a survivor from one of the raids. He's alleged to say the Cayuga's medicine men poisoned the land against the white man.

"May the land feed off the blood of your children."

Fifty-ish years later, the town of Horseheads came into being. A hundred years after this, the department of transportation broke ground for what would become New York Route 13. They say the construction workers found the bones of the headless horses under the earth, and ground them into the concrete used to lay the road's foundation.

I don't think the curse has ever cared about the white man clause. If a curse exists, it's indiscriminate, and executes its directions with extreme prejudice, in spite of a person's race. The indigenous peoples living along the highway suffer from as much poverty and tragedy as the colonists.

Some say the first victims of the curse were the husband and bride in an intertribal marriage on the shores of Cazenovia Lake, in modern day Madison County. A few years later after the Fort Reid massacre, a contingent of Oneida warriors, unhappy with one of their own marrying an Onondaga princess, invaded the proceedings. With the husband wounded in battle defending his new bride, the couple attempted to escape the carnage in a canoe. The husband died in his wife's arms before it sank halfway across the lake. When you ride through Cazenovia today, you might hear the bride's cries at night.

Traveling north, up Rt. 13, you can't go through a town without some disaster or tragedy coming to mind. But people brush it all off and attribute it to life as normal. I think there's a simple reason why no one thinks the road is cursed, it's because the things happening, they don't always happen on it. The curse feeds on those near it, or to former residents after they move away.

The great flood in Elmira back in 1972 is a good example, and weather related disasters are common along the highway's length. The region is notorious for record snowfalls, averaging twelve or more feet of snow a season. The blizzards of 1966 and 1993 stand out as two of the most impactful.

Snow brings out snowmobilers, especially in the northern hills, and if you don't go down a groomed trail, the odds of you hitting something in the snow are high. Oh, and I tell you I'll never forget the tragedy in Hogh's Field in Madison County. That was when Kristine DeFio's fiancée, David Barton, on a guys' weekend snowmobiling adventure on Oneida Lake, lost his head to a barbed wire fence.

And she lost her love.

Back down Rt. 13 we come to the city of Ithaca. Two colleges, the Ivy League's Cornell, and Ithaca State, reside here. The city is a world leader in student suicides, many of whom are jumpers into one of the prolific glacial gorges cutting through the campus. The death toll rivals the Sea of Trees in Japan. Students say you can hear the last screams of the victims when you walk across any bridge.

Serial killers are rampant, even if they aren't hunting along the highway. One comes to mind, involving Josh Wetzler, who grew up alongside Rt. 13 in Chittenango. He moved away from the region in the early 2000's with his family, only to succumb to drug addiction. His ultimate fate? Being one of a handful of victims eaten alive by Satanic Cannibals in North Carolina in 2009.

Then there's Lewis Lent, back in 1993 he took a detour east to Rt. 8 and abducted Sarah Woods, the pastor's daughter. He's not the only serial killer to hunt along Rt. 13's expanse.

The Foothills Slasher in the hamlet of Tinker's Falls also comes to mind. A half dozen victims and no leads leaves this one unsolved. At least the news gave them a memorable nickname.

Vehicular tragedies are common on the winding road. The Top of the Hill accident back in the late 80s, near where Rt 13 shares some time with Rt 48. A tractor trailer didn't notice when a motorcyclist slid under the trailer's Mansfield bar at the hill's crest, trapping the unlucky motherfucker underneath. The truck dragged him down Rt. 48 through Constantia before anyone noticed something was amiss. Some say you can still see the skid marks left by his body in the road, even though the blacktop's been replaced a few times since.

People still talk about how 1980, when the motorcycle driven by Bill Guifre cut through the trans-am coming around the bend by Rt. 31. The impact killed both Bill and the car's driver, Jimmy Zupan. No one could believe the carnage. Jimmy's body was in one piece. Bill? Not so much. The first responders to this one found the biker's feet a football field away, still in his boots. The rest of his body coated the surrounding road and the remains of the trans-am in a crimson sheen.

Locals remember 1985, and the pre-graduation accident in Canastota, just off Rt. 13 on a road the locals call the Oxbow. The drunk driver, a teenager whose name is still protected by a sealed file, lived. But his passengers, a classmate and their girlfriends from Oneida, and the driver of the other car he hit, they all died.

Teenage tragedies of this ilk are a staple of the curse's impact on the region. The Canastota class of 1985, for example, continued to suffer many more queer accidents than would be typical of a graduating class. Eddie Smith still remembers when the push-mower he was cutting the lawn with exploded, mangling his face. Or Kelly Hilts who fell to his death from atop a Ferris Wheel during the field days. A class of hundred and thirty-eight students has whittled down to less than half this number in less than thirty years.

Sylvan Beach itself is reputed to be haunted, but who am I to dispute this? We're talking about a curse here. Once part of the stomping grounds of the infamous 19th century bandits, the Loomis Gang, the waterfront properties on Lake Oneida were developed into a lakeside resort and penny arcade in the roaring Twenties.

Through the 1950s and 60s, it was the place to go with your cool car. By the mid 1980's the place had transformed into a theme park with video arcades and thrill rides. And some say the haunted house attraction is indeed haunted. I can say the bridge over the canal has attracted far too many suicide jumpers through the years. I swear I can hear their cries as I go over the bridge at night.

The region is full of examples. Everyone remembers 1987, when Billy Blake pulled Bernie Meleski's sidearm out of his holster on his way into court in Dewitt, NY. Billy gut shot deputy Dave Clark, and Bernie, a giant of a man, took bullets in arm and chest. Blake surrendered in the parking lot and died of cancer in Auburn twenty-five years later. Why do I bring this up, you ask? The Meleski family camped off Rt. 13 at Verona Beach State Park every summer.

A plethora of campgrounds, both State Parks and privately owned, line Route 13's rural pathway. In fact it ends at Selkirk Shores, a State Park on Lake Ontario outside of Pulaski, NY at Route 3. Pulaski is another economically depressed town, with its biggest attractions being fishing, snowmobiling, and Brennan Beach campgrounds, a few miles up Rt. 3 from the end of 13. I won't tell you how many campers have been sucked into the under tow on the eastern shore of Lake Ontario. But they're mostly children, or a parent attempting to save their drowning kid.

I'm sure that you, a simple person out trick or treating in the snow with her neighbor's kids in Sylvan Beach, NY, would wonder why I know about all of this. Who is this guy on a snowmobile, with his helmeted head in his hand, sitting at the light while you ponder if a road with a name like Route 13 is cursed or not.

It's because I ride up and down the infamous cursed highway every day, and night, on my sled. Winter, spring, summer and fall, the season doesn't matter. The snowmobile I'm tethered to doesn't need powder to move. But it's on Halloween when I can cross over, and see you. It makes what remains of my soul weep with bittersweet joy.

The light changes color, the throng of costumed kids, patiently waiting with you, springs to life. Together, you cross the street, walking right through me and my snowmobile. I place my head on the stump on my neck, and squeeze the accelerator, continuing on my daily trek along the highway's expanse.

My head remains attached to my body somehow, because I know I'm as dead as the other spirits and ghosts I see and hear along this cursed highway. But the one thing I've learned? The curse, no matter what it may be or how it started, you know what it hasn't done? It hasn't stopped what remains of me from loving you, Kristine.

THE RAINBOW'S END

"**T**im?" Treading water and remaining in place, Abbey called for her boyfriend. He didn't answer. She couldn't say she knew when Tim disappeared. Whatever sucked him out of the lake took him fast. None of their friends saw it, they were preoccupied, doing their own things. One moment, Tim was swimming next to Abbey, alongside the boat, broad stroking like a champ. His arms and legs, driving him across the glacial lake, cutting a slight wake in its pristine surface. And the next? Tim evaporated without any more than an extra ripple or two on the glassy water. It was impossible to discern if he was taken down, into the depths, or launched into the sky.

Abbey noticed the moment her boyfriend transformed into a missing person. It didn't alarm her, at first. She assumed he doubled back when she closed her eyes, something she always did in the water. It was the only explanation for his disappearance. Abbey would swim back to the rented pontoon boat, Tim would be on the deck drinking a beer with Jenn and Ross, and all would be well. There was no reason for her to believe otherwise.

Everything leading up to this moment seemed to play out as part of a divine plan. Abbey met Tim on a Norwegian cruise the year before, and the two became lovers, and friends. He spoke perfect English for being from Iceland, and this amazed Abbey. She became smitten with her exotic, world traveler.

Tim was the walking, talking, stereotypical perfect European man. He fit right in with Jenn and Ross, her best friends. Oh, and the best thing? Tim shared their love for adventure.

The two couples sought extreme vacation spots, holding fast to the theory of YOLO. When the ad for Örlög Travel popped up on Tim's social media, he showed it to the others. They knew it was meant to be their adventure of a lifetime. A private island in Iceland promised a secluded lake with a perpetual rainbow arcing across it, and miles of hiking trails. It was perfect and a steal at only a few hundred bucks for each of them.

Passing around a bag of cheesy poofs, staining their fingers and lips an unnatural orange, the couples jumped at the opportunity and vetted the locale. They found the lake on Google maps, hidden from civilization and nestled near an air strip in Iceland.

"Örlög Travel, can you believe it? Double umlauts! So metal!" Jenn said, flashing devil horns with her fists, giving this her seal of approval.

"I grew up near there," Tim pointed out a small city near the mainland, "so this will be like going home!"

"Did you know about this place?" Ross asked.

"No, it looks like this was opened up after I moved, but the perpetual rainbow over the island makes me think of the Norse gods and their Rainbow bridge, the Bifrost, guarded by the watcher of Asgard, Heimdall. Did you know Icelandic is the closest language to Old Norse remaining in the world?"

"Yeah? Well what's your name in Old Norse?" Abbey posed the question as she popped a cheesy poof in his mouth.

"They call me," he paused for dramatic effect as he chewed and quoted Monty Python and the Holy Grail, "Tim." They all laughed, "well, Timoteus." He added.

"And what does that mean?" Jenn inquired.

"Tim?" he said, then smiled, his lips, tongue, and teeth stained orange by their snacking.

Cheap airfare both ways and roughing it by camping out on the shore in tents made the trip affordable. They chose the following weekend, putting this in the middle of summer, which made the days incredibly long and the nights as short. Tim and Abbey booked their flights on Norn Airways through the agency, made sure their passports were in order and packed for the trip.

The flight into Iceland was by jumbo jet, but a charter plane ferried them to the island. Modern satellite technology, and a small landing strip, made this place accessible to the masses. Before, travel to the lighthouse was a treacherous journey by ship. The only safe way to reach the lighthouse with tourists was by plane. The seas were too rough for a ferry, this close to the Arctic Circle.

Except for the Air traffic controller/Lighthouse attendant and his matronly wife, it occurred to Abbey they were the only living beings on the island. The couple was more than gracious, and a whole lot of creepy, in welcoming them to the island paradise.

What was his name? Vindlér or something like that? And she was Mardöll, right? Abbey tried to recall. *Weird names.* Like Tim's full first name. *Timóteus.* She wondered what their names meant.

To the couples' benefit, both of the caretakers spoke perfect English. The man squinted constantly, and a mouthful of tarnished teeth smiled at them. His wife, a frumpy blonde matron, explained to them how the volcanic vents heated the waters, making it a perfect secret swimming spot any time of the year. Oh, and who could forget the Northern Lights and the rainbow.

The never ending rainbow.

•

S itting on the deck of the boat, Jenn, too, believed this was truly a dream vacation. Right up until moments ago, when she joined Abbey and noticed Tim had gone AWOL.

At first, they didn't have a clue, being too preoccupied. Her fiancé, Ross, stood next to her, his shorts down to his knees, with his cock in her mouth. She loved to suck dick, the control it gave her over Ross. And since they were mostly alone on a secluded lake, and it wasn't like they had never fucked in the same room with Tim and Abbey, she figured why not? Jenn worked his unit for a good fifteen minutes before his eyes rolled back in his head and he climaxed. She skillfully milked him dry with her tongue.

The pop and fizz of a beer can opening followed. Jenn popped Ross's dick out of her mouth. He pulled up his drawers and Jenn guzzled down the beer, chasing down Ross's semen with hops and barley. She gasped, smacked her lips and crushed the can with her hand. Jenn could see Abbey under the surface, her tattoos glistening in the crystal clear water.

The glittering of something shiny and gold below Abbey caught her eye. She hyper focused on it, zoning in.

Was that Tim underneath her? Or could it be a reflection of the sky? Maybe it's the volcano's bottom? Jenn wondered all these things until Ross broke her concentration.

"You drink like a trucker, and suck dick like a champ." Ross told her.

"You're damn right I do. We all have to have some skills. Where's Tim?" Jenn asked Ross as he zipped up. Her legs now dangled off the front pontoon, into the water. Her hand was dipping into a cooler, and when she withdrew it, she grasped another can of regional beer. *When in Iceland, do like the Icelanders do!* This was her motto no matter where they traveled. Jennifer always drank the beers made locally.

"He was right there," Ross pointed, then stopped talking and grunted. Abbey was swimming alone.

"Exactly." Jenn said, affirming something was amiss. Next to them, a mane of blonde hair broke the surface, followed by a woman in a slim bikini leaving nothing to the imagination. Abbey was pushing her half naked body back onto the boat, getting out of the water. Tattoos covered most of her torso and arms, the latter sleeved with yellow lilies and rose petals. Scattered across her legs were flash pieces, the largest a giant crab with a yin-yang "69" at the center of its round shell. Abbey's zodiac symbol, Cancer. Tim would make non-stop jokes about the sexual connotations of the tattoo's symbols, something Abbey would never dispute.

"Tim?" Abbey called for her boyfriend. He didn't reply, of course. How could he? He wasn't there anymore.

"Tim?" Jenn repeated, in spite of the act's futility. When there was no answer, she made eye contact with Abbey. Both women appeared frightened. Jenn absently pulled her feet up, out of the water. "Ross, can you -"

"Tim, where the fuck are you?" He interrupted her and shouted out. His words echoed off the lake's surface. "Stop fucking around, you're scaring the broads!"

"Broads?" Jenn said, tossing a stern eye at her fiancé. Abbey joined her in solidarity, equally offended by his chauvinistic statement.

"You know," he replied, shrugging his shoulders. He saw Jenn take a deep breath and he knew a rant about his choice of verbiage was coming. Rather than endure further admonishment from her, he dove into the lake, looking to see if his friend was playing a game. He opened his eyes under the surface. Only the boat's double pontoons floated above him, and a black abyss spread out below.

No Tim.

The waters of the glacial lake, nestled in a volcanic caldera were warm and crystal clear. On a sunny day, a deep rainbow hue cut across the crystalline depths, creating a perpetual rainbow emanating from the lake's surface. Under it, you could see the black void of the lake's bottom. How far down, how deep, was anyone's guess.

•

Ross's head rose up from the water. He blew snot out of his nose and shook his mop of blonde hair dry. The calcium level, boosted by the hot springs feeding the lake, left a chalky residue on his face as the water evaporated. He looked scared. He didn't speak until he hopped back on the boat's deck.

"He's not here. Not down there, either. I don't know. I think Tim's fucking gone. Maybe he drowned? Hit his head? And sunk? I don't know."

He put his head in his hands. Water dripped from his head, though his fingers onto the deck. Each droplet splashing into the already saturated all weather carpet.

"Don't say such terrible things, Ross! He can't be dead!" Abbey shrieked as she ran from port to starboard, screaming his name as she hung her head over the gunwale. "Where could he have gone?" She made a valid point. The lake was isolated, as far from society as they could manage. There was one other person there, was he a kidnapper? And people knew the couples were here. Not to mention the control tower and lighthouse were on the far side of the island, too far away for the creepy Lighthouse Keeper to interfere. Odds are he was sleeping in his tower. Effectively, there was no one else here but them. "Do you think Tim's pranking us and swimming back to shore already?"

"Abbey, it's over a mile to the shore. He was just fucking there, there's no way he could have..." Jenn tried talking sense into her friend. Abbey turned her head away from Jenn, not wanting to listen to the truth.

"I don't know, I mean," Ross stuttered, not sure what to say, "I guess he could have."

"So what are you waiting for?" Jenn said to her fiancé, sitting down. She grasped the gunwale with one hand and hung her other over the side, tapping her fingernails on the hull. Ross stared back at her for a moment, before comprehending her hint. She pulled her hand back in, reached into the cooler, and took out another beer. Jenn cracked it and drank the can dry before Ross could move.

"Yeah, sure." He replied, and turned the key in the ignition. The 900 horsepower engine roared to life, spinning about the submerged propeller. Oil and water cycled out through a siphon as a cloud of black smoke rose about the stern. The Pontoon boat built up speed, the bow tilting up slightly, raising off the surface as it did so. Abbey tripped and fell as the deck inclined. She rolled back, bouncing between the rows of seats in the cockpit, slamming her arms and legs into the seats before coming to a stop.

One of Abbey's legs kicked Jenn in the face. Her neck snapped backward.

"Fuck!" Jenn yelled. Blood flew out of her mouth as she spoke. She closed her mouth and threw both hands to her face. Jenn felt around the inside with her tongue. She thought she saw a tooth in the mess of blood and spit. She smiled when she determined they were all there. This was hilarious.

"I'm sorry." Abbey said, crawling up to one of the benches. "Slow this fucking thing down some, we aren't in a race, dude."

"Oh, sorry." Ross replied, and pulled back on the throttle. The engine slowed in response, and the boat leveled out some.

"You okay?" Abbey asked Jenn. "Sorry about that. If your dipwad boy toy wasn't such a shitty captain."

"What the fuck, that fucking hurt. You're lucky I didn't lose any teeth!" Blood streaked across her pearly whites, as she tried hiding her laughter. "Want a beer?"

"I want to get to dry land and find my boyfriend." Abbey pointed to the shore. It was further away.

"Hey dimwit," Abbey smacked Ross in the back. "You've got the boat in reverse. We moved away from the land."

"Uh, no I don't." Ross replied. He gestured to the throttle. It was in drive, second gear, no less. "See." He said, further pointing it out with his hands.

"Then why are we moving away from the shore? Because it looks to me like we did move away." Jenn interjected.

"No, we're moving to the shore." Ross held up a bandanna. It fluttered to stern. The boat was indeed cutting wind in a forward motion, it's bearing heading it straight to the camp on the beach..

"This is fucked up." Abbey shook her head and stepped to the stern. She grasped a long, stainless steel cleat, and looked over the gunwale. The engine was bubbling and splashing the water, moving forward. She turned to her friends. "This can't be. Something is wrong here." Abbey focused on the boiling torrent near the outboard motor.

Is something holding us? She imagined the fingers of a gigantic hand pinching the boat's motor, keeping it in place. Abbey stared at the froth for so long, at one point she thought she saw actual fingers underneath the surface.

"I'm giving it all it's got, I don't know why it looks like we're moving away from it. It's some optical illusion from it being a volcanic lake or something." Ross said.

"That's bullshit. Something isn't right." Abbey barked back.

"You're telling me!" Jenn responded. She drove her hand into the cooler for another beer. "Come on, sit down and have a brewski, it'll calm your nerves.

Here, take it!" The drunk woman hiccupped to end the imposing request, pulling a dripping can out of the receptacle. Her arm extended out, presenting the cold beer to her distraught friend. When Abbey again refused the offer, Jenn slithered an arm around Ross, gave him a kiss and placed the opened beer in his free hand.

"Really, Jenn?" Abbey said. Jenn's free hand gave her friend the finger. She detached herself from Ross, turned around to return to her seat.

"Listen here, girl. Just because your boyfriend is a bad practical joker who just happens to come from these parts." Jenn stopped.

Abbey wasn't there.

Seconds ago she was sitting by the engine. Now she was missing, no different than Tim.

"Abbey?" Jenn went to the stern, looking over the guard rail. "Ross, stop the boat! Abbey might be overboard! Stop the boat!"

"What?" He turned around and saw Abbey was indeed missing from the stern. Ross slammed the boat to a stop. The engine died and a moment later all was silent and the pontoon boat drifted forward. "This can't be fucking happening! Where the fuck did she go, babe?"

"How do I know? She was there and now she isn't." She looked over the gunwale. Nothing, she could see nothing, only the reflection of the rainbow in the crystal clear depths. Abbey was nowhere to be seen.

"Do you think something is in the lake? Maybe something took her and took Tim?"

"Something like what?" Her face was drawing pale from the alcohol and fright.

"How the fuck do I know? What lives in volcanic lakes in the arctic circle?"

"You mean you didn't research that before we came here?" Jenn guzzled down the beer and dropped the can on the deck.

"Woah!" Ross put a hand out. "How the fuck was I supposed to know to check for carnivorous lake fish? Is this my fault now?"

"Abbey!" Jenn screamed for their friend. Her cries carried across the surface of the lake and echoed off the walls of the caldera. "Find her Ross!"

"Are you fucking crazy? I'm not getting in that water. No fucking way."

"Whatever, then put this thing on full speed ahead and get us off the water!" Ross responded by pushing the throttle open, launching the boat into full power. The engine came back to life. The boat skipped across the surface to the mainland. The speedometer read 50 knots. The boat was at its maximum speed. It was getting no closer to the land. Ross was starting to feel panic set upon him.

They saw movement on the beach near their tents. Ross felt his heart jump in his chest, Jenn felt a brief moment of hope.

"Tim?" Ross asked, pointing at the distant figure. Jenn squinted her eyes.

"No, it looks like the fucking lighthouse keeper. It looks like he's...wait. Is that Tim with them?"

"Holy shit, I think it is. What's he doing on shore?" Ross was holding the helm of the boat with one hand, and shielding the sun from his eyes with the other. He couldn't focus. It almost seemed as if the boat was moving away from the land. "Wait, Jenn. Something ain't right here. This boat hasn't moved at all."

"Damn if I know." Jenn replied and withdrew another beer from the cooler. "Wait a minute. Holy shit. What the fucking hell? He is. They're tearing down our tents."

"He's what?" Ross was shocked.

"Holy shit it *is* Tim. And he's tearing down our fucking tents. What the actual fuck!" Jenn stepped out of the cockpit onto the deck, throwing her middle finger in the air. "Fuck you, you fucker! Stay away from our shit, mother fucker!" She stomped on the deck in anger, throwing out enough f-bombs to fill a swear jar at a BINGO hall bar with quarters. "Ross! He's taking our shit." She turned around. The boat was pulsating and skipping forward without a pilot.

Ross was fucking gone.

"No! Ross!" She sobbed! Jenn called his name until her tongue and lips stumbled over the word. "Abbey! What happened to you?" She looked across the bow and saw the land was finally getting closer. Jenn staggered, the beer finally catching up with her motor functions, and fell into the cockpit and empty helm. She lurched forward, grabbed the twisting and turning wheel, breaking her fall while she failed trying to stabilize the craft. She didn't fall down or overboard, so it worked, a little. Despite having something to hold onto, she still found it more than difficult to stand. The vibrations from traveling at such a high rate of speed were so violent, Jenn wondered if the pontoon boat would stay in one piece. It reminded her of an ancient carousel.

And then the penny arcade ride stopped.

The engine sputtered and went quiet. The pontoons splashed back down as the boat leveled out on the water. Jen found her footing and stabilized at a vertical base, as the vessel listed in the water, softly rocking from starboard to port. She looked across the bow. The shore still looked too far away.

"Ross! Abbey! Help me! Help!" Jenn screamed. She grasped the gunwale until her nail cracked on the fiberglass. Her reflection shone back from the surface of the water, the sun glaring out her face. The site blinded Jenn with a flash of white light. She felt her pulse raise as panic set in. She was alone, on a lake on a remote island off the coast of Iceland.

Where did Tim bring us?

Why did he bring us here?

Why? Why was this done to us?

Jenn didn't like her chances. She knew she was fucked. She reached back into the cooler for another beer. It was empty. In a fit of rage she threw the container. It skipped across the deck and off the bow, splashing into the lake.

Jenn felt *something* pull her out of the boat from the stern.

Jenn tumbled, becoming completely disoriented as she did. She felt herself splash into the water. She opened her eyes, no longer blinded, everything around her was distorted and obscured by the water. She held her breath until she couldn't anymore. Mentally preparing to drown, she sucked in her final breath.

It was air. She could breathe.

The tumbling soon stopped. She regulated herself and adjusted to the weightlessness of the expanse she floated in. She was trapped within something organic, some sort of translucent membrane. Jenn could feel the edges of it, a rubbery, malleable material. She could also see it was plummeting into the depths of the lake. The light of the sun fading to the familiar track of a rainbow courtesy of Roy G. Biv. Whatever trapped her was following the rainbow down. Jenn looked up, her eyes tracing the path of the rainbow, and found she wasn't alone.

"Son of a bitch." She whispered.

Ross.

Abbey.

They were here floating about, but unconscious, above her. The four of them were trapped together... but how? She went to Ross. He lived, but at what cost? His eyes were frozen open and all expression was gone from his face. Something he saw scared the life out of him. He wasn't alone. Abbey, too, was catatonic. Jenn felt tears well up in her eyes. She didn't want to know what drove them to this state. But she knew she would, and sooner rather than later. They all learned the answer, somewhere over the rainbow.

●

Someplace, next to this place, no place the human psyche can comprehend, a sentinel stands a lonely vigil. Giant in stature, it watches the expanse of the multiverse and those who would cross its path, standing guard as it does, at the foot of a massive prismatic rainbow.

Hearing all.

Seeing all.

Hungering... as it does so.

A cauldron sits aside the being, and from it the rainbow extends as far as its eyes can see. It is a pot of gold to some, and to others, much more. It's a gateway, a portal through the cosmos. From this multi-purpose receptacle, the solitary sentinel seeks nourishment, pulling it from the Nine Realms where it is still revered as a god. For this, the gateway between worlds, the Bifrost, remains open. There is always nourishment, it comes here, drawn here by the power of the Yggdrasil.

An offering was due from Midgard, the plane's tithe. It would satiate the being's hunger, for now. The thing reached into the cauldron with a gelatinous appendage, pausing for a millennia, then withdrawing it a lightyear later. Within its grasp it holds a clear pouch of ether. Inside, a handful of frail beings float about. One is active, resisting their fate.

The guardian of the gates to Aesgaard ignores the prey's cries, much like you would ignore those of boiled shellfish. The thing considers having remorse for its actions, then rejects the notion. It knows how much of a delicacy they are, pink fleshed with brittle bones. It holds them high above the void of its hunger, twisted golden fangs protruding from its black lips

237

circling the rim of the thing's gums. Before dropping into the elder thing's gaping maw, it hears the creatures scream in agony, as they are consumed through space and time. It relishes the savory morsels as they melt away for an eternity in torment, satiating the elder thing.

And before they become nourishment to an ambivalent deity, its suffering victims gain the wisdom of the ancients. An unwavering truth, affirming you do, indeed, only live once. The secret of what lies at the end of the rainbow is...

Nothing.

SEIZURE

rip. Drip. Drip.
Paralyzed, Corry Jackson watched the liquid bead and fall from the ceiling of his trailer. A puddle of it surrounded him on the floor. It amazed him how much of it saturated the tiles and how the color shifted. Black in the moon's glow, and crimson in the flickering lights. A coppery taste filled his mouth. Corry, as well as the rest of the Jackson clan, weren't too bright, but he knew the taste. Every time Pa would slap him in the face, he tasted it.

Blood.

It bubbled and frothed about his lips and out his nostrils as his labored breathing became shallower with each exhale. Next to him, his brother, AJ, or at least what remained of AJ, lay in an unrecognizable heap. Moments ago, Corry watched that fucking thing rip off AJ's head and fuck the stump with its giant cock. Goo and guts and pieces of AJ's insides covered the walls and ceiling of the trailer as the creature went to town, humping away at his chest cavity.

Corry took a shot with the twelve-gauge and it succeeded in stopping further desecration of his sibling's corpse. Other than this, it only pissed the creature off. The thing swiped at Corry with one long arm, and sent him flying into the trailer's kitchen island. He heard the vertebrae in his back crack and then he stopped feeling. All he could do now was loll his head and barely breath.

Across the room, huddled in fear, Corry and AJ's Momma, shielded their other brother, Toot, the two of them sobbing and crying. The shadow of the thing fell across them, menacing his horrified kin. And there wasn't a Goddamn thing he could do about it with a broken back. He still couldn't believe his ears when it would speak, guttural and terrifying.

"Eye for eye. Tooth for tooth. Head..." the thing paused, obviously relishing the moment with some dramatic flair. Then it picked up AJ's head with one of its long, sinewy arms, and bit into it like a piece of fruit. Instead of juice, cranial fluid squirted out and covered Momma Jackson's face. She squealed in shock, flailing her arms as she attempted to wipe the insides of her son's brain off. "...*for head,*" it finished, speaking, crunching down on gray matter and bone with its long, wicked teeth in the process.

"No! Please no! We don't deserve this! We didn't do nothing wrong to deserve this!" Momma Jackson said, pleading for their lives.

But Corry, his Momma's baby boy, knew the truth. So did big brother AJ before he got roto-rooted. And so did little brother Toot, shitting himself behind his Momma. Corry may not have the brains to pass fifth grade, but he understood cause and effect.

Piss on the 'lectric fence, you gonna get a shock up your pecker and your balls will tingle.

Corry Jackson knew the Jacksons bought and paid for every ounce of flesh and blood strewn about their trailer on this night.

Drip...

*E*ARLIER...

In the empty parking lot of a long-closed Big M grocery store, a Suburban sat under a blown street lamp. Within the vehicle, the Jackson family boys filled the SUV to the brim with kin, waiting for the person they ignorantly called Ali Baba, and his family, to get home. They had some business to attend to with the *Ay-rabs*, as the senior Jackson, Andy Junior, would pronounce the word.

Andrew Jackson Jr. loved his name so much he wore the motherfucker out. His pappy did, too, which is why he gave it to Andy Jr. in the first place. Junior, in turn, passed this name on to not one, but two of his own children, Andrew Jackson III otherwise known as AJ, and Andrew Jackson IV, aka "Toot." The three of them, along with their other brother, named after their mamma's pappy, Corry, didn't give a rat's ass fuck about social distancing. Nor did they care about any lives, let alone the lives of anyone of color. All they cared about was themselves.

"Listen up here, boys," the senior Andy Jr said to his sons, "For two fucking months, the Godamned Governor-in-Thief's been telling us we can't go outside because of that fake ass pandemic, shutting down the titty bar we worked at and all your side gigs that put food on this here table."

The sons mumbled in concurrence, doing odd jobs meant they didn't file taxes to the fucking IRS. This also meant they were fucked out of any pandemic aid, at least in their eyes. With no money coming in, the Jacksons found themselves destitute. And desperate.

"We ain't gotten none of that welfare stimulus money or Unemployment promised by the filthy Democrats. Now that crook in Albany wants us to shave our beards and wear masks in public like we're the Chinese or them Antifa commies!" His sons cheered him! Andrew Jackson Jr. smiled and said, "Fuck all to all of that there shit!" Another cheer followed. "But that fucking Ay-rab mart in town could sure as hell stay open and price gouge the fuck out of us. Fuck them, fuck all of them," the senior Andrew believed his words.

Today he and his sons were going to fix the problem and exercise their rights as Americans. They followed the family from their convenience store to their home in the suburbs. A two-story Colonial, with a big back yard and a wooded lot as their neighbors. This burned a hole in Andy Jr.'s ass!

How could this family of asshole illegals-*they had to be illegals*-live better than Andy and his kin? He punched the steering column of the big truck and drove away, to wait for nightfall when they could catch their victims by surprise. Now with the sun falling, the time came for the Jacksons to even the score.

•

Zana Turani and his wife Leila ate dinner in the quiet of their home with their children. Sam, the toddler, held a square of cooked chicken in his hand and smiled as he devoured the food before him. Their newborn daughter, Arina, gummed a green pepper from the safety of her highchair.

Fresh-grilled kabobs of lamb, chicken, and beef, with grilled vegetables and husked corn on the cob. When in America, eat like an American, Zana believed. And so his family did. Second-generation Americans, both Zana and Leila's parents immigrated to the United States from Iran before they entered grade school. Fleeing the tyranny of the Ayatollah's religious state in the early eighties, the family now had established roots in the greatest country in the world.

"Could Aunt Frida not join us tonight?" Zana asked Leila in English. Though they kept their Farsi tongue alive, the family spoke English. They reserved the ancient Persian language for readings of the Quran, or small talk with Aunt Frida. The matriarch insisted on speaking the language of their homeland.

"She is not well today. Earlier, she made herself sick. I don't know, husband. Should we call *the home*?" Leila hated saying the last words. She cursed in Farsi.

"English, please, Leila. I know," Zana's empathy for his wife matched his love for her and the family she provided to him. But they were Americans, and English would be spoken at the dinner table.

"Son of a bitch," Frida relented, "is that better?" She punched the table. Little Sam dropped his chicken, "what do we do Zana? Tell me? If we put her in a home she dies. The virus is killing people."

"I know. Anyplace, other than our home, is out of the question until the pandemic is over."

"Momma, Papa, why are you arguing?" Sam asked.

"We're not, we're only concerned about Auntie Frida's health," his father replied.

"But I saw her up earlier today. She looked okay to me," the boy said with earnest sincerity written on his face.

"Aunty Frida always puts a happy face on for the young ones, she doesn't want to alarm you." Zana rebutted his son.

"But she was playing with me in the back yard after school while you were still at work. We played catch," Sam insisted.

"Samah, why are you making things up? You know she can barely make it out of bed to eat with us let alone throw a ball around outside for you. Do you want to be pun-"

A roar of concentrated thunder rippled through the house. The loud clatter interrupted Zana as he admonished his son. Someone or something blew out their front door. The baby screeched on cue, terrified by the sound. Leila grabbed her daughter from the highchair as Sam flew under the dining table, seeking its relative protection.

"Shhh, it's okay, shhh," Leila said to little Arina as she tried to calm the child. The baby's screeching pierced their ears.

"Would somebody shut that dirt-eating baby up before I shut it up for them?" Announced a disembodied voice. Zana and Leila looked about for the person speaking. Standing in the remains of their foyer, a stranger with a red bandana covering his face raised his shotgun and pointed it at Leila and Arina.

•

*T*he *'Umm Ghulah watched the lair of her prey from the woodline. A full and bright moon filled the late autumn night with silver light, heralding the feast to come. Obscured by branches and their relative shadows, she trembled in anticipation. The feast of sacrifice, promised to the 'Umm Ghulah by Allah Himself so long ago, awaited consumption. And so the 'Umm Ghulah waited for the time to come.*

The flash and bang of an explosion brought the 'Umm Ghulah out of her trance. The lights in the sacrifice's home no longer blazed. Instead, darkness surrounded the building inside, and out. The smell of spent gunpowder and burned wood drifted on the wind to her sensitive nostrils. Another predator sought her prey.

How could this be?

The 'Umm Ghulah sprang into action, her powerful hind legs launching her out of the tree line. In leaping bounds she crossed the lawn, reaching the backyard of the house in moments. She stopped, flared her nostrils and sniffed the air. Her ears raised to points, and they cocked to either side of her head … listening. Sobbing from within the building caught her attention.

She did not like what she heard.

The crack of a gunshot rang out. The flare of the muzzle lit up the interior for a brief moment, long enough for the 'Umm Ghulah to fully understand the gravity of the situation. She saw her sacrifice, bound, and men, dressed in black and carrying weapons, surrounding them.

For nearly a generation, the 'Umm Ghulah had been denied her sacrifice. She would not let these barbarians stifle this opportunity. She jumped and landed on the rooftop. On all fours, she scurried across the tar and paper shingles, and across the roof's peak to the front of the building. High above her, the clouds dissipated and the full moon came back to life. It cast its lunar gaze down upon the 'Umm Ghulah as she stretched out to complete length, and hurdled off the building.

•

"**N**ow you three can sit right there and not move. My boy AJ here is going to tie you up. Now don't be making no sudden moves or bang bang! You're all dead and stinking. And quit yer crying, lady. Ain't no one gonna try and grease your mustard flaps. We ain't into fucking your kind."

"And just what is our kind?" Zana challenged Jackson. The husband found relief in the man's admission but knew the alternative was death.

"The towel head illegals kind, there, Ali Baba."

"My family has lived in America for fifty years. We're citizens, Americans."

"Not in my book you ain't. Your kind took down the two towers. Your kind took the hostages at the embassy," he stopped giving examples when a loud thump resonated through the house. Andy Jr. gave it a moment of thought before acting. "Corry, go upstairs and see what that was," Andy Jr. told his youngest son. The boy, who sported a poorly sewn up cleft lip, ran up the stairs without hesitation.

"Look at what I found, Pa, another one!" AJ pulled little Samah out from under the table. The boy fought and kicked as the redneck dragged him out. The boy broke free and ran to his father's side.

"Now isn't that special. How many more of you are hiding in this place? Are we gonna find anything upstairs?"

"No, no one else. It's just us," Zana lied. He feared for Aunt Frida's life. Zana hoped Frida hid when she heard the commotion. If she could hide.

The old woman could barely move of her own volition.

"All clear up her, Pa" a distant voice shouted from upstairs. Zana thanked Allah in private for this miracle, sparing Aunt Frida from experiencing this nightmare.

"Very good. Now, where the fuck were we, Ali Baba? Oh, that's right, you scumbag American hating sand eaters from a country that hates us."

"Fuck you and your racist bullshit. My family has never supported that bullshit regime. It's why we came to America in the first place! That's like saying all Germans are bad because of the Nazis. Not every German is a Nazi."

"They should be."

The man's terrifying reply shocked the shit out of Zana. Andrew Jackson Jr. spoke the words without a single bit of sarcasm in his tone, and Zana could feel the seething hate accompanying each syllable. Zana knew at this moment this night would be his last in the mortal form, and he would soon join his ancestors in Paradise.

"You're a fucking lunatic. The whole lot of you."

"You know you shouldn't use language like that around little kids. You're a bad father."

"Fuck you!" Zana cursed back. He never expected the result of those words.

"What did I just say about language?" Andrew Jackson Jr. turned the shotgun on Zana.

And squeezed the trigger.

Leila screamed in terror as she watched a lunatic murder her husband in front of her eyes.

Zana Turani's head exploded in a thunderous roar, covering his wife and children in bits of bone and brain. His body followed the trajectory of the blast and slammed into the wall. It left a bloody trail on the floor. The man's body slumped down, and he appeared to be sitting up, his chin the only part of his face still attached to his neck. Twin fountains of blood, one orange, the other deep red, arced up from the larger arteries and veins in the jagged stump.

"Would ya get a load of that!" Andy Jr. declared, "fuckin' bullseye!"

"Pa it looks like you spilled some of Momma's Tomato soup and rice all over them," Andrew III said.

"Zana!" Leila shouted and charged at Andy Jr. The senior Jackson rammed the buttstock of the rifle into her face. The blow sent her reeling backward, stunning her. She fell on the floor.

"There we go, now you can say whatever the fuck you want." A crash of metal and glass from outside interrupted the redneck home invaders.

"Pa, what the fuck is that?" Corry yelled.

"What are you talking about?"

"A monster just landed on our Suburban and fucked it all up!"

"What do you mean, *a monster*?"

"Exactly what I said, Pa, a monster. Come see for yourself!"

The Senior Jackson ran to the door and saw, much to his dismay, the monster.

"What the fuck is that?" He stood, frozen in terror as his eyes beheld a chimera of horrifying proportions.

On top of their truck's caved-in roof stood a bipedal, dog thing with a cat face. A rack of antlers with enough points to make any hunter proud to mount in his den sprung out of the thing's head. He was sure it was a female, it didn't have any balls. Six drooping breasts with gigantic nipples lined each side of its chest. A giant, erect pseudo-cock hung between its legs, sticking out of the thing's hoochie. The feline head sported razor-sharp teeth, and a forked tongue slithered out between the fangs. The creature's hind legs, though similar to a satyr's, were clawed and not hooved as expected.

Andy Jr. couldn't be sure, but the thing looked pissed.

Really pissed.

"Boys! It's a demon straight out of the Holy Bible! Sweet Jesus! Shoot that fucking thing and now!" Andy Jr. ordered his sons.

The men opened fire with their shotguns. A hailstorm of buckshot and slugs littered the truck.

Not a single spec of lead touched the thing.

Before any could, the monster disappeared, jumping out of their line of fire. The men emptied their magazines, and silence followed with a cloud of spent powder. Andy Jr. and his boys stood in a semi-circle in front of the house, each frantically reloading his shotgun.

"Oh fuck this!" Andy Jr. declared as something in the sky captured his attention, "*incoming!*" He shouted to his sons.

A screeching roar accompanied a loud thump as the monster landed in front of the door. Its claws scraped and dug into the concrete walk. It hissed and growled, showing its fangs. Then it spoke in broken English.

"Move," the word rumbled from the beast's mouth.

The Jackson brothers dropped their weapons and shells without hesitation. Wood, plastic, steel, and brass scattered across the cement as the brothers ran off. But their daddy stayed his ground. He popped one last shell into his shotgun.

"Fuck you!" Andy Jr. said as he cocked it and aimed the weapon straight at the monster's face.

"No," it replied, *"fuck you."* With one powerful blow of an arm, the beast batted the senior Andrew's gun out of his grasp. The rifle slammed into the side of the house and discharged. It grabbed Andy Jr. by the shoulders and pushed him down onto his knees.

"No, please! No!" Andy Jr. screamed, begging for his life. His pleas fell on deaf ears. The thing held his head in place with one clawed hand, the nails biting into his scalp. He closed his eyes and pursed his lips sealed. It didn't stop the inevitable.

The beast thrust its hips forward and jammed its foot-long pseudo penis down Andrew Jackson Jr.'s throat. The force of having his face fucked smashed his nose in. It pulled back and a gushing blood, snot, and teeth smoothie followed. The gore dripped down Andy Jr's dislocated jaw and smeared across his chest. A loud, cackling laugh followed.

Andy Jr. might have screamed-

He wanted to scream!

But his larynx was destroyed. Instead, a bubbling gasp of air hissed out of his wrecked mouth and throat. The creature held the man's face in place and continued to fuck it. Laughing, it humped and bucked, driving its phallus in and out, deeper and deeper, impaling the man on it.

•

The 'Umm Ghulah tossed the dead man's body aside and wept. Tears of blood poured down its cat face, staining her orange hair in crimson and pink. It stepped into the home of the Turani family. The trio shook in terror until the beast addressed them in Farsi.

"My curse has brought me to this New World. I have come to take what will sustain me. But I cannot, I will not take the living. These heathens have already stolen my sacrifice from me," the creature picked up Zana's corpse, tears dripping into crimson puddles on the floor as it walked away with it.

"Papa!" Samah screamed and struggled to escape his mother's clutches. But Leila wouldn't let him go.

"My poor, poor sweet boy," the 'Umm Gullah said, folding back the remaining portions of his skull, making his head as complete again as possible, "I was to take you to sustain me, but now you have passed, and what remains of your life still warms this shell. Is it enough to satisfy the curse? Only Allah knows."

Leila covered Samah's eyes.

"Today I played ball with your son, he laughed and filled my ancient bones with mirth. And now tonight, you honor me, the first born of my first born."

The beast opened its mouth wider than nature dictated, and lifted Zana's corpse high above its head. Then it dropped the man's body into the gaping maw. Zana's body disappeared into a void that could not exist, but did, within the 'Umm Ghulah.

"What do you want with us?" Leila cried out in English.

"Please, we will not speak with the tongue of the barbarians," the thing corrected her in Farsi, the same manner as Aunt Frida would if you dare speak English in her presence, "I cannot bring myself to put this generation of my kin through any more pain and loss for my satisfaction. Because of this, I will allow time to pass before I call again. I have much more pressing matters at hand," before Leila and the children's eyes, the creature's features morphed from a monstrous chimera into the form of an elderly woman.

Aunt Frida. Kindly, bed ridden Aunt Frida, who always spoke Farsi and never English.

The transformations continued, and Aunt Frida grew young before their eyes, stopping as a striking raven-haired beauty in her prime. Leila could see her eyes in the woman's, and in turn, could see the lineage they shared. She could only stare at the being she believed to be her elderly Aunt for so long. Her mind desperately tried to hold her sanity together.

"Yes, I was once very much like you, Leila. Now I must go and you must be strong for your children.

The kin of the man who came tonight and took Zana from us will pay for their sins. Eye for eye. Tooth for tooth. Life for life."

Weeping, Leila nodded and held her children tight to her bosom. Outside, the distant sound of sirens resonated while red and blue lights lit the horizon. The 'Umm Ghulah stepped out of the house, through the shadows, and disappeared into the night.

THE ROCKER

Sophie sat on the rocking chair in the antique shop, staring at her smart phone as she scrolled through some form of social media. The technology she held seemed out of place in the chair. The former an antiseptic, almost alien device. The latter, a sturdy and practical piece of furniture, cut from walnut with a tall slatted back and elaborate scrolling notched into the headrest. Character scratches from decades of use pocked the wood's surface, adding to its antique aesthetic. But to Sophie it was a place to park her ass as she stalked her acquaintances, approved of selfies and placated the anxieties of her friends. An annoying itch under her thigh brought her out of her trance. She reached down to scratch it through the fabric of her blue jeans and came face to face with a shop keep, startling her. She ignored him and went back to her phone.

"That chair is a hundred and sixty years old, ya know," said the middle aged man in a smock and overalls. He wore a name badge, but the ink had smudged and faded, concealing his identity.

Sophie wasn't paying attention to the elderly shopkeeper speak, her focus on a meme featuring a cat with bad grammar.

"Not to mention it's cursed," he added.

The words caught Sophie's attention. She clicked her phone off without closing the app and jumped out of the chair as if it had been struck with a pox.

"It's cursed?" She said and looked back at the innocuous piece of furniture with a cautious eye.

"Ayup," he replied, "it's got a dark history. Anyone who owns it is doomed to die when they sit in it. Or so they say."

"I think they got this one wrong, sir," Sophie countered, "unless you're a ghost haunting this barn.

"Oh, I'm quite alive," he chuckled in response, "it's on consignment from an estate. I don't own it."

"Of course not," Sophie looked at him and raised her eyebrow, "I suppose you're going to tell me its dark history of murder."

"I could. But why waste it on someone that wouldn't believe the tale?"

"Try me," Sophie replied.

"Then sit back down, don't worry, the chair won't bite. It's only wood," he paused for dramatic effect, then added, "on the outside." She shook her head, disapproving of the poor attempt at humor, and sat back down. The shopkeeper pulled up a stool, sat next to her and began his weird tale.

"They say the chair was built by an Amish caner, living up north on the river, just before the Civil War broke out. It was his first rocker, built as a gift for his wife during her first pregnancy. In this very chair her water broke, they say, but sadly the child was still born. The Caner cursed the chair in grief, blaming it for taking his child, blighting the wood.

'By the Word of God, a pox on thy frame and all who possess thee!' he screamed, words that would have an effect he would regret the rest of his life. His wife passed in her sleep that night, the curse's first victim. He found her sitting in the chair when morning came, though she had gone to bed with him. The distraught Caner tossed the chair from his home in rage. He left the community, exiling himself to a life of drink, telling wild stories of curses and their results to those that would listen until he choked on his own vomit in a gutter only a few years later.

"The other Amish had no knowledge of the curse, so they took the chair and placed it in their Sanctuary in honor of the Caner's wife. The chair sat in the Amish church until the turn of the century when an English collector purchased it for a healthy sum. No sooner had he arrived at his home with the chair, then he suffered a stroke and died. It wasn't long after that rumors of a curse started circulating and reached collectors of oddities. Over the next decade the chair passed through dozens of hands, each with the same result, a dead collector left in the chair's wake. It went from dealer to dealer on estate consignment until then the chair found its way to Harry Houdini. the magician bought it for his mother as a gift. She died shortly after, as did Harry. Both deceased were found in the chair, cementing the chair in morbid legend."

"Wait a second," Sophie interrupted, "you're telling me this chair was owned by Harry Houdini?" Sophie's tone betrayed her disbelief in his statement.

"Yes," he replied.

"But he died after getting punched," she returned, "in the hospital."

"Lies," he countered, "the chair was discovered in the hospital room. Someone had brought it there, apparently."

"OK, then," she grinned, playing along with his game, "please, by all means, continue."

"The chair disappeared again, for nearly 50 years, until it is found in the Jungle Room of Graceland with the dead Elvis Presley."

"Elvis, too? This is too fucking funny," Sophie again interrupted, this time soliciting an unhappy frown from the shop keep. "I'm sorry," she giggled, "carry on."

"The King was discovered hanging upside down on the chair, in some sort of weird 50 Shades of Grey bondage gear. In fear that public knowledge of the true nature of his death would stain The King's legacy, Ginger Alden covered up the circumstances surrounding Presley's death from the media. He hid the chair, along with other occult artifacts and curiosities."

"Oh, like finding him on the toilet was any better?" Sophie interjected. The shopkeeper looked at her with a stern eye, then continued.

"At a secret auction in 1979, the chair and other occult items were purchased by a consortium of private collectors, where they remained until two years ago. The imminent and quick succession of the consortium's collectors passing away one by one in a short time led to a decades long battle that has since been fought by the heirs of the consortium. Eventually, I was contracted to liquidate the assets by consignment," he stood up and pushed the stool out of the aisle way and headed back toward the sales counter.

"That's it?" Sophie shouted as he walked away. The shopkeeper ignored her, reached his destination and went about tidying up his work station. Sophie got up from the chair and charged the desk.

"That's it. Now what can I help you with, it's evidently not a chair," he said, annoyed with Sophie.

"Nope. That's where you are wrong. I do want to buy the chair."

"Even after the story?"

"Your bullshit salesman tall tale? Yeah, whatever. It's not for me, anyhow, it's a gift for my mother."

"Why would you want to do that?"

"Because it's her birthday later this week and I came here to buy her a gift with a story, that's why," she pulled her credit card out of her pocket and placed it on the counter.

•

Baby u wont believe this
?
I found the chair it was right where we thought it would be
OMG did u buy it for her???
YES!!!!!
Can u say $$$?
How much was it?
Only 500
Thats it?
Are u sure its the chair?
Yes
When will u be back?
The day after tmrw if it is the case, I dont want to be around
k bae luv u
When this is over u can fuck my a$$ on a bed covered in dollar bill$
Hah! Kk! You asked for it!!!

•

Ding Dong The Witch Is Dead blared on eleven, waking Sophie up from a deep slumber. She stared at the ceiling as the alarm on her phone kept playing, thought about stopping the song, but let it play. It was the best night's sleep she had gotten in some time, which surprised her. The chair was scheduled to be delivered to her mother today, according to the tracking program. In Sophie's mind, that made today a figurative Christmas Eve, and typically she couldn't sleep on the night before gifts were handed out. Finally, she would be rid of the bitch and the money would be hers. Well, hers and Donny's. She dreamed all night of beaches and fast cars and expensive dresses, all the things mother kept from her over the years. But not anymore. Being the sole heir, upon Nancy's death, Sophie would get it all. But the wait was excruciating.

Her trust fund was nearly depleted, and Nancy was a tight ass cunt when it came to giving her anything extra. Sophie had learned of the cursed chair through an episode of Coast to Coast AM. A bit of research on a Reddit board narrowed down the chair location, and she saw her potential out. Maybe it was a real curse, maybe it wasn't. If she learned a single thing from her late father, it was "nothing ventured, nothing gained." It wasn't hard to track the chair down in the grand scheme of things. And now, the chair should be arriving at Nancy's house sometime this morning. The thought that this could all be over soon got her excited, and she contemplated masturbating. She grabbed her phone to open up her photos and her collection of Donny's cock shots, which always got her wet. Her bottom itched for his manhood. She reached down and ran her fingers over her panties, the elastic pinching her thighs as she stretched them. She felt herself getting wetter.

Without warning, the song stopped and her phone rang. She looked at the caller ID. It was her mother, calling from Albany. She rolled her eyes, sighed and pressed the green icon to answer the call.

"Hello, Mom! Happy birthday," Sophie spoke into the phone, putting on her best fake happy voice.

"I got an email with a tracking number for your gift. And just how much did you spend on this? When will you ever learn, Sophia? If your father was alive -"

"He isn't alive, Mom. And he would probably tell me I did good for thinking of my mother."

"What is it?" Nancy's voice seethed in contempt of her daughter.

"An antique rocking chair."

"Well, I'll put it on the porch. It won't match anything in the living room or den."

"That's fine, Mom. A nice rocker on the porch will do you good. You can sit on it on nice summer nights."

"The nights we don't have mosquitoes. Are you coming by for dinner tonight?"

"I'm still out in Utica, I'll be back in town tomorrow."

"That's a shame. I'll see you then, Sophia?"

"Sure, Mom."

"OK, bye, Sophia."

"Bye, Mom. Happy birthday." The phone went dead midway through her words, and Sophie knew her mother gave less fucks than a honey badger about birthday wishes. She sighed, and realized the call hadn't totally ruined the moment, fact, the knowledge that the chair would soon be in Nancy's possession thrilled her even more.

She dug the pocket rocket vibrator from her purse and opened her phone's photos. A quick scroll and she found what she was looking for, a shot of Donny's huge, glistening penis; dripping in semen and covered in her juices. She licked her lips and pressed the vibrating bullet to her clitoris, her mind losing itself in carnal fantasy as she swiped the phone left.

•

Sophie liked to drive at night on the New York State Thruway. Aside from tractor trailers, no one was on the roads and she could get lost in thought. She cranked some nineties era band, tonight it was the Goo Goo Dolls, and drove.

She was mentally spending her mother's money, the expenses adding up faster than the mile markers on the highway. The lights of a rest area beckoned, and she felt her bladder calling. She pulled off into the parking lot, the BMW roaring to a stop. Within a few moments she was sitting in a stall in the sterile and surprisingly clean rest stop lavatory, pissing her brains out. Sophie made a mental note, the coffee hadn't been a good idea, and her phone rang, its shrill tone echoing through the lav. She didn't recognize the number on her screen, but it had her mother's area code in Albany. Hesitant, both afraid and excited, she answered.

"Hello?" She inquired.

"Is this Sophia Bennett?" The voice was cold and as sterile as the bathroom.

"Yes. Who may I ask is calling?"

"This is Sgt. Mitchelini from the New York State Police in Albany, Ms. Bennett. I regret I have some bad news. Your mother, Nancy Bennett, passed from a heart attack about 45 minutes ago. I'm sorry."

"Oh my. Oh, no," Sophie faked shock and grief as best she could.

"I'm so sorry, ma'am, please accept our condolences."

"Thank you, sir. I'm at a rest stop on the Thruway. I should be back in town in a few hours. I was on business in Utica. Her birthday was this week! This, this is too much. I can't believe it! No!" She feigned a weep and sob on the phone.

"I'm very sorry, ma'am."

"Oh, fuck," Sophie continued to weep, "I have to go."

"O.K., Miss—" and she hung up on the trooper. She sat in the stall for a few more minutes, wiped the fake tears from her face and gathered her composure. It was real. The curse was real and the bitch was dead and Sophie was rich beyond belief. She made her way to her car as fast as possible, and once in the Beemer she sped off from the parking lot, squealing her tires as the loud music leaked out from within the car.

•

OMG! Donny! Shes dead!!!
What?
Heart Attack! Baby! We're rich!

OMG!
Im on the road now
Im gonna tap dat a$$ when u get home tonight
with that cock?
Yeah bae with this 8====D
Oh yeah! Better be ready 4 me

•

The hilly Mohawk Valley loomed about her on the highway, a point where the Thruway followed a pretty steep incline. It is also a cell phone dead zone. Her phone went dead and she got no replies from his end for a good fifteen minutes. She had traveled about 20 miles down the highway when the phone went ape shit. Text after text coming in from Donny, then another, and another, blowing her phone up. Service came back and the phone was catching up. The screen lit up with a swipe of a finger, exposing another dick pic, courtesy of her man.

Sophie's gaze remained on Donny's impressive manhood. It was a unit to die for, she had said many times before, and right at this moment she couldn't think of a better place for Donny's cock than one of her orifices. She was sure she'd have to pull over at the next parking area. She swiped it away to see what was next.

A picture of a rocking chair.

The rocking chair she had bought for her mother. Why was it in her house? How had Donny taken a picture of it? She tried replying, but the backlog of messages kept coming in faster than she could swipe them away.

Then she felt something near her crotch other than her own lust. A sharp pinch bit her inner thigh. She reached down to itch what she assumed was a bug bite. Instead, she pulled out a long splinter of wood, wedged in the seat.

"What the hell?" Sophie wondered out loud, "where did this come from?"

The car seat turned stiff on her back and legs. It was changing, morphing. The fabric was becoming dense, almost wooden. Sophie was struck with fear as wooden chair arms rose under her elbows. She grabbed the steering wheel with both hands, her knuckles white from the pressure. The safety belt constricted on her chest as the seat continued to metamorphose from cloth and vinyl into wood. She took her hands off the wheel for a moment, pulling at the seat belt, but it grew tighter. She desperately attempted to shake herself from the chair, but it kept growing under her, taking over the car's seat. The highway curved to the left, but her Beemer continued going straight. Sophie felt her stomach drop into her diaphragm.

"Oh, no! Oh, no!" She cried, struggling with the straps. She felt a sudden shock as the car landed with a loud thud of metal on rock. White light erupted inside the car. It was a blaze, dazzling and confusing the already stressed Sophie.

"It shouldn't be that way," she thought, and looked behind, to find the back of her seat had become caned, and she saw through the wicker lattice. There were no cars, only darkness and a trail of reflectors as the BMW was thrown forward. She looked at the chair back and recognized the top finial from the rocking chair she had bought her mother. This couldn't be happening. She wasn't sitting in the chair. She couldn't be. But somehow she was.

Shocked with fear, her bladder let go and Sophia pissed herself as she turned forward and saw only blinding white. Her hands shot back to the steering wheel in a death grip, her feet trying to find the brakes, but to no avail. The rising slats of the seat had lifted her legs up and the pedals were out of her reach. There was a deafening roar followed by the sounds of thunder and a high pitch screeching. Sophie felt an immediate, strange sensation of weightlessness.

Sophie didn't register what had happened until her head was laying on the seat of the tractor trailer rig, staring at the terrified truck driver. His face and lap were covered in blood and his face was a visage of gore blanketed horror.

Her thoughts raced. She had hit a big truck head on, and in turn her body was launched out of the car, through the windshield of her BMW. Sophie tried to move her head but she couldn't. She was paralyzed? That couldn't be.

Donny? she thought she said.

Sophie turned her gaze from the trucker and saw her cell phone lying on the seat next to her face and a headless body hanging over the dashboard, blood pouring out into the cab, flooding the floor and splashing the seat and driver.

Her body.

Text messages from Donny were still coming in, her phone chiming and lighting up with each. Sophie screamed but her breathless mouth formed words no one would ever hear as the white light returned, even brighter than before.

•

Bae Why did we get this?
Is this the chair u bought 4 ur mom?
Bae?
Bae where r u?

•

The shopkeeper wiped the last of the furniture polish off the rocking chair and slid it back into its place in the antique shop. The shop door opened, triggering a dangling bell. He looked over to see a young couple, the lady many months pregnant. He went back to the sales counter and watched the young couple search for the perfect piece for this next chapter in their lives. Within moments, the woman saw the rocking chair.

"Honey, this would be perfect for the nursery!" Her eyes lit up at the site of the rocker. The husband rushed over to see her discovery and nodded in approval. The shopkeeper saw this and made his way to the couple, standing between them and the rocker.

"That's not for sale," he said. The woman's smile left and she frowned, "I'm sorry. It's going out tomorrow for restoration. But, if you come with me, I think I've got exactly what you're looking for over here."

MON MORTE
L'AMOUR

1: ROADKILLING

Opening his eyes, Marty Kavanagh is greeted by the stench of forty tons of animal carcasses festering in the midday sun fills the air. The northbound lane of I-476 in Pennsylvania is held to a standstill, a result of an eighteen-wheeler expurgating its fetid load. Trapped within this traffic, Kavanagh idles his rental Camaro. The sun shines off the Chevy's candy apple red paint job as his right leg throbs in agony from tendinitis.

Other than a finger of black smoke tracing into the sky on the horizon, there's no indication of what may have caused the disaster. High above, flocks of turkey vultures and crows circle in the air. Marty watches as they swoop down, feeding off the carrion.

For the love of fucking God, what died? Marty thinks, then resolves, *At least there's no flies.* The malodor of festering meat is thick, permeating the air. Any passerby could likely taste the rotting flesh while breathing through their mouth, and Marty is no different. He suppresses the urge to vomit, shifts his weight in the seat, shakes his head, chews his lip, and punches the Chevy's steering wheel. A quick scan of the carnage spread as far as his eyes can see, gives him the answer to his question:

Everything.

Pieces and parts of dead cows and horses line the median between the north and southbound lanes. He'd been inching through, past the carnographic scenery and taking in the glorious aroma of decaying meat, for going on a mile. The disruption of traffic already set him back an hour on his road time. All he could do was watch the time of arrival on his GPS app rise by each minute that passed.

The entire trip down to Pennsylvania turned out to be a disaster, with a week of rain and humidity preventing him from enjoying outdoor activities during his solo vacation. The end result was the walk of shame back to his hotel room after losing on the gaming floor. As his bad luck would have it, the day he checks out of the Rivers Casino resort in Philadelphia, the rain stops. *Of course it does!* Marty thinks, chews his lip, and punches the steering wheel again, recalling his other morning discoveries.

As if the rain wasn't bad enough, he woke up to his foot exhibiting the symptoms of a heel spur on the ball just under his toes, which made the process of packing the car a chore in and of itself. By the time he'd finished, he could barely walk or put any pressure on his right foot and knee.

Then, as fate would rub it in, it's also the day this car's air conditioning decides to quit. On the first day of a projected heat wave. But the additional fuck you of a never-ending traffic jam, with a roadkill attraction main course, makes this the most memorable worst vacation Marty's ever experienced.

At least I'll have stories to tell at the bar, he thought. *Zero fucking Stars, would not recommend.* The comedian fancying itself as his inner monologue dealt with stress through humor, and it worked overtime at the comedy club in his mind today.

He craved a cigarette for the first time since quitting six years earlier. Instead, he dragged off the THC vape he brought with him. The little stick filled with concentrated THC was the only thing working today. Not that it mattered, the heat being so oppressive, he found himself sweating away his buzz as fast as he caught it.

"Holy shit, it's a fucking miracle!" Marty shouts out loud when he sees the first sign of emergency and rescue vehicle flashers on the horizon. The closer he gets, the faster the traffic moves, while the cars zipper away from the median. As vehicles move into the right lanes prematurely, it allows traffic to move in the left most lane. Kavanagh takes advantage of this. He flips his blinker on, and depresses the accelerator. The tendinitis sends a stabbing jolt of pain through his leg. He winces.

You go and be a bunch of ducklings and get in line, he thinks, sweat creeping down his neck and soaking his back. The heat is making him impatient, and Marty speeds the car forward, actually hitting twenty miles an hour. The act creates a brief breeze, airing out the car for a moment, until the red brake lights on the car in front of him forces Marty to do the same. Pain shoots through his foot as he moves his ankle.

"Goddamnit!" Everything on his passenger seat, which amounts to a vape pen, fast food bags filled with wrinkled food wrappers and stained paper napkins from his breakfast, slides forward onto the floorboards. Kavanagh shakes his head in disgust as the stench of the offal rises. The urge to wretch up said breakfast returns. The traffic slowly moves as the lanes zipper into one. He eases off the brake and the pain subsides, much to his relief.

"Almost out of this bullshit." Marty says to himself. He notes the emergency vehicles are in the median, just ahead. He can make out an ambulance, a flatbed wrecker with a Subaru on it, and a trio of Pennsylvania State Trooper cruisers. The back end of the import is caved in, telling all someone hit them from behind and it wasn't good. This all culminates in the remains of an eighteen wheeler's trailer and cab. The scene is horrifying as he slowly rolls past. The cab is charred, likely the source of the black smoke, and he stares at it with morbid fascination. The trailer is on its side, the wheels pointing to the road. He notices the truck is sitting at an odd angle. Underneath it, crushed, are the crumpled, blackened remains of what Marty assumes was once a sports car.

Damn. Whoever was in that didn't make it. His internal monologue laments. Then something catches his eye. On the far side of the median, away from the emergency vehicles. Kavanagh sees a black tractor trailer, with a pair of gray horses at full gallop air-brush painted on the door, sitting parked in the median. A stylized logo for *DULLAHAN TRANSPORT* is stenciled on the side of the trailer.

The truck's tinted windows reflect the strobing, multi-colored lights, making his view difficult. But at the rear of the trailer, there is clear movement. Raising his sunglasses, squinting to avoid the L.E.D. and strobe lights, Marty can make out a trio of people with a large, black dog- a Marmaduke-style mastiff. There's a tall woman with them, whom Kavanagh immediately finds to be gorgeous. She's wearing black cowboy chic and it turns him on.

Goddamn she's hot! Marty thinks as his eyes absorb her. She's every bit a sight to see, from the Stetson with a mop of hair hanging from it, down to the boots, with a shirt and jeans hugging her voluptuous curves.

"Ain't you a looker," he says, "wow. I'd bend you over and stick my dick in your dirt hole in a heartbeat." Then he makes eye contact with her and his heart drops. Her eyes are as black as the lenses in a pair of sunglasses. And though she's half a football field away, he swears he can see his soul reflected in them.

And he also swears she knows what he said only moments before.

The thought sends a chill through his body, causing him to jerk from the palpitation. Marty breaks his stare and notes she's holding a clipboard in her hands, while directing a pair of scrawny workers dressed in dingey overalls. The giant dog sits at her heel, observing the workers.

What are they doing? He briefly wonders, then he realizes what is going on. The helpers are carrying something. In tandem, they swing their arms and toss their load into the trailer. Marty extends his neck and his eyes grow wide, as if the added inch will clear up an ambiguity about the scene he beholds. It doesn't, but he comes to the only logical conclusion to what he is witnessing.

They're loading a body into the trailer?

As Kavanagh continues to stare at the woman, her alluring, aquiline features make him forget about the stench... until she turns and stares back. Her gaze is cold, and those black eyes are infinitely deep. She keeps the stare down locked in for a moment, long enough for Marty to get a chill up his spine. Then she drops her gaze to her clipboard, scans it, and makes a note on it with her free hand.

The traffic starts to move again, picking up speed. Marty is still mesmerized by the woman. She raises a hand with a finger pointed into the air, and swirls it around before whistling. The dog follows her, the huge beast's shoulders level with her chest. Marty rolls out of view as her assistants close up the back of the trailer, then climb into the back of the cab. In the rear-view mirror, Marty can see her behind the wheel of the rig, the dog in the passenger's seat. The reflecting sun provides Marty with a horrifying optical illusion as the glare covers her face.

The end result is a headless truck driver.

The reflection shows her going through the ritual of firing it up, culminating in plumes of black smoke pouring out of the truck's dual exhaust stacks. Marty returns his gaze to the road ahead as a loud, screeching air horn blares behind him.

He doesn't have to look in his mirror or turn his head to know the source.

2: TICKETS

Driving up the turnpike at full speed, well, in this case, a few miles above the legal limit of seventy, Marty no longer minds not having air conditioning. With the windows down a nice, albeit loud, breeze roars through the car's interior.

Despite this distraction, he can't get the thought of the lady trucker out of his head. The woman's whole being has consumed him, and every little thought of her causes his groin to stir.

The rush of air soothes his upper body, but underneath, his calf aches as he feels each inflamed tendon pull in his leg. The tendons cause the bones and muscles around them to ache. Cruise control helps some, especially when he's not in the stop and go of a traffic jam, but Marty can't extend his leg out straight, which adds to the discomfort. A partially hard cock, trapped within the confines of his briefs, makes it worse.

He looks into the rear-view mirror and sees the skull-like visage of a Dullahan Transport tractor-trailer staring him down from behind. It's a good seven or eight car lengths away, and he can't make out the driver, but he's certain it's the same truck he saw at the accident.

And the same driver.

As much as he'd like to see her again, as much as he'd like to bend her over and fuck her silly, he's not sure the circumstances merit him propositioning a random person for sex. That dog, for one, would probably have something to say about it, if not the helping hands. Marty accelerates his Camaro, hoping to put some more distance between him and the truck.

He passes a Pennsylvania State Trooper, tagging speeders. "Where's your buddy?" Marty ponders, taking a moment to search for the trooper's speed trap tandem partner. He comes round a bend, and a set of blinking and flashing lights on the right shoulder answers his question. "There you are." He pulls into the passing lane and slows until he passes by the trooper and ticket recipient coincidentally in a cherry red sports car, this one looks to be a Mustang.

Is that an omen that I should slow down? Marty wonders. His eyes dart from the rear-view mirror to the road and back. He notes the eighteen-wheeler is still barreling down the turnpike, it's not getting any closer, but it's not slowing down. Marty waits for the reflection of the patrol car's lights to disappear from his mirrors, and smiles.

"Naw!" Marty shouts. He winces as he presses down on the accelerator, pushing the car's speedometer to ninety miles an hour. The Dullahan Transport truck disappears on the horizon, and for the second time today Marty feels some stress relief as the miles separate him from the truck. He drags off his vape, closes his eyes, and imagines the lady trucker naked, riding on top of him, her hips slapping on his thighs.

He opens his eyes and his heart jumps. Red and yellow flashing lights reflect off the mirror. He sees the trooper's car grow in size as it nears him.

"Are you fucking kidding me?" Marty declares, pulling into the slow lane, before coming to a stop on the shoulder. He slips his THC vape into his pocket, unsure of Pennsylvania's weed laws.

Should I make it so this asshole needs to stand in the road? He ponders, then opts against the call to someone else's void. *Best not to make it any worse than it already is.* Marty thinks while taking his license out of his wallet. *Where's the registration? The insurance card?* He doesn't know if it's in the car or not. Opening the glove compartment, he shuffles through its contents. Nothing resembling a registration or insurance card is found. A look up to the mirror verifies the cop's patrol car is still parked behind him. But Marty thinks he can make out the profile of the rig on the horizon. A chill runs through him.

"Shit!" He declares in response to a tapping at his door. Marty looks up and sees the trooper staring down, his eyes covered by dark sunglasses. The name *Swierat* is embossed on a lapel pin. His eyes see himself, haggard and tired in the reflection while Marty's mind briefly flashes back to the alluring lady trucker.

"Hello there. You're sweating pretty hard, nervous at all?" The trooper asks.

"No, officer, um, how do you say it?"

"Swierat. It's Polish, no ski. New York plates I see. In a hurry to get home?"

"Not really. Was I speeding?"

"I was about to ask if you know why I pulled you over, but yeah, that's it. Ninety in a seventy? That's twenty miles above."

"I wasn't doing ninety! No way!"

"Well you were, and I think you know you were, and that's why you're sweating. Haven't had anything to drink, have we?" He watches as the trooper's demeanor changes from jovial to professional, and it scares Marty. He decides to make up another lie. He looks at the rearview mirror and sees the truck is closer.

"No, no, sir. I'm sweating because this car's air conditioning decided to die on me on the first day of a heatwave." *All good lies are rooted in truth, right?* Marty makes a mental note, "But you're right, officer. I was trying to get away from a tractor trailer that's been tailgating me. I don't know what their problem was but, yeah. I lost it a few miles back."

"Is that so?"

"That's so."

"Well, I can't smell any alcohol on your breath, so we'll forget about a sobriety test. However, I will need your license, registration and insurance," the trooper instructs Marty.

"This is a rental, I couldn't find the registration and insurance, but here's my contract." Marty hands the trooper his license and the rental agreement.

"I can get all that off the plate. Hang tight. I'll be right back."

Before Trooper Swierat walks away, the screeching roar of a speeding eighteen-wheeler whizzes by, reminding Marty of a TIE-fighter from Star Wars. It's the same truck from Dullahan Transport, a black and chrome streak hurtling down the turnpike. It shakes the car and the wake of its tailwind forces the trooper to hold onto his hat.

"That's the truck." Marty points to the speeding rig. "See what I mean?"

"I see that. I'll never catch him, but he's not faster than a radio. You hang tight. I'll be right back." The trooper leaves Marty alone for a good ten minutes. The heat makes him sweat more.

And the time allows him to develop further carnal thoughts about the driver of the truck.

3: EMPTY

"Tickets between New York and Pennsylvania are reciprocal. You know what that means?" Trooper Swierat asks when he returns.

"I don't," Marty replies, taking back his papers.

"It means this is points on your license and if you don't pay the fine your license will be suspended." He hands Marty the ticket.

"Great. Thanks for the good news."

"My pleasure. Now, keep it within 10 of that speed limit, please. You're in a red car, we're always going to tag you."

"Good to know."

"Have a great day Mr. Kavanagh."

"You, too, officer." Marty nods to the trooper. Once he sees the police officer in his car, Marty crumbles up the ticket and throws it on his seat. He waits for the cop to drive off and disappear before getting back on the road. Paranoid of getting another ticket, Marty makes sure he uses the cruise control and sets it for the exact speed on the signs, which happens to be seventy on this stretch of I-476.

With the windows down, it's not long before he's back in the swing of things on the road, listening to the radio on full blast while carnal thoughts of what he might do with a lady trucker in a rest stop shower run through his brain. The music is barely audible over the roar of the car's open windows, but he's not sweating. At a steady speed of seventy-five, cars are passing by him like his car is parked, but Marty doesn't care. His throbbing knee and ankle have numbed him to giving a shit about anything other than getting home. And as far as the speedsters go?

They can get the fucking tickets and the points on their license, he thinks, hoping to see at least one of them pulled over.

He doesn't, which is of no surprise to him.

One thing does happen to bring Marty relief. At least there's no sign of that creepy truck. The only car that stands out is one in front of him, a Subaru Outback with fake wooden paneling and a canoe strapped to the roof. The driver pisses him off for no reason other than their windows being up, and the assumption their A/C is blowing on high.

The longer he paces behind the Subaru, the more he becomes irritated with the thought of them having operational air conditioning. The worry of having a *Final Destination* moment with the canoe makes up his mind. Marty decides to take the gamble and presses down on the gas and shifts into the left lane. The pain from daggers stabbing his ankle causes another wince, but the boost of speed does as he wished, and he catches up with the Outback. On the way by, he notices the driver is wearing a black hoodie. And it's pulled up, over their head.

In a fucking heatwave.

Marty is baffled and he shakes his head, before edging the car to go a bit faster, and finally pass the Subaru. He waits to be a few car lengths ahead, before settling back into the right-hand lane. He sets the cruise back to seventy-five, and stretches his aching foot and ankle.

The next car to pass him is the Subaru. Marty shakes his head in disbelief.

"Whatever. You wanna play hopscotch? That's fine. I'll play."

The Subaru is a few lengths ahead when Marty see's the right blinker come on and the Japanese SUV drifts back into the slow lane. Marty shakes his head, mutters an "Oh, no," and accelerates, sending the Camaro past the Outback. He stays in the passing lane for a bit longer this time, at least until a sputtering takes him by surprise. The warning lights on the dashboard come to life and he feels the engine die.

"What in the ever-loving fuck?" Marty declares, and looks at the dashboard and realizes he's run out of gas. *How in the fuck did I run out of gas?* Then he realized he must have missed the alert. The car's momentum is enough for him to guide it to the shoulder, where the Chevy comes to a stop. Marty Kavanagh punches the steering wheel and screams out loud in frustration.

"Can this day get any fucking worse?" Opening the door and stepping out of the Camaro, Marty cries out in pain as his leg gives out under him. The turnpike is less than three feet away and Marty realizes quickly if he tumbles into the road he could very well become the victim of what the news would call a "tragic accident." To prevent this, he drops to a knee and falls into the sports car's frame.

"Christ on a broken fucking crutch!" The words do nothing to stop the pain. Tears stream down his face while the sweat on his brow drips into his eyes, burning them. "What else are you gonna do to me today?" He throws a middle finger up, flipping off the sky, and God in turn, one could assume.

Pulling the door closed and resting his forehead on the steering wheel, Marty has no idea how he'll get gas. Should he call roadside assistance? Does he have any with the rental agreement? He can't walk to get it; he knows that much is true. The beeping of a car horn breaks him from his trance. In the rearview mirror a familiar car is parked behind him with its four-ways on.

The fucking Subaru? Are you kidding me?

4: EXITS

"Hi, I'm Karen, everything okay?" The tall woman in a hoodie says, standing outside the passenger's side of Marty's rental. She's pale, nearly chalk white. The hood is pulled over her head, covering a mop of blonde hair. She has more than a few errant chin hairs growing, long, blonde, and barely visible. They're not quite a goatee, but close enough, and Marty's almost embarrassed, because he can't stop staring at them.

"Hi, I'm Marty, and I think I ran out of gas." He replies, diverting his eyes from the woman's chin to her dark eyes. They're not quite the void the lady trucker's eyes were and are set back into a gaunt face.

"Oh man, that sucks. The next exit is less than a mile from here, need a lift?" She asks him. Marty can't believe his stroke of luck.

"Hell yes, I'll give you gas money."

"That won't be necessary. You were helping me stay awake by playing hopscotch, so I feel like I owe you one."

"You're too kind for being a Karen."

"Hah! I didn't pick the name, you know. I just live with it and try not to act like the stereotype."

"That's good." Marty laughs and Karen chuckles in return.

"Hop on board!"

"Um, that's not going to be as easy as we'd like. I'm afraid my hopping days are on time-out. I'm a little lame from tendinitis in my driving leg."

"Oh shit, here, let me help you." Karen steps around the side of the Camaro and offers a frail, almost skeletal hand. Marty takes hold, concerned he might snap the bones—to his relief he doesn't— and pulls himself up and out of the Chevy. Her grip is stronger than Marty anticipates. "There you go, buddy!"

"Thanks," he replies, limping along in agony. It takes a few minutes, but they make it to the passenger's side of her Outback and Marty eases into the seat.

"So I'll buzz you down to the next exit, fill up a can, and bus you back. Are you down with that?" Marty nods and Karen continues to talk while walking around the car to the driver's side. "I've got a spare gas canister in my trunk you can use. You never know when you might need one."

"You never know." Marty replies, extending his leg as far as he is able. It's not much, but it's enough.

"You can slide the seat back as far as you need. Marty it was, right?"

"Yes, Marty. And you're Karen?"

"Yes, yes I am. Seat belt, please, Marty." The woman says. Marty complies, and she drives off. The air conditioning in her car is a relief, the interior of the vehicle is ice cold, allowing Marty to understand why she has the hoodie up over her head. The exit is closer than Marty thought, less than a mile. A PILOT with an attached Taco Bell is within spitting distance of the on and off ramps, and it's apparent to him the truck stop is Karen's destination.

"I guess it was close."

"Absolutely." The woman replies. Marty notices she's sliding something into her mouth, sucks on it for a moment, then asks, "NECCO wafer?" She extends a hand. Grasped within it is a roll of quarter-sized NECCO wafers. Marty recalled his grand-mother loved these confectionery treats, and he hadn't seen one in the real world in years. His grand-mother also had a little chin beard. Marty snickered aloud at the thought before answering his new friend.

"Sure." He replies and Karen slides one of the discs off the stack. Marty takes it and places it in his mouth. He's not sure of the flavor. *What are they supposed to taste like anyways?* He keeps to himself before asking, "Where'd you find these?"

"Cracker Barrel this morning. They had Moxie, too."

"Moxie? What's that?"

"This." She holds up an empty soda bottle. MOXIE is written in white across the bottle's orange label.

"Never heard of it."

"It's a New England thing."

"What's it taste like?"

"Black licorice soda." She says and Marty grimaces.

"No thank you. You can keep it. Not a big fan of licorice."

"Yeah, I get it. It's an acquired taste," Karen answers as they pull into the PILOT and park next to one of the pumps. Marty sits up and opens the door, but Karen protests. "No, no. Your leg is bad, remember, I'll pump it for you. You got a bank card?"

"Are you sure?" At this point, Marty is baffled by her continued kindness. *Ain't you the ultimate Good Samaritan. What's next? Is she gonna ask me for some weird sexual favor in return for her hospitality.*

"I sure am." Karen informs him. Marty shrugs in response, digs his bank card out of his wallet, and hands it to her. He leaves the passenger door open and extends his leg completely, stretching the tendons. The thought of sticking his leg in a bucket of ice is the most appealing he's produced all day.

Across the parking lot of the PILOT, Marty can see a plethora of tractor trailers. He scans them, looking for the Dullahan Transport rig. It's nowhere to be found, and this pleases Marty. Mostly. Residual thoughts of the sexy truck driver still linger in the recesses of his mind, and he feels a little disappointed. Meanwhile, Karen fills up the little two-gallon gas can and places it in the trunk of the Subaru before returning to the car's driver's seat.

"That was quick," Marty tells her as she settles back in and hands him his bank card. He takes it, "thanks a bunch for all this. If there's any way I can repay you, let me know."

"That won't be necessary. I enjoy helping people. You just pay it forward to the next guy stranded on the side of the road. So I saw a trooper turn-around we can use to get back to your car quicker. You down with that?"

"Works for me!" Marty replies as the Outback leaves the rest stop and Karen navigates it on a return course to Marty's Camaro. He gives his savior an appreciative wink. She answers it with a silent nod.

Karen sticks to the plan, finds the turn around, and they're back to the Camaro in a flash. Marty limps back over to the Chevy, opens the gas cap, and Karen pours the two gallons of gas into the tank.

"There you go!" She says, and slaps the cap closed on the car.

"Thanks, again."

"My pleasure, at least you've got enough to get back to that rest stop and get back on the road. Speaking of which, I do need to get going to my destination."

"I totally understand." He waves goodbye and she replies in the same manner. Then, the gaunt woman, Marty's roadside saint in a black hoodie with a little blonde chin beard, gets back into her Subaru Outback and drives off. He waits until her rear lights disappear down the turnpike before he drives off himself.

It's not long before Marty fills up the Camaro at the PILOT, and decides to take advantage of the rest stop's pisser before hitting the road. Limping in, he doesn't expect what awaits him when he enters the lavatory. The first urinal he sees is overflowing with matter. He's not sure what it is at first.

It's brownish black, resembling partially stirred fudge brownie batter and Black Forest cake mix coagulated together. Chunks of something semi-solid the color of dark chocolate inhabit the mixture, and it's dripping onto the tile floor with audible *plips* and *plops*. The odor is sickly sweet, reeking of sulfur and ammonia. It wrinkles his nose, waters his eyes, and makes Marty wish for the roadkill traffic jam earlier in the day.

"Someone shit in the urinal?" Marty asks no one. He'd heard the legends, the same as anyone else, of the wild stuff people do in rest stop restrooms, but this fecal batter mixture took the dogshit cupcake challenge to a whole new level. Marty didn't believe he could piss now, as much as he wanted to minutes before. He makes a quick about face—

And sees the helpers of the Dullahan Transport. lady trucker, shopping in the convenience store.

Son of a bitch. Marty thinks. If they're here, he knows it means one thing—*She's here? Someplace? Walking that dog, maybe?* His lust for the curvaceous truck driver temporarily blinds his judgment, until the scent of the shit filled toilet behind him and the throbbing in his leg shock him back to reality. *I need to get the fuck out of here,* he resolves.

And he does so.

5: TUNNEL

Sitting at the stop line of a red light at the intersection of the I-476 northbound on-ramp and whatever road the PILOT sat on, Marty feels anxious. He couldn't find the Dullahan Transport truck in the lot, but this means nothing. *The helpers were there, and that math adds up to two and two make eighteen wheels,* Marty's internal monologue affirms. His leg bothers him, and the lack of air conditioning contributes, he is certain. But something more than these factors is throwing him off. *Is it the allure of the truck driver? Is it the ticket, or maybe the whole ordeal of running out of gas?* His mind fails to settle on a catalyst for his nervousness.

The crossing lanes get the green light, and Marty's heart jumps out of both fear and anticipation. The familiar sound of air-brakes engaging catches his attention.

"Are you fucking kidding me?" He says as the Dullahan Transport eighteen-wheeler rolls up to the intersection at Marty's right—

And stops at the green light.

Horns blare behind it, as irritated rush hour commuters express their displeasure at this unannounced delay in their travel plans. The truck doesn't move. Marty's vantage point again has a glare of sun striking the windshield of the rig, blotting out the driver's face. He can see the mastiff clear as day sitting in the passenger's seat next to her. What twists Marty more is the lust building within his person. The presence of the lady trucker is enough to send enough blood to his groin to stiffen his cock.

Does she not see the light is green? Marty ponders. *Or is she waiting for me to go?*

The question is answered when the lights change. Marty ignores the pain in his ankle and guns the Camaro's engine. His tires squeal and the car races through the intersection to the interstate on-ramp. He hears the blaring of an air-horn behind him, followed by the chirping of more car horns, and knows the rig is making a right-on-red.

She's following him, without a shadow of a doubt. And it's getting him off.

"Well ain't this some bullshit!" Marty declares and presses the accelerator all the way to the floor. The Camaro's V-8 revs into the red as it is projected by the force of motion down the turnpike's northbound lane. The car reaches traffic speed and then some in seconds.

Marty feels his cock orgasm in his pants, filling his boxers with semen. But he remains hard. The chase is getting him off.

Screaming down the on-ramp behind him, the Dullahan Transport tractor trailer isn't fucking around. The air-horn blares and cars in its path not moving fast enough realize they have two choices: be pulverized or move to the right lane and let the rig through. All of them wisely choose the latter.

"Where's a fuckin' cop when you need one?" Marty shouts and punches the dashboard. On cue, the Camaro's air conditioning springs to life unannounced, blasting cold air through the car. "Son of a bitch!" Marty declares in elated surprise, and clicks the automated windows up. It drowns out the blaring of the rig's horn, and allows Marty a valuable second to determine the correct course of action. *Speed.*

Speed so Goddamn fast the cops can't help but chase you, and let them do so until they see that fucking truck!

Within moments the Camaro's tachometer is redlining and its speedometer is flirting with triple digits. Cars moving at seventy seem to be sitting still as he passes them. Marty knows the car will hit nearly two hundred miles an hour, and he also knows excessive speed won't be necessary.

A hundred and twenty-five is just fine.

A glance at the rearview mirror reveals the rig is still in pursuit, but ahead, it's a different story. The road is narrowing down for the northbound portal of the Lehigh Tunnel. A little over three-quarters of a mile long, the subterranean underpass cuts through the base of Blue Mountain.

Follow me through here, bitch!

The speeding Chevy reaches the entrance in record time, and is greeted by a flashing sign informing him of his speed. "*00*," the maximum speed a two-digit sign can declare, flashes on the radar board.

Marty doesn't take his foot off the accelerator. He whips into the tunnel and within seconds he can hear the air-horn of the tractor trailer blaring. He sees cars pulling over, making room for the Camaro and eighteen-wheeler. The horn echoes off the tunnel walls, it's nonstop. Like the truck.

What the fuck did I do to deserve this? Marty wonders. He looks to the rearview again, and sees the truck isn't giving up. The Camaro exits the tunnel when Marty returns his attention to the highway in front of him. The natural lighting of the sun glaring off the Chevy's windshield temporarily blinds him.

"Motherfucker!"

He closes his eyes and can still see white dots.

It's enough of a distraction to cause disaster.

Still flying at a buck-twenty-five, the Camaro strikes the back of an all too familiar Subaru

Outback. The impact catapults the Japanese import onto the turnpike's shoulder. Marty presses on the brakes and throws his arms up in front of his face as the canoe on top of the Subaru slides off.

Transformed from a water vessel into a deadly battering ram, the wood and aluminum boat slams into the sports car's windshield and pierces the glass. The airbags in the Camaro deploy, providing Marty with a shield from the canoe, which misses his face by inches. With his head now pushed to his left, Marty is looking directly at the side rear mirror. What he sees drives him mad as time stops.

The Dullahan Transport tractor trailer finally catches up. Sitting behind the wheel is the lady trucker, almost as beautiful as Marty Kavanagh fantasized. Almost because her face is smiling back at him from the dashboard. Where her head should be, there is only a bloody stump of neck. The mastiff sitting next to her drools, its spittle splashing into the hair on the trucker's disembodied head. The mouth speaks words Marty can't hear, but he can clearly make out...

"Who's fucking who in the ass?"

A long tongue snakes out from between the head's lips, licking them, a cheek, and a black eyeball. The mouth opens, revealing horrible fangs, and it laughs—no, it screeches—his Christian name...

"Máirtín Caomhánach, glaodh abhaile thú!" The headless woman stands in the cab, lifts her head, and throws it through the windshield of the rig.

Time starts back up as the truck barrels into the Camaro.

"Jesus, no!" he screams his last mortal words as the woman's head flies at him.

There is an epic explosion as metal and glass are torn apart by the force of the impact, but its occupant doesn't feel it. The mercy of shock and the remaining dopamine in his body prevents the poor soul from experiencing the agonizing pain of being crushed and burned. Rather, Marty Kavanagh finds himself in the throes of his final orgasm, within the embrace of his love... and closes his eyes.

ACKNOWLEDGEMENTS

After reading my first short story collection, the now out of print A BOOK OF LIGHT AND SHADOWS, Armand Rosamilia made a poignant statement. *"Will be interesting to see which genre the author ultimately finds his groove in and builds a long and successful career in, too!"* My love of Sword & Sorcery, splatterpunk, and fantasy came together shortly after these words were written. My teacher, Garrett, once told me my horror comes from fantasy. So I wrote THE GOD PROVIDES and two reviewers referred to me as a "splatterfolk" author, a combination of the genres I've fallen into, the counterculture splatterpunk and folk horror. I'll go a step further cand call it "Cottage hard-core."

The baker's dozen of stories you've just read encompass all points in my thus far short career, the oldest being The Rocker, a story included in that previously mentioned volume. The most recent is The Breeders, my 'What if John Wick met the Sawyer Family" misadventure. Not only is it an expose on where I've come from and where I am headed, it's also an Easter basket filled with various folk horror tropes. In between the pages you saw stories ripe with werewolves, vampires, witches, druids, cursed objects, death gods, ghosts, and bogeymen of all sorts. We've revisited the McEntire family from THE GOD PROVIDES with Giants and Concrete Harvest.

I want to thank Francois Vaillancourt for the wonderful cover art and my friend and mentor Garret Cook for his lovely foreword. And, of course, the editors who streamlined these stories at the various small presses these first saw the light of day through, including but not limited to FROM THE ASHES, CARNAGE HOUSE, DARK MOON RISING, and ST ROOSTER BOOKS.

As many of my fans and friends know, I love a band from England named GREEN LUNG, a newer folk horror doom metal ensemble. The woodcut branding style done for me by Deborah Coldiron is directly influenced by Richard Wells' work for the band. The title of this collection comes from a verse in a GREEN LUNG song, Upon the Altar (which you can hear on their second full length release, BLACK HARVEST). This band is responsible for my transformation into a folk horror author. Hell, a misconstrued verse from the song Old Gods (on the same LP, BLACK HARVEST), has transformed into my catch phrase "Beneath the autumn dark." I won't stop you from bingeing their library of music while reading this collection. In fact, I encourage the activity.

THOMAS R CLARK
January 2025

ABOUT THE AUTHOR

Thomas R Clark is a two-time Splatterpunk Award Nominee (Best Novella, 2021 for BELLA'S BOYS and Best Short Story, 2022 for FIREFLIES & APPLE PIES). His most recent release, IMMORAL DILEMMAS, is available through Nightswan Press. His journalism and entertainment critiques have appeared in Memento Mori Ink, Rue Morgue, Stranger With Friction, House of Stitched Magazine, This Is Infamous, and miscellaneous internet outlets. Tom lives in Central New York with his wife and their canine companions.